GILL WOMEN OF THE PREHISTORIC PLANET

a novel

by Brad Warner

Joe,
Rock on!

ELAY Press

2013

ELAY Press, ul. Graniczna 17,
PL-43-384 Jaworze, Poland
http://www.elay.media.pl

ISBN-13: 978-1482712155 (CreateSpace-Assigned)
ISBN-10: 1482712156
BISAC: Fiction / Science Fiction / General

GILL WOMEN OF THE PREHISTORIC PLANET

1968, directed by Ben I. Goldman
Reviewed by Stuart M. Ryfle VI
for *The Complete Guide to Psychotic Psinema*

To some, Ben I. Goldman is a legend, coming dangerously close in certain cases to an object of worship. It would be difficult to find a science fiction film director who inspires more devotion or who is, conversely, more unknown. He made few films, and even those are impossibly difficult to find. And among the obscurities, Gill Women of the Prehistoric Planet must rank as the most obscure. I've never seen it, nor has anyone else I know. There is some doubt the film even exists at all. I've decided to list it here because I believe it to be a real film, though the evidence is scant. The film itself hasn't been available in any format for decades and I have been forced to construct this entry based mainly on reviews published when the film was new, as well as slightly dubious articles published by a Xeroxed, Ohio-based Ben I. Goldman fanzine briefly available in the mid-1980's.

Constructed from bits and pieces of little-known Japanese and Russian science fiction films supplemented with new scenes shot by Goldman himself, Gill Women tells the story of an intrepid group of explorers who are the first to set foot on the planet Venus. The imported effects footage, which show flying saucers touching down over a lake, as well as prehistoric beasts roaming through the Venusian jungle, were quite impressive for their day, so say the few who've actually seen the film. Only Goldman's own magnified lizards with fins stuck on their backs failed to measure up. The biggest of many problems in this film was apparently its rambling storyline.

4

The plot reportedly involved not only the Venusian landing, but somehow worked in the American government's testing of an advanced propulsion system found in a crashed UFO, and its devastating results. Even fans say it was a confusing mess. Critics at the time found John Agar's closing speech about the dangers of "meddling with things beyond the scope of human comprehension" heartfelt, but completely incomprehensible.

The dubious legality of the director's "borrowings" from foreign films is perhaps why Gill Women is no longer seen today, though a small group of rather fanatic fans of the sci-fi underground like to believe some kind of deeper conspiracy is at work. According to these sources, the government has deliberately suppressed the film because, they say, certain parts of the Soviet footage contain actual images of real flying saucers.

Goldman never made another movie after this. And though aficionados of fine cinema might feel this is no great loss, we here tend to look upon Goldman's early retirement as a great tragedy for fans of trashy special effects, wooden dialogue and confusing plots. Ben I. Goldman, wherever you are, we salute you!

had to go to The Grind, despite knowing right from the outset the whole night would be a disaster. It's not very often The Cramps come through Akron, Ohio. I mean, the last time they showed up was at JB's out in Kent, which'll tell you how long ago that was. JB's hasn't had a show in a decade, not since they became a biker bar in the late 80's. Lux Interior and Poison Ivy are both originally from Cleveland, but they avoid Ohio like the plague. Who can blame them? Fucking shithole of a state. The 1990's have been a shithole of a decade. Thank god they're almost over.

Despite the fact they were playing at The Grind, just down the street from Doctor Bob's house in Highland Square and despite the fact that that fat, hippie, dolt loser Jay, who threw me out of The Subterraneans' reunion show last year, still books the place, I could not *not* go. If you know what I mean. And if you don't that's pretty much your problem now isn't it?

I knew Charmaine would show up. What I didn't know was that Nicole would show up with her. The sight of her hanging all over Nicole like she was Nicole's pet or her personal property or something was nauseating. Guess Charmaine's that type, though. Fine.

In full display mode, Charmaine had on this little white tank top and no bra, so her nipples, which could pop your eyes out if you got too close, were spotlighted, up front, center stage. Get 'em while they're hot.

What Charmaine sees in Nicole is anybody's guess. Trendy, pretentious, wants to be very butch with her United States Marines crewcut, but looks like a girl in spite of it. You'd never make it as a real bull dyke, Nicole, so you might as well forget it.

Whatever. Who cares?

I got to The Grind just as the opening band, The Zen Luv Assassins, were starting their set. Logan was doing his whole I-wanna-be-Iggy-Pop-or-is-it-Danzig-I-can't-decide-right-now routine - black leather jacket and hair dyed to match. Linda had her old sea foam green Fender Precision bass slung half way to her knees; she knows you're jealous of it and you want to grab her tits, but her husband Jim is the guitarist so you better just stay away. Mark, the drummer, who is Charmaine's brother, was pretending not to notice his sister and her new "friend."

The whole place was packed with sweaty, mindless teen punks who weren't even in junior high when I used to play at these kind of shows, every one of them acting like he owned the whole shit-up-the-ass world. I was squashed up against some big gear-encrusted machine from when the place used to be part of the B.F. Goodrich tire factory. That was before the Japanese came and bought all the tire factories in Akron, and left the city a smoldering memorial to the dead dreams of the industrial age.

Smoke and noise and heat and kids.

No-one was talking to me anymore, apparently. Which was well and good as far as I was concerned. I must "bring them all down" or something. God forbid anyone should ever say anything that wasn't entirely positive and cheery. You'd think so-called "alternative" types would be better. But they aren't. They strive for the same kind of brain-numbed conformity as anybody else. They just have a different dress code.

Nicole pushed her way through a pack of brain-dead college boys comparing their tattoos over to where I was standing. "Hey Joe! Fancy meeting you here. Get you something to drink?" she said, looking all superior. Her in her stupid Ramones-type leather jacket with the big decal stuck on the back. It's Vince Rancid's cover drawing for the old Millions of Dead Cops single, the one with the tank shaped like a human skull grinding starving children into the dirt. It's been 15 years since any of that stuff was as "cutting edge" as she seems to believe it is. Charmaine slipped crossways through the tattoo boys and entangled herself around Nicole, clinging there like a roach on a garbage can and giggling, like maybe she was on nitrous oxide. Rubbing those maddening brown boobs of hers all over her new Mistress, all the while acting like she didn't even notice me standing two feet away from her.

"I'm fine," I said, trying to act casual and unaffected. Who was I kidding? They could read me like a Xeroxed flier for a Hammer-Damage show stapled to a telephone pole on South Water Street. Anyone can. I've got one of those faces like I might as well have a neon sign on my forehead announcing whatever emotional state I'm feeling to passers-by.

"Hi Nicole!", "What's up Charmaine?", "What's new with you two?" they're all saying. Ignoring me like I'm not even here, as usual. All Charmaine's old friends, who used to pretend they were my friends. Whoop-dee-doo-dah. Like I need friends like that anyway. They ended up talking to each other and left me alone. Thank God.

Bash, bash, clang, scream, thud, thud, went the Zen Luv Assassins. How many times have I heard these same stupid songs? Every Tuesday and Thursday evening for the past three years, that's how long. They practice in The Clubhouse's basement. I live on the second floor.

The Zen Luv Assassins finished with some Julian Cope song I couldn't recognize, and Mark came over to talk to me after he'd packed away his drums. "I knew you couldn't stay away."

"Yep. My mistake." I nodded over at the couple of the year, who were now off in a corner by one of the pool tables.

"Charmaine's always been a little bit flighty. She'll come around in the end," Mark said, leading me down the bar and out of sight of the two of them.

"I'm not so sure I want her to," I said.

He gave me this look like he knew I was lying. Maybe I was. How was I to know what I was really thinking anymore? Seemed like everybody else could tell and I was the only one left in the dark.

"Zeta Reticuli," I said. Mark just gave me a puzzled look. The sound system at The Grind was turned up to pile-driver volume, just to make sure nobody's ears got a chance to recover between bands. It wouldn't have been so bad if they weren't playing the lamest music possible. I mean, who in their right mind thinks ancient ABBA songs are hip? "Planet X. Fourth planet from the star Zeta Reticuli 2," I said.

"What did you do, rediscover some new lost treasure from the 50's?" Mark said. "I always liked the movie where Ghidorah the three-headed monster is controlled by the little guys with new wave sunglasses and black leather skull caps. Then all the monsters go berserk and blow up like half of Yokohama before they blast them with some kind of ray or something."

Yeah, go ahead and make a joke of it, I was thinking. Just wait till the aliens show up at your door and start dictating what clothes you have to wear and what your ration of energy wafers will be for the week. And don't come crying to me when it happens. I'm not part of this universe anyhow.

Of course I didn't say any of this. Mark got me a beer and ordered a Kahlua and milk for himself. I said, "Mixing caffeine with a depressant like alcohol is not really a good idea, and the fat content in one of those is triple..."

"Look, I don't need nutrition advice from a guy who lives on instant Cajun Beans 'n' Rice out of a bag," Mark said, and gulped down half his drink in one go.

Whatever. It's your body. Anyway, Cajun Beans 'n' Rice contains a complete protein, which is important for a meat-free diet. And besides, it's very cheap and easy to make. Just add water and a half a stick of Parkay margarine, the one made from 100% canola oil, and there you go.

I didn't say this either. People don't like to hear the truth. So it's best not to tell it to them. The Cramps came on after 45 more minutes of woefully inappropriate music played over the house system. "I'm a human fly, I spell F-L-Y!" Lux Interior sang. If that doesn't totally encapsulate everything there is to say about life here at the end of the 20th century, I don't know what does.

After the show, Mark and I decided we'd walk back home. It was warm outside and it'd only take about half an hour to get from The Grind to The Clubhouse.

We crossed the Y-Bridge, which was built after the old Akron Viaduct crumbled to pieces back in the '70s and smashed a bunch of projects in the valley below. Pretty soon we were in North Hill, a former Italian neighborhood that's now what's called a "mixed area." This has always been just fine with me. I was there with Mark, who's very big and very black. I'm very skinny and very white. Perfect, right? There should be no hassle at all walking through North Hill, right? Wrong.

We turned the corner onto Chalker and walked through just a normal residential area. Not the projects. Not even a particularly poor section. Of course the entire city of Akron is "The Poor Section" these days; everybody with money moved out to Cuyahoga Falls or Fairlawn decades ago. Me and Charmaine once shared a place just down the block - speaking of racially integrated neighborhoods. Ha! She lives there with Nicole now. But I don't want to go into that.

I noticed these two guys following us at a distance. All of a sudden I could hear they were running up from behind us. One of the guys was shouting something that sounded like "What's up, Lokes?" or maybe "What's up, blokes?"

I turned around and these guys started circling us. One of them was big and stocky like Mark; his friend was a little smaller. It was dark and they were both Black guys so it was hard to see their faces. Mark put on this fake Black accent, which I'd only ever heard him use as a joke before. "Be cool, man. Be cool."

"Don't be tellin' me to be cool," the bigger guy said. "I axed you, what's up, Lokes?", or "blokes", I still couldn't tell. There was something weird about the way they talked. Their use of inner-city Black slang was about as smooth as mine. They dressed like they were from the projects down below the bridge. But they weren't, their clothes were wrong somehow. They had weird accents too, not American.

So I kind of patted the smaller guy on the shoulder and said, "It's all right man. We don't want any hassle..." - which was a major display of bravado on my part because I was scared shitless. It was also a major mistake.

"Don't be touching me!" he shouted, pronouncing the "g" at the end of "touching" much too clearly for a real inner-city kid. I pulled my hand away like you would if you touched a hot stove or something. That's when he punched me hard in the side of the head.

I saw stars just like in a cartoon. I was dazed for a second and then he punched me again, so I did what any intelligent person would do. I ran.

The bigger guy was hitting Mark. Mark landed a nice one in his stomach. But that just made the guy mad. Mark's big, like I said, but he fights like a girl.

Meanwhile the other guy shouted at me, "We don't like the color of your skin either!" Now I'm thinking, *what the fuck?* Who said anything about the color of anyone's skin? And they're saying this to me. I probably know more about and have more respect for real Black culture than any of these guys. You think they ever heard of Blind Lemon Jefferson or Charlie Patton? Besides, who did he think Mark was, Al Jolson?

By this time some people in the neighborhood were out on their lawns watching. One middle-aged Black guy came out smiling and tried to get between us and the guys who were beating us up, attempting to calm them down. There were a couple of girls out on their porch yelling at the guys to stop it. Seemed like they might have known them. Even though this was a mixed neighborhood, the only people doing anything to try and help us were the Black people. I'm sure all the whites were hiding in their houses with the doors locked tight, peering at the scene through their blinds. Useless pieces of shit.

At this point the little guy had caught up with me, so I couldn't see what was going on with Mark, being too busy getting smashed in the face. But I heard one of the guys say, "You ain't asleep yet?!" He sounded like Bob Marley. But not exactly.

I shouted to the girls, "Call the cops!" But all they did was keep standing on their porch yelling at the two guys to cut it out. Meanwhile I was taking all kinds of blows to the head. I didn't throw any punches myself because I knew I couldn't do any damage, and I'd just end up pissing them off even more. So I got an idea. I broke away, ran over and jumped up on the girls' porch. They screamed, "Don't bring them over here!"

I kept yelling, "Call the cops! Call the cops!" I figured they'd only call if I got them directly involved. I felt bad about it because they were trying to help us out, but what could I do? The girls ran inside. Mark must have seen what I was doing because he jumped up on the porch too. I noticed he was carrying something. It turned out to be this three-foot tall metal lantern from somebody's garden. He'd ripped it out of the ground and was holding it down at his side, so the guys who were after us couldn't see it.

"What the hell?" Mark said to me. I noticed his bottom lip was bleeding.

"One of 'em picked something up!" the bigger guy yelled. Somewhere I heard glass break. The middle-aged guy was kind of holding the bigger guy back and the smaller guy was circling around the porch but not getting too close.

"This is for the people of Planet X!" the smaller guy yelled.

"What?" I said.

"Something about Malcolm X," Mark said.

"Planet X! He said Planet X!" I shouted.

"Zeta Reticuli, muthuh fuckah!" the bigger guy shouted.

I turned to Mark and said, "You heard that! You heard him say Zeta Reticuli! You must have heard him!" I finally figured it out. The guy's accent was African! I know African accents because I've seen every Tarzan movie there ever was. He was trying to hide it, but I could hear it.

"Come on, let's get out of here!" Mark shouted back at me.

"He said Zeta Reticuli! And the other guy said Planet X! Not Malcolm X! Planet X! Planet X!" I yelled back.

Mark grabbed me by the arm and pulled me off the porch. The neighborhood people were between the crazy guys and us by this time. We ran through a bunch of back yards, zig-zagging all over so they couldn't follow us. After we got about a block and a half away we stopped and rested. Mark turned to me and smiled, which was when I saw he had a chipped front tooth. Then we heard somebody yell "Busted!", but I couldn't tell if it was one of those guys or not. So we took off running three more blocks all the way back to the Clubhouse.

Mark and I sat there with the doors locked and all the lights off for about twenty minutes on The Couch of Doom, which always smelled of beer and cigarettes, in the Living Room, which always smelled like cat shit. In the Clubhouse the "Living Room" means something similar to "Living Doll" or "Living Skeleton." The room is alive and therefore it is a Living Room. Mark said, "They're gone now. Let's turn the lights on."

"You heard him say Planet X," I said, being careful to keep my voice low so as not to be heard from outside. "You had to have heard that. And I am not turning the lights on. They're probably still lurking around out there."

"Shut up, Joe," he said. "I'm going to bed." He got up and went on upstairs to his room.

He probably figured this was just some isolated incident. Just some fucked up kids looking to start a fight with somebody. Me, I knew better. The people of Planet X had made their first major move against the one man on Planet Earth who had the goods on them.

They'd be back. That much I was sure of.

*   *   *

Carl ¶Walters, General Manager of the Cuyahoga Falls Johnny Teagle HyperMarket, thinks there is something very strange about the new store owners. For one thing, he's never actually met any of them, they communicate only by fax.

When the Cuyahoga Falls Johnny Teagle's HyperMart was taken over by Marutani and Associates of Yokohama he wasn't even sure if he'd have a job. Instead, the Japanese seem to be going out of their way to keep him on as manager and to convince him that their odd way of doing things is simpler and more efficient than what he'd been doing before. They're especially interested in the store's seafood section. Well, they are Japanese after all, Carl thinks. He once read that Japanese people eat a lot of fish. Otherwise all he knows about Japan is that the streets of Tokyo are always filled with bicycles, they all practice Kung Fu, and they all meditate for two hours every day.

The Japanese have imported some kind of special lobster and provided a specially modified live lobster tank with all kinds of complicated filtration systems to make sure it stays fresh and healthy. All of this and they only sent in one of the things. A whole big expensive filtration system and what-not for one lousy lobster. Someone is going to eat the bastard anyway. So what's the point of going to all the trouble? The thing looks weird too, like it's some kind of mutated Oriental samurai creature, gray with black stripes all over its body. Plus it's way too highly priced for any of the low-lifes from North Hill who shop at his store. The people with money in Cuyahoga Falls all shop at Fresh Foods of Fairlawn. That lobster is going to be in the store for a very long time.

Stupid, thinks Carl. But it's their store now, so what can he do? If they want to run the place into the ground, that's their business.

It's eleven o'clock at night and Carl has finally got the tank all put together and set up. A thick red kitchen mitt on his hand, he carefully takes the lobster out of its plastic box and drops it into the water. Johnny Teagle's HyperMart is still open. It's open till midnight, seven days a week, three hundred and sixty-five days a year, and sells everything from pomegranates to pets.

*   *   *

The Cramps are finished and Charmaine is still drinking gin and tonics. Nicole wonders what she's going to have to deal with at home. The crowd is thinning out. "Maybe we'd better go?" Nicole says.

"Oh come on," says Charmaine. "Don't be such a wimp. Maybe if you get me drunk enough you can have your way with me." She winks and licks her thick luscious lips. She finishes her drink in one gulp, slams the empty glass down on the bar and calls for another. The bartender shrugs and gets her a refill. The music on the sound system gets lamer and lamer: old Culture Club and bad disco hits of the '70s.

God, she's sexy, Nicole thinks. And she knows full well where this is going to lead. Heartache and despair. On the other hand she hasn't gotten laid in ages. And Charmaine is too seductive for words with her tight round ass and impossibly shapely legs shoehorned into a pair of black jeans that leave nothing to the imagination. She knows she should never have moved in with a woman like that. There was no way she could live with someone so incredibly sexy and not end up lusting after her. No further, she thinks. This will go no further. She orders another gin and tonic for herself.

*   *   *

"We need more paper towels in the men's room," Abraham Kidman, president/CEO of the American Mills Corporation says to the janitor, wiping his wet hands on his dark green khaki trousers. The whole Goofy Feet° ordeal has left Abe with mountains of paperwork and he's been in past midnight every day this week trying to finish it all. Who'd have known every retailer in Northeast Ohio would return the stuff by the truckload? He should never have given them the option. Christ, he should never have even made the stuff in the first place.

What was he thinking, anyway? A sugar-sweetened breakfast cereal in the shape of feet? Who wants to eat feet - even if they are feet in chocolate brown, lemon yellow, cherry red, and peach-flavored peach color? Why did he ever expect the people of Northeast Ohio to get excited about a breakfast cereal that tried to celebrate racial harmony and equality? He curses himself for being far too idealistic.

"But who's gonna use them towels?" the janitor replies.

Abraham rolls his eyes. Who hired this guy in the first place? He'll have to go down to personnel and have a talk with those people. Maybe it's some kind of quota thing, maybe every cereal factory has to have at least one crazy old Black man in its washroom. "I will use the paper towels," Abraham says.

The janitor's dark eyes twinkle in the fluorescent light of the warehouse and he smiles. "And who might you be?"

"Look," says Abraham, spotting the man's nametag, "Charlie, you know who I am. I own this place. I don't have time for pointless discussions with my janitor. I have a company to run. Just get some more paper towels, all right?"

"Yes, sir," says Charlie with a little salute.

Moron, thinks Abraham, I am surrounded by morons. He turns to walk back to his office and his paperwork. "Hey, chief," Charlie calls from behind, Abraham turns. "From when you born to when you die it's jes' like this," he says with a toothy grin, and laughs heartily.

At that moment Abraham Kidman suddenly recognizes the Truth of the Universe.

*   *   *

Nicole helps Charmaine through the door of her apartment, then lets her go. Down the street she can hear some kind of fight going on. Typical. Charmaine stumbles forward and lands in a sprawling heap in the center of the living room floor. She has a terrific ass, Nicole thinks. A completely amazing body: legs like a gazelle, perky brown tits, skin like chocolate milk, and all that long, thick black hair. She's beautiful and she's trouble.

Why do I always get involved with girls like this, Nicole wonders as she steps over Charmaine to get to her dingy bathroom with the bullet hole in the ceiling. How come there are no real gay women around anymore? Why is every good-looking woman she meets "bi" or "curious"?

She was blatantly using me to make her ex-boyfriend Joe jealous, Nicole thinks. Nicole likes Joe, from the little she knows about him. And she hates public displays of affection. Her attempts at trying to be sociable to the poor guy by buying him a drink came off totally wrong after Charmaine decided she just had to put in an appearance by her side. How much more obvious can you get? Not just to him, she thinks, to me as well. Was I too stupid to notice, she wonders, or just to horny to care?

Nicole realizes that instead of making Joe feel better, she ended up looking like she was gloating and only made him feel worse. Good going,

Nicole, she tells herself as she looks in the mirror. My skin looks like sour milk, she thinks, running a hand through her spiky red hair. She decides she'll go and maneuver Charmaine onto the couch and then go to bed.

She opens the door and Charmaine is standing there unsteadily with a sexy smile on her face, her shirt and jeans crumpled on the floor by her feet, while only a pair of pink silk panties with lace trim remain. Her eyes twinkle and she licks her thick brown lips with a tantalizingly tiny strawberry tongue.

What am I getting myself into, Nicole wonders. But she was right before, she's too horny to care.

*   *   *

The following day Carl Walters, manager of the Cuyahoga Falls Johnny Teagle's HyperMart drives his rusty old orange Toyota downtown to the Akron Public Library to try and find some books about Japan. After six months the Marutani Corporation is finally sending someone to see him. He hopes that this Ken Suzuki can understand English. He should be able to, or else how could he be their Northeast Ohio representative? But then again, so many immigrants come to America and still speak terrible English. If they want to live in this country they should at least learn the language and customs of their hosts, right?

Up till now Carl's impressions of Japan have not been good. Even the movies that try to make it look good do not succeed as far as he is concerned. Jackie Chan is supposed to be their national hero or something, but he just goes around beating people up with Kung Fu. Carl's father fought against the Japanese and afterwards told him lurid tales about his days with the occupation forces. You could have any woman you wanted over there, if you had a Hershey bar to pay with. It's probably still the same. He hopes he won't have to study too hard.

Inside the library he finds some books on the Orient. Jesus, there are a lot of countries over there. He figures he better look for one specifically about Japan. There might be differences between places like Japan, Korea and China. They could probably tell each other apart just by looking. God only knows how.

Carl notices another man looking at the same shelves who looks like he could be Japanese. Maybe he could ask him about what his country is like. He smiles at the man, but gets a stern look in response. Maybe I shouldn't ask him, Carl thinks. Maybe he would hit me with Kung Fu or some kind of judo thing.

He takes a book about Japan from the shelf and sits down to look at the pictures. The people there all look exactly the same,but he can't find any pictures of all the bicycles riding through the streets of Tokyo. Maybe those are in another book. He memorizes a few phrases in the glossary at the back. *Ohio* means "hello", and *origato* means "thank you." He hopes that will be enough to get by with.

He goes over the papers that the Marutani Specialty Foods Corporation faxed him. Basically they only care about three things: making sure he knows who's boss, making sure their precious lobster is being taken care of, and getting him to order from that mad man down at American Mills Corporation. They must get kick-backs or something from the guy. It's all thoroughly weird, Carl thinks. But he wants to keep his job and to do that he has to cooperate with these people.

*   *   *

Soon Park goes downtown to the Akron Public Library to try and find some books about Japan. He's not sure who the Marutani Specialty Foods Corporation is or why they need him to pretend to be one of their representatives, but they are paying him a lot of money to pretend to be Ken Suzuki, their man in Northeast Ohio. He does not like the idea of perpetrating such a deception, but things have been going badly at his Tae Kwon Do studio. His American visa was always dodgy at best, and now he's being investigated by the State Department. He had to shut the studio down two weeks ago and has retained only three students who he now tutors at home and who pay him in cash.

Soon doesn't know the first thing about Japan. His parents and grandparents suffered so much during the Japanese occupation of Korea, being forced to learn the language and work in near slave labor conditions, that they instilled a deep hatred in Soon of all things Japanese.

Soon comforts himself in the knowledge that he won't have to study too hard. The average Ohioan doesn't even know that Japan and Korea are two separate countries. Most people Soon meets assume he's Chinese, even after he explains to them very carefully that he was born and raised in Busan, South Korea - a country the Americans defended in the 1950's. South Korea, like in *M*A*S*H,* he explains again and again. "Oh really? I just love Chinese food," is the usual reply.

He finds the section with books about the Orient. Of course they've got every country in the Far East all bunched up on one little shelf. Typical. A man with incredibly fat legs and a huge ass smiles at him. Soon looks him over. What a specimen. The whole country seems to be made up of people like this. He gives the guy a brief uninviting look, grabs a book and goes over to a table to read.

He checks out some of the pictures. Disgusting morons with cameras around their necks and high and mighty attitudes. He thinks about all the idiot Japanese tourists he used to see shopping for imitation Louis Vuitton bags in the markets back home, and how the only Korean they ever bothered to learn was "make it cheaper." He closes the book in disgust. It's just one meeting with a grocery store owner after all. How much studying does he really need to do? Just for good measure he memorizes a couple of phrases from the glossary at the back. *Ohio* means "how are you?" and *origato* means "you're welcome." Or something like that. He really can't be bothered.

He closes the book and goes over the papers that the Marutani Specialty Foods Corporation faxed him. Basically they want him to do three things: make a strong impression that they are in control now without offending the supermarket manager's pride; make sure the lobster tank renovations are going as planned and that the new imported lobster is being looked after properly; and finally encourage the manager to do more business with a company called the American Mills Corporation. It's all thoroughly weird, Soon thinks. But he needs the cash.

As if he didn't have enough troubles, earlier today a friend of a friend called to tell him he'd heard that Kim Yong Lee was living in Akron now. If he and Kim Yong Lee meet again, only one of them will walk away alive.

*   *   *

One day Zen Master Seppo Gison received a letter from Zen Master Shibi. While on his way to deliver a sermon, Master Gison opened the letter and found that it was only a blank sheet of paper. He showed it to his students and said, "Don't you understand this? Haven't you heard that excellent people, though separated by thousands of miles, have a common attitude?" But Master Shibi, upon hearing this, did not confirm Master Gison's understanding.

Abraham Kidman, president of American Mills Corporation and creator of Goofy Feet˚ cereal, puzzles over this one for a while. He has been reading the book of Zen stories given to him by Charlie the janitor, trying to get some perspective on what he experienced last night outside the washroom. He feels that he has just about gotten the one about the dog having Buddha Nature and the one about the shape of your nostrils before your parents were born. Charlie confirmed his understanding of the former, but seemed a little reluctant about the second one.

The one about the letter is a little tougher, but it has a kind of beauty to it that he wants to share. He calls his secretary in to his office and dictates a memo. "Interoffice memo, to all employees," he says. "From Abraham Kidman."

His secretary waits for him to continue, but he says nothing. After a time he says, "Print that up and post it in all departments." She gives him a puzzled look. He lets it pass.

"By the way," he says, "what time are those toy sales people supposed to arrive today?" She tells him they've been waiting around for twenty minutes but she has not disturbed him because he gave her strict orders this morning not to disturb him when the "Meditation in Progress" sign was hanging from his doorknob. She then asks if she can go home - the only reason she agreed to come in on a Sunday was to set up this meeting. Abe asks her to usher the guests in, then tells her to "Depart and be free."

Abe's secretary rolls her eyes as she leaves the empty factory. Everyone who works at American Mills Corporation knows that Abe Kidman is losing it.

*   *   *   *

Ngugi and Msoto do not like America. They do not like the job they've been asked to do and they do not like each other. Why is it so incredibly hot and humid here so early in the day? Nairobi is only a few kilometers from the equator and it's not nearly as hot as Akron, Ohio. Last night they failed in their mission. They had beaten a man who they had never met before without even extracting from him the item they had been ordered to obtain. Both Ngugi and Msoto know they are working for a greater good or else they could not do such a thing.

Ngugi is wearing a baseball cap that says "LA Raiders" on it and a pair of blue jeans that have been deliberately designed to fit poorly. Msoto has a pair of sneakers that, for some reason he cannot fathom, have a small rubber object on the side which inflates a series of tubes inside the shoe lining. What is an "LA Raider" anyway? Is it another name for a person who enjoys wearing clothes that do not fit his body, and shoes with idiotic looking designs on them like they were made for children?

After a long search and several arguments about the lousy map they've been given, they find the shop they have been instructed to visit to get material to study the local culture. This city is dark and dirty, Ngugi thinks, as a crushed beer can rolls by. Nairobi is much cleaner and more modern once you get out of the bazaars and the places where people like Msoto hang around. Msoto is a low life.

Msoto thinks Ngugi is an elitist scoundrel. Simply because he is a Kikuyu, Ngugi thinks he is superior. The Kikuyus are no better than the Whites. So what if they formed the Mau Mau and fought the British? That was a very long time ago. Now they have become just like the Whites.

Msoto is proud to be a Masai, part of a culture that has not forgotten its roots nor adopted the degenerate ways of the Whites. It pains his heart to be in this place. But the money he makes here will be of great use to his family. Besides, he is on a mission much greater than even the elders of the Masai could understand.

Msoto resents having to work with Ngugi, but they have a common cause. Soon their work will be finished and his association with Ngugi will be over.

"Let's get this finished quickly," Ngugi says. For once Msoto agrees with him.

*　　　*　　　*

"I don't see the point," Abe Kidman, president of American Mills Corporation says to Ljes and Milena, the two sales people from the Dogs On TV Corporation of America sitting across from his desk.

"They are so cute. Don't you think they're cute?" Milena says with bubbly enthusiasm. Her accent is sexy beyond belief and she has absolutely the biggest set of boobs Abraham has seen in years. And those gigantic brown eyes. He is having trouble not being distracted in spite of his new depth of understanding.

"This will increase your sales by many fold," says her partner Ljes in the same accent, except that when he uses it, it just sounds dopey. With his bulging biceps, thick neck and blond crew cut, he reminds Abe of some kind of idealized Aryan dreamed up by a Nazi propagandist.

"I don't know," Abe says. He looks through the lens on the back of the little plastic toy television set again and clicks the little shutter button on top. The first picture is a basset hound wearing a bow tie. Next comes a dachshund with an apron tied around its waist pushing a baby carriage. "It's a bit big to fit in a cereal box."

"But then you can put less cereal inside the box and save money, no?" Milena coos.

"Look at the blister card," Ljes says passing the package across the desk.

What is a "blister card"? Abe wonders as he accepts the package. It sounds nasty. All toy industry words sound nasty. The blister card, as it turns out, is a three-by-five-inch printed card to which the Dogs On

TV toy has been attached. On the front of the card is a picture prob-ably taken around 1953 of a young woman watching television. On the screen is a collie. The woman is smiling. The words "Dogs On TV" are printed above the TV set.

"On the back is a history of all the famous dogs on TV," says Ljes. "I wrote it myself."

Abe reads, *The dog on television is the part of American culture. Many of famous dogs are remembered well by people of all aging. We present to you many good faces of dog to be enjoying again and again with all family members and a friend.* Below that is a list of trivia about Lassie, Rin Tin Tin, Benji and some other TV dogs Abe is not famil-iar with. None of these famous TV dogs are to be seen when he looks through the little lens on the back of the toy TV set. He asks why and Ljes says, "The rights are very expensive. Anyway these dogs are more cute."

These are boring, Abe thinks. And they make no sense at all. He can't understand why anyone would bother to make them at all. And yet there is something compelling about this stupid toy, it's almost hypnotic. There's something in them that feels like it's almost pulling him toward some unavoidable conjunction of influences.

Against his own best judgment Abe says, "We can't put the blister card in the cereal boxes, but maybe we can put the toys in." He needs *something* to help sell those damned boxes of Goofy Feet˚. "Leave me your number. I'll get back to you."

*　　　*　　　*

Mark knocked on my door in the morning wanting to show me his tooth before he went out to have it fixed. I refused to be seen. He called me paranoid, said that those guys were long gone, that they wouldn't even know us if we stared them right in the face. They were too drunk or too high, and probably didn't even remember last night at all. I wasn't buying it. What did Mark have to worry about? After all, he wasn't the real target. He wasn't the one the creatures from Planet X were out to get at any cost. He did not have the one item that could expose the whole scam, and rewrite the history of the past fifty years. Mark gave up and went away.

Being rudely awakened at an indecent hour on an indecent day with severe bruising about the face and neck, I decided the least I could do was put the time to good use. I set up the two VHS recorders I'd purchased for five dollars each from the Salvation Army, and edited some special effects stuff I'd done a long time ago into something a bit more coherent. It was some videotape of a friend of mine's pet iguana walking around amongst a bunch of miniature buildings I'd made out of cardboard and old laundry baskets. I dubbed over some music from the *Plan 9 From Outer Space* soundtrack, and some screaming crowds from a Beatles live tape. It looked all right, really. I originally shot the scenes for a film that I wrote with Charmaine. It was going to be called *Escape From the Vampire Planet of Dinosaurs and Prehistoric Women*. I still have the script somewhere. It would have been brilliant. Among my many other talents I am a born special effects genius.

Johnny Phlegm called at about noon saying he was trying to get together all the old Slam magazines. Slam was the Xeroxed rag he put out in the early 1980's. He wanted to release it as a book. Punk nostalgia. Who would have believed such a thing could ever exist? Johnny knew about the mountains of moldering junk Steve, who lived upstairs, kept in the Clubhouse basement, and asked if I'd mind digging through it to look for some stuff he could use.

Johnny Phlegm's a good guy. He used to be the drummer for the Bursting Brains. I kind of owed him for a lot in the past, so what the hell. I left my room.

The Cat With No Name was sitting on the landing cleaning himself. He stopped and stared at me for a long time, shocked at my appearance, no doubt. I said hello and went past him. He was still staring at me contemptuously as I walked down the steps. Critic.

The basement smelled like beer, cigarettes, mold and old guitars. Given the damp, it was amazing none of the bands that practiced down there had ever gotten electrocuted. Jerry Apathy was the only one who ever died in that basement, and he'd done that himself quite deliberately.

In the back of the basement there was a little room stuffed with Steve's collection of ancient magazines, dead PA equipment, splintered drum sticks, old guitar strings and a thousand crushed cans of Red White and Blue beer. I sifted through the magazines looking for old copies of Slam, Boredom, Oops! or The Slathering Reptile, or any of the other Xeroxed things that had come out in those days. There were loads of old Trouser Presses and a couple of copies of Penthouse, but not much of what I was after.

While I was down poking around the basement I checked to make sure *Gill Women of the Prehistoric Planet* was still safe and sound in its secret hiding place. It was.

As I re-deposited the film I heard the doorbell ring upstairs. I was the only one home: Mark and Lesa were out doing god-knows-what on a Sunday afternoon, and Steve was off painting houses or something. I knew it wasn't Johnny Phlegm; he never stirs before nightfall. I could have just hidden down in the basement. But I knew that if it was the beings from Planet X they'd probably break down the door and come looking for me. The basement was the worst place to be since there would be no way out of there.

So I went upstairs and tiptoed up to the door. I looked out through the peephole. On the porch stood a wiry young Oriental man wearing a really cheap looking blue suit with a red and blue striped tie. Next to him was a short, tubby white woman with straight blonde hair wearing a flowered dress. I knew exactly who they were, of course. The resistance. Those who, like me, chose to oppose the will of Planet X. Who else could they be? But I had to be careful. Every move I made was probably being monitored. I couldn't let on that I knew why they were here.

I opened the door. "Oh, hello!" the tubby woman said. "We were afraid everybody might be away." Sure you were, I thought. You knew exactly where to find me and exactly when I'd be at home and alone. I didn't say anything, though. Let them go through their piece, I figured.

The tubby woman cleared her throat. "My name is Wilma Fierson, and this is Kim Yong Lee. We're from Christ the Crowned King church." She pronounced "crowned" in two syllables, crown-*ed*. "Do you know Jesus Christ?"

"Well, I don't know him personally..." I said.

"Well, you can know him personally. What's your name, by the way?"

"Joe Nofziger."

"Okay, Joe," she said, that smile still frozen on her fat face, "have you ever wondered what will become of you when you die?"

I looked her and her partner over. Unusual-looking types. The resistance, I knew, would never say anything directly. Too much risk of detection. The message would be delivered in code. So I said, "No. What *does* happen when I die?"

She beamed a big smile up at me, I must have said the right thing. Maybe that was the special response the coded message required. She nudged the Oriental guy who reached inside this leather satchel he had hanging over his shoulder. It actually looked more like a purse. He pulled out this little comic book–type religious tract which had the title "What Happens When You Die?"

Nice comic, I thought. Exactly what I need today, more horror and death. "Interesting reading, yes?" said the Oriental. He wasn't playing the part very well. The little spin he put on the word "interesting" gave the whole game away.

The chubby girl must have realized it too. She quickly cut in. "Do you have any hobbies, Mr. Noftsinger?"

"Hobbies?" I said. Why did she call me *Noftsinger* and not *Nofziger*? I had said my name quite clearly. Did that mean something?

"Yes. Things you like to do, like drawing pictures or sewing or music."

"I dunno. I play guitar. I used to be in a band called..." I almost said The Bursting Brains, but I decided to spare her. "I was in a band. And I also make movies. Just amateur things on video and eight millimeter."

"Oh really?" said the Oriental man, tilting his head and sucking air through his teeth.

"You make movies?" the chubby girl said. "That's interesting. Our reverend makes movies too. Movies about Jesus. At Christ the Crowned King we believe that the Lord gives a talent to each and every person, and the true use for that talent is to serve and glorify Him."

"That's what you believe, huh?" I said. I always figured that if there was a God and he gave you some talent, the only purpose was to make you suffer and agonize because there is no way you can ever earn a living from your talent, unless you're a complete and total sell-out and you compromise your true beliefs in order to produce crap for mass consumption. All that my considerable talent had done for me was make me miserable.

"Yes, we do believe that," she said. "In fact, our reverend is looking for someone to help him with his new picture. If you have any VCR tapes of your movies I could show him what you do."

Now if that wasn't a sign, I don't know what was. "Hold on a second," I said and shot upstairs to my room. I fished through some of my videos. The Zen Luv Assassins live show probably wasn't appropriate, neither were the dodgy tapes of some of Charmaine's "performances" from the time we were dating. Finally I picked out a copy of the tape I'd put together of the giant-iguana-attacking-a-city special effects footage. I went back downstairs and handed the tape to the chubby girl at the door.

"Thank you, I'll show this to the reverend right away. Please accept the tract as our gift." Tract? I thought. What's a tract? She must mean the comic book. "If you have any questions about it our number is printed on the back. We hold a special service for newcomers every Monday. The church is just a few blocks away. Hope to see you there!"

She and her friend - her partner in the resistance - got out of there as quick as they could after that. They knew I had gotten the message and must have been worried that we'd be seen together.

I sat on The Couch of Doom in the Living Room and studied the comic for a long time. Before I knew it, it was getting dark outside. No matter. This was important.

I didn't even notice the stench of the litter box, which was normally so overpowering it propelled you right out into the Kitchen of the Forever Damned. The Cat With No Name officially belonged to Mark and Lesa. Cleaning up after it was their job, not mine or Steve's. They never cleaned up after it and Steve never left his room, so as usual, I was the only one who suffered.

The title of the comic was especially interesting. I figured they'd probably hide the message in there.

"What Happens When You Die?"

Taking every third letter it became: Aaewnue

Avenue, perhaps? Something important would happen on a certain avenue?

Maybe every other letter: Wahpeshnode

A Polish name, maybe? Some Polish person named Wahpeshnode was to be my special contact? Maybe the W sounded like a V so he'd be Vahpeshnode. Or was it their V's that sounded like W's? Or was that German, not Polish?

Maybe the letters were scrambled.

"The wops new pad, ah yuie."

"Edne is the happy hun, wow."

"Thaw pap hens. We do hynie."

Now I was getting somewhere. "We do hynie" was obviously a reference to someone into anal sex. It could be a reference to gay people, although not all gay people are into anal sex. "Thaw pap hens" could be a coded reference for the way the aliens embryos were stored in frozen form in a kind of pap, or gelatinous material.

I had been contacted. The next move was up to me.

*   *   *

Abe Kidman sees Charlie mopping the floors near the dispatch center. "You're very diligent at your work," he says.

Charlie turns and smiles up at him. "I don't know, chief. There's some folks that don't work so hard. Maybe I'm one of them."

"If that's so," says Abe, holding his mind steady, paying attention to this very moment alone, disregarding nothing, "there is still some division between worker and work."

Charlie lifts up his mop and stands straight, looking Abe right in the eye. "You see any dirt on this pretty floor, chief?"

Defeated, Abe turns and goes back to his office to meditate some more.

*   *   *

Mark sits back. It looks like another slow night. He checks under the counter and picks out a good Traci Lords tape to watch. Then he calls Joe to tell him the videos he ordered are in.

Just then a couple of black guys dressed in Raiders jackets saunter into the store. "Gotta go," he says to Joe and hangs up. Mark hates dealing with neighborhood people. They're never interested in anything but porno tapes. No taste for Electronic Eye's wide selection of obscure cult films, Hong Kong action flicks, Japanese animation and old monster movies. And besides that far too many of them seem to think he owes them something just because he happens to be black.

Just then he realizes he's seen these two guys before. They're the men who attacked him and Joe the last night in North Hill. Mark goes over to the phone and gets ready to dial the cops, but then realizes the two of them don't look so much menacing as lost. He catches one of the guys' eyes, but the guy doesn't seem to recognize him at all.

The other guy swaggers up to the counter, like a bad parody of a rap singer. "Do you have any films which show the real life of black men in America?" the guy asks in this weird Jamaican-type accent. Maybe Joe was right - which would be a major first - maybe they really are foreigners.

Mark smiles. "You bet I do," he says. So they want to learn how to pass for Americans, do they? This is going to be good. He goes over to the Blaxploitation section and picks out a couple of Rudy Ray Moore's mid-seventies Dolomite movies in which he plays a jive-talkin' detective, a copy of *Blackula*, and just for good measure, some Stepin Fetchit movies from the 1930s. Fetchit was famous for playing shuffling, dimwitted negroes and his films rarely get shown these days. Fetchit was subtly subversive and actually very funny. He was also the first black millionaire in Hollywood. Mark hands the tapes over to the guy. "Just watch these and you'll learn all there is to know about black people in America."

"How much?" the man asks.

Mark thinks a minute. Like every tape in Electronic Eye Videos, these are copied in the back of the store from VHS masters of dubious quality onto tapes the store gets from Johnny Teagle's HyperMart, five for seven dollars. With crude Xeroxed covers Electronic Eye Videos usually sells them for twenty bucks a piece. These guys don't look like they have that much money. But what fun would it be if they didn't get the full treatment? "Tell you what," Mark says. "I'll give you the whole bunch for ten bucks if you promise you'll come back in a week and show me what you've learned."

*   *   *

Charmaine awakens the next morning: eyes bleary, head stuffed with cotton wool, completely naked and in someone else's bed. It takes her a long moment of bringing the Björk and KD Lang posters on the wall into focus to realize where she is. The scent of perspiration mixed with perfume and beer hangs in the air. Nicole is lying on her back next to her, fast asleep with her mouth hanging wide open; she's wearing a Cleveland Indians T-shirt and a pair of checkered boxer shorts.

Charmaine crawls out of the bed and pokes around on the floor for her clothes. She remembers what happened last night only in brief flashes. Out in the living room she finds her jeans and shirt and pulls them on. Her underwear hangs from a floor lamp, and she shoves it in her pocket. What have I done, she thinks. The question is rhetorical: Charmaine knows exactly what she has done.

Pieces of the night before float through her mind at random. Her thigh muscles ache.

In the other room, Nicole rolls over and mumbles something. Charmaine looks in. She is still asleep. Charmaine can't face Nicole, not yet. The best thing to do is to leave quietly. It was a mistake to have Nicole move in with her, she decides. She's going to have to stay somewhere else until this thing cools down.

*   *   *

I put on my army coat and got ready to go down to Electronic Eye and pick the tapes up. Then I paused at the door.

At present the potential dangers facing me in the outside world were 1) agents of Planet X, dressed up as "urban youth," 2) an ex-girl-friend and her new lover, the sight of which would depress me to no end, 3) the resistance forces, who may be expecting that I'll have deciphered the code by now, and 4) the usual collection of mundane city terrors like guys with mustaches and pick-up trucks with big ol' stereos stuck on Aerosmith.

On the other hand there was the entire publicly known filmography of Ben I. Goldman including *Death To All Monsters*, *Earth vs. Count Dracula* and *Space Zombies vs. The Aztec Mummy* waiting for me.

Mark had managed to get them all in at the video store he worked at downtown. They came from some guy in Wyoming, he said. A likely story! Anyway, it was worth risking your life for, so I cautiously ventured out into the mean streets of Akron, Ohio.

And there they were. The very same two Planet X-ian operatives who had attempted to take my life for having in my possession the one item that would expose the whole nefarious business. They were coming right towards me, swaggering around with several unearthly looking little black boxes in their hands, strange weapons of unknown destructive force, no doubt. I dove under the crumbling awning of the Diamond Bar and Grill and hid in the shadows.

As they passed I heard one say to the other, "Now at last we shall understand these people." I knew it all along! Alien infiltrators. Space usurpers.

When I was sure they were long gone, I sprinted the rest of the way to Electronic Eye Videos.

"It was them! I saw them!" I shouted breathlessly to Mark behind the dusty counter, adjusting the *It Conquered the World* poster. This place was no commercial superstore like Ballbuster Videos. It was a mess of disorganized video boxes and bizarre display items from the worst films ever made - a yellowing poster for the underground super-hero classic *Rat Fink A Boo Boo*, a partially ripped up standee of Jackie Gleason made to promote the '70s trash classic *BJ and the Bear Part 2*, and toy Godzillas in every corner of the store. But if you were willing to search through the rubble you could find films and TV shows you would never find anyplace else in the world.

"You saw 'em, huh?" he said, casually. "They were just in here."

"Just in here?" I said. "You know who those guys were?"

"Yeah," said Mark. "Those were the guys that beat us up last night. Morons. Must have been so high on crack or whatever they were on, they didn't even recognize me."

"They're not from our world," I said.

"Get off it, Joe," Mark replied. "They're just a couple of assholes from some other country. Their accent was like Jamaican or something. What did you say it sounded like to you, Africa?"

"Africa," I repeated, completely dumbfounded that Mark could take the whole thing so casually.

"They were in here, trying to buy tapes to study African American culture," Mark said. "So I gave them the biggest pile of racist horseshit I could find. I can't wait to see what happens!"

He laughed. That was funny? I was stunned.

"Where did your sense of humor go? Did they whoop it out of you? Anyway, here's your tapes, as promised," he said plunking down the Ben I. Goldman videos. My God, they were beautiful. I told Mark I'd pay in three weeks.

"That's what you always say," he said. "Go on, before I change my mind. And don't forget to buy a box of Kleenex on your way home. That Holly Marshall in *Girls of Dinosaur Valley* is one hot babe!"

I ignored him and went home to be alone with my VCR.

*   *   *

Abraham Kidman decides to buy a case of Dogs On TV and insert them in the packages of Goofy Feet˚, his great cereal disaster. The whole idea of cereal shaped like feet was stupid to begin with. But, like all American Mills' cereal concepts, Abraham had only himself to blame for that. His staff had warned him. But Abraham had been too captivated by the idea of promoting racial harmony with his multicolored feet mingling happily together in the cereal bowls of kids all across the nation, popping and crackling with glee as pure white milk (or chocolate for an extra taste treat) was poured all over them, melting them into an ideal colorless, racially blind society.

Idealism, pure and simple. And idealism was an extreme, to be avoided just like its opposite, materialism. The man of the Middle Way avoids all extremes.

In the warehouse were thousands of Goofy Feet* boxes as well as a storage bin out in Brimfield full of the damned stuff. The ad campaign had been a wipe-out. They should have used cartoon or Carlmation feet, or even computer-generated ones. Real feet equals realism and that's what Goofy Feet* was about, Abraham had insisted. What an idiot, he told himself now. Abraham figured he'd sell off the last batch and be done with the whole sordid enterprise. If he stuck some free prizes inside, the crap might sell a little quicker.

*   *   *

Nicole wakes to find that Charmaine has left the house and taken most of her stuff. No note. No good-bye. Nothing. She sighs. It was to be expected, really. She wonders if she'll ever see Charmaine again. Probably not. It's happened all over again: someone's just used her as an experiment and then left without a word. As she shuffles over to her tiny kitchen to make herself some toast and coffee, she thinks about how she should know better by now. But she knows she will never learn.

God damn it, she thinks, she took the toaster too!

*   *   *

"Build your walls," the manager said to me as I packed several boxes of Ralston Corn Chex into a grocery bag, a hawk-faced housewife with a skunk stripe of silver in her black hair looking on critically as I did. Over at the other check-out counters a couple of the regular workers were complaining about how non-union employees always did inferior work. I should have just taken the phone off the hook this morning, I thought, but I was running seriously short of cash. The last time

I went to my cash station, I couldn't even take any money out since you have to withdraw your money in denominations of $10. So when Vector Temporary Services asked if my car was running yet (I'd told them it wasn't when they'd called last Friday), I said yes. I'd signed up with them when I was even more financially desperate than I am now.

So there I was bagging groceries for $4.50 an hour at Johnny Teagle's HyperMart in Cuyahoga Falls, one of those awful cavernous nightmare stores that sold everything from fresh fruit to live pets. Meanwhile the fate of the world was on my shoulders. I had to figure out to do next. Bagging cereal was not a real concern.

"No, no, no! You never put tomatoes in when you still have heavier items such as bread and TV dinners! Mr. Hoftsinger, are you paying attention?" the manager said, startling me and thereby causing me to drop a bunch of grapes. They went bouncing and dancing across the floor around the register. I ended up squashing half of them as I tried to chase them all down. "Get a broom!" the manager screamed.

I went off in the direction the manager pointed to try and figure out where they might store the brooms. He'd called me *Hoftsinger*. Those resistance members yesterday called me Noftsinger. Why? Who was this Noftsinger person anyway? And who was Hoftsinger? Was it a clue of some sort?

I went around the produce section where some other guy from Vector Temps was showering the lettuce with a little green hose. He kind of waved at me as I went past, as if we had some kind of special bond by virtue of both being members of Vector Temps. The pitiful fool. At the end of each aisle there was a security guard, some burly jerk who was probably an ex-high school football star now reduced to wearing a pathetic red and white striped vest with a nametag on it while trying to look serious and threatening. Life is so sad for most people.

I went by the butcher's area, and the egg area, and the place where they keep the live lobsters in the big tanks so that sadistic cretins with brains the size of walnuts can take them home and boil them alive. They had one particularly ugly-looking mutant lobster in its own tank separated from the rest. Poor guy. I gave him a thumbs-up sign for what it was worth. He did not respond. Probably too depressed about his future.

I opened up a couple of doors marked "Employees Only" - oh, the power and privileges I had as one of that elite class - but there were no brooms in any of them.

Then I heard the manager's voice over the PA. "Joe Noftsinger to register four please. Joe Noftsinger to register four."

I started rushing back over there. And then I thought as I was running, what the hell am I running for? To impress the manager of the Cuyahoga Falls Johnny Teagle's HyperMart? Do I want to make a career out of this or something? I walked the rest of the way. Plus he was calling me *Noftsinger* now not *Hoftsinger*. Why?

When I got back to the register, my fellow Vector Temps worker was there with a broom, sweeping up the rest of the grapes. How did he get the broom? How did he get to the register before me? Maybe I spent more time looking at the lobsters than I thought. That mutant one kind of reminded me of Ebirah, the giant lobster that Godzilla fought in *Godzilla vs. The Sea Monster*. A very Oriental-looking lobster, that one. I wonder if anybody ever made a movie with a live lobster on a miniature set. That would be kind of cool. It'd be cheap to do, too.

"Don't you know where we keep the brooms?" the manager said. "If you don't know something, you should ask. You know we have an arrangement with Vector Temporary Employment Services. If you temps work out here for a couple of weeks' trial period, we can arrange for a raise above minimum wage and then after that we can even hire you full-time. Didn't they tell you that at your introductory briefing?"

They might have, I thought, but don't ask me. I never pay attention to those things. "All done, Mr. Walters!" my fellow temp said in a perky voice, a great big smile on his face, the kind of smile stupid people called "winning." It was then I noticed he was wearing a retainer. Not a good sign. Communications devices can so easily be hidden in those things.

"Very good, Eric," the manager said. "I think there may be a place for you with us."

"I hope so, sir," he replied and trotted off back to his appointed task.

"Now, Mr. Noftsinger, do you know where the grapes are?" the manager said.

"Yes, sir," I said. I don't know why I threw the "sir" in there. It sounded good, though. Maybe he was part of the resistance too. Maybe this was a test of some kind.

"Will you please go and pick out a very nice bunch to replace the ones our valued customer bought?"

"Nice ones," the woman with the skunk stripe in her hair said. "Make sure they're ripe and very firm."

"My name is Nof*ziger*, not Nof*tsinger*," I said, raising my eyebrows and hoping the message that I did not understand the current use of the code word *Noftsinger* was clear. Nor why the mysterious Mr. Hoftsinger had suddenly disappeared.

The manager scowled hard at me, his face turning red. An act? I could not say. "Just get the grapes." he scowled. Off I went, dutifully. Soon all mankind would be slaves to masters like this, unless I could complete my task.

As I looked for the fruit section I thought about the manager's statement. "Just get the grapes." Grapes might have been a reference to something. Wine, perhaps? Wine is made from grapes. Wine is the blood of Christ and I had been contacted by resistance members posing as Christians. Maybe "Just get the grapes" was a veiled suggestion that I was to work more closely with them. Or the manager could be working for the enemy. In which case I should do the opposite of whatever he ordered. It was very confusing.

I ended up in the lobster section again. If you made a movie using a lobster as your monster, you'd probably have to get several of them. I imagine they can't stay out of the water too long. Do they breathe air? Probably not. Then what would you do with it afterwards? I know that when Ben I. Goldman made *King Gorilla vs. Gorgosaurus* in Japan they ate the live octopus they used in the scene where the giant octopus attacks the natives on Farou Island. But Japanese people eat tons of octopus. It's like Japanese potato chips or something. I couldn't do that, I'd have to let it go. But where could you let a lobster go in Ohio? Maybe you could sneak it in to Sea World and let it go in one of the big whale tanks. But then Shamoo would probably eat it. How many killer whales named Shamoo were there in all the Sea Worlds all over the world anyway? A lot, that's for sure.

"Joe Nafzinger to register four please. Joe Nafzinger to register four." The manager sounded angry even over the tinny PA system. And now they were calling me Nafzinger. Obviously a different code name was in use. Why? This time I jogged back. Somebody else had apparently already gotten some grapes for the woman with skunk hair because she was gone. I noticed that my fellow Vector Temp employee was now bagging at register four.

"I'm taking you off of bagging for a while," the manager said. "Go over where Eric was and spray water on the produce for a while. I'll come over there in a few minutes to check on your progress." Then he walked off toward the back of the store, probably on urgent business.

"All right," I said and walked in the general direction he had been indicating. After a while I found myself in the cereal aisle. I started reading the ingredients on a package of Lucky Charms, trying to find out if they used any gelatin in the marshmallow treats. Gelatin is made out of cow bones, hooves, teeth and skin so you shouldn't eat it if you're a serious vegetarian. And I am very serious.

It turned out there was gelatin in the marshmallow treats, which was grievously sad, since I like Lucky Charms. There was also gelatin in Kabooms and all the

Count Chocula–related horror cereals.

I justified what I was doing as "work related," reasoning that if any vegetarians came by my register with boxes of Frankenberry or whatever mixed in with their Egg Beaters and their Healthy Links, I could say something like "Sir, did you know that this product contains gelatin, which, as you know, is made of cow bones and hooves?"

"Why no, I did not," the customer would reply. "Thank you so much for informing me of that. You are very thoughtful and helpful." Maybe I'd get to be Check-Out Person of the Week or something. An honor like that is not to be viewed lightly, you know. Feh!

I noticed that Goofy Feet˙ - the lightly sweetened corn cereal in the shape of feet from around the world - now had a free prize inside. It was a little plastic toy TV set called "Dogs On TV." Apparently you looked through a lens at the back of the TV and saw View Master–type slides of dogs dressed in "wacky" outfits, like fireman hats with matching raincoats or striped pajamas. What sort of mentality would even come up with a concept like that? I wandered back over to my register to see if anything might be going on there.

*   *   *

"I will not say you won't regret this," says Abe Kidman to Carl Walters as they stand beside the loading docks behind Johnny Teagle's HyperMart watching a two-ton American Mills Corporation truck unload 45 crates of Goofy Feet® cereal, "because the mind of the future is ungraspable." He pauses. "As is the mind of the past. And indeed the mind of the present." He pauses again. "But I will say I believe you've made a fine choice."

"Yeah, whatever," Carl says. "Put it all in section D!" he shouts at his stock people. "We'll figure out where to shelve it later." The loading dock whirrs and clanks into place and three former stars of the Cuyahoga Falls High football team, now dressed in Johnny Teagle's HyperMart's distinctive red and white coveralls, begin unloading the boxes. Two others from the team are cutting up old produce boxes and sailing them into a nearby dumpster, their only chance left now to use the skills they so carefully honed for four years.

"Goofy Feet® represents a step forward in sugared-cereal evolution," Abe shouts over the roar of the loading dock lowering back down.

"Look," says Carl, "I bought the stuff. Maybe it'll sell, I don't know. It's Monday, and I really can't deal with any of the far eastern guru bit."

"Right," says Abe, nodding rhythmically, his graying ponytail sweeping the back of his neck. "I reach." He puts his hands together at chest level, fingertips touching but palms apart. An employee sends a cut-up cardboard box whizzing by into the dumpster beside him. He quietly acknowledges its presence.

Carl rolls his eyes and winds his way through the boxes into the store to check on how the idiots from Vector Temporary Services are doing on the promotional material he assigned them. That dumb-ass Nofziggler, or whatever his name is, seems like he's on drugs and the other guy is a complete goofball. You get what you pay for, though, he thinks. Nofziggler looks artsy, Carl thinks. Maybe I can get him to make me some free advertising for this garbage.

Why did I even go into this business at all, he wonders as he makes his way inside, I could have been…he stops for a minute. He's not sure what he could have been. Something other than a grocery store manager, though, that's for sure. A cardboard box sails by straight into the box. One of the ex-football stars shouts, "Goal!" But Carl is too lost in his thoughts to notice.

*   *   *

It was odd being asked to make a sign about Goofy Feet* cereal, when I'd just been thinking of that very subject. But that's time for you. Flowing in both directions at once, making things as confusing as possible for ordinary people like me.

I followed the manager to a grimy stockroom at the back of the store and got to work on the sign. This is where our food comes from? Remind me not to eat.

I used to do all the flyers for The Bursting Brains shows as well as the layouts for The Slathering Reptile, so making signs for the store was right up my alley. Where did that phrase come from, anyway? Why an alley? Outside the burly guys in coveralls were hooting and giving each other high fives as they pitched old boxes into a dumpster. I suppose people have to find their meager triumphs somewhere.

I swept away some crushed lettuce leaves and dead roaches, then laid a big piece of stiff paper on the floor and drew a picture of the cereal box. Beside this I put another picture of the Dogs On TV free prize. On the top I wrote "Dogs On TV Now Availible in Specially Marked Packages Of American Milk Corporation Brand Goffy Foot™ Cereal!" I looked and looked and looked at the word "Availible." Something wasn't spelled right. But there weren't any dictionaries around as far as I could see. Whatever. It's not like anyone else in Akron, Ohio knows how to spell. Someone yelled, "Heads up!" A cardboard box sailed by. They laughed a lot about that. I guess that's the kind of thing stupid people think is funny.

"All baggers to the front, please. All baggers to the front," came the manager's voice over the tinny loudspeakers. I supposed I was included in that. "Baggers" sounded vaguely insulting when you thought about it. Maybe there should be a more P.C. term for the job, something like "Packaging Assistant." No. Nobody wants to be anybody's assistant. Everyone's got to be a leader. How about "Packaging Specialist"?

When I had made my way through the maze of the store and up to the front, it looked like every housewife, night-shift worker and out-of-work former tire company employee in the city had suddenly decided to descend on Johnny Teagle's HyperMart in unison. There were huge lines of sad, fat people behind every check-out counter. So I went back to register four and started bagging their Pop Tarts and Oscar Meyer wieners again. I was very careful to "build my walls" and not crush any bananas underneath cans of lard or boxes of Kraft Macaroni & Cheese.

One pale, bloated guy with a sorry attempt at a beard bought a box of Kabooms, and I was about to warn him of the gelatin content when I noticed he was also buying several tins of Armour Deviled Ham.

After a few more bags I noticed that I was packing a bunch of Grillers and veggie sausages in with several varieties of Kraft Macaroni & Cheese and a six-pack of Red White and Blue. Obviously someone I knew. I looked up. It was Charmaine. She noticed me and shot me one of those "Oh Jesus Christ it's you, please don't talk to me" looks.

"Charmaine," I said, ignoring that look, "I've got to talk to you."

She grabbed her bag away from me. "We have nothing to talk about."

I followed her out past the candy machines. The skinny middle-aged lady running register four yelled, "Hey! Where the hell do you think you're going?" I secretly hoped I would not find such a question important when I reached her age.

"Just a minute. This is urgent!" I shouted to Charmaine. I went through the automatic doors, sneezing when the sunlight hit me. I always do that. Why? No time to wonder. Maybe I'd look it up at the library later.

I caught up with Charmaine over by the Dr. Pepper machine next to the shopping carts. I grabbed her arm. She jerked away. A housewife grabbed her little kid and dragged him away from us. "Will you wait a minute please? I have to talk to you right now."

She turned around and glared at me with those big, black, slightly slanted eyes. God, she was gorgeous. "Make it fast. I have a lot of things to do today."

Half running out of breath as I spoke, I told her about the people from the church and the coded message in the religious comic book and all the veiled references to *Noftsinger* and *Hoftsinger* and *Nafzinger*. Charmaine was the only person to whom I had ever revealed the facts about my owning the one thing which could bring down the current regime of lies and disinformation. I had to let her know.

"Look, Joe," she said, very seriously now, the cruelty gone from her face. "You need help. Professional help. I can't do anything for you. You should talk to someone, a counselor or something."

"I am not in need of professional help," I snapped back. Someone slammed a shopping cart into the row of carts behind us. I didn't care.

"Joe, can't you imagine for just one moment that maybe these ideas about alien conquest of the Earth and you being the only one who can thwart their plans might be just a little bit far-fetched?"

"But I have proof now," I said, in a tone a bit more whiny and desperate than I'd intended. "I've met the resistance forces. Just meet them once for yourself and if you still don't believe me, I promise I'll drop the whole thing and never bother you again."

She paused. "And if I meet them for you, you'll talk to someone about this, someone professional? Will you promise me that too?"

"All right, I'll do it." Maybe I was lying, but I knew she'd call me in on it and force me to go. So I guess I wasn't lying.

She thought about it for a minute, staring into her grocery bag. Then she said, "I'll be at home tonight. Call me." She turned and walked out into the parking lot to where her old orange Chevy Nova with the rust holes by the left front tire was parked. Not too many of the other cars in that lot looked a whole lot better. The Ohio winter takes a toll on steel, and few can afford to repair it these days.

When I turned around to go back inside, the manager was standing right in front of me. "There you are! Just what on earth do you think you're doing?"

"I'm sorry," I said. "Something urgent just came up."

"Something urgent?" he said, rubbing his graying temples. "Listen, mister, I'm paying for your time here, and while you are under my supervision, there is nothing, and I do mean nothing, in the world more urgent than the smooth functioning of this store. And that smooth functioning is something you have disrupted more than once today. Your private life is something to deal with on your own time, not on mine. Am I being clear?"

That did it. "Private life?" I said, looking him right in the eye. "Listen, friend, I happen to think that preventing the enslavement of the entire planet by malevolent beings from a distant solar system is a little bit more important than the smooth functioning of the Cuyahoga Falls Johnny's Teagle HyperMart."

His piggy face turned red. "Get out of here!" he shouted. "Turn in your apron and your nametag and get out!"

"I will!" I said and stomped back inside. A couple of skinny homeless guys standing near the door looking for handouts applauded.

"Vector Temporary Employment Services will be hearing about this!"

I turned around, blocking the automatic doors. "Fine by me!" I shouted, tearing off my nametag and attempting to untie my apron. He was walking away. I shouted, "You and these so-called 'Noftsinger' and 'Hoftsinger' and 'Nafzinger' people who you are obviously working for, will be hearing from me as well. You can rest assured of that!"

I couldn't get the damned knot out of my apron. I wanted to tear it off and fling it at him. Failing to undo the knot, I wriggled my shoulders free, slid it down my legs and stepped out. Flinging would have been inappropriate after that. I put my apron on the conveyor belt on register four and left the store. I got in the Wheezing Dragon, the '79 Chevy Celebrity my dad gave me ages ago, and tore out of the parking lot.

*   *   *

Abe Kidman, president of the American Mills Corporation, makers of Goofy Feet* cereal, and recently enlightened being, finished his

42

walk around the streets of Cuyahoga Falls, where he had been con-
templating the void while enriching his consciousness with the sights,
sounds and smells of the city.

He walks back into the parking lot of Johnny Teagle's HyperMart
to get his car and go back to work. A madman screeches past him in
a banged-up old Chevy Celebrity. Abe feels compassion for the poor
man's restless state. If only there was some way to help him.

He looks at the front window of the supermarket and sees a sign
advertising Goofy Feet* cereal. Only it's spelled *Goffy Foot* with a "™"
instead of an "*," the word "available" is spelled wrong, and his company has apparently been renamed the American *Milk* Corporation.
But Abe does not mind. He can tell by the way the letters have been
drawn that the man who made this sign is at once deeply disturbed
and yet in some way in touch with that which is terribly profound. It
is truly a beautiful accomplishment. He makes a mental note to find
the artist and thank him personally for embodying the spirit that he
hoped his cereal creation would represent.

*   *   *

"I got a *dawwwnng* as *lawwnnnng* as King *Kawwwnnnggg*," says
Msoto.

"No," Ngugi replies. "You are completely off the base. The word
King Kong must be said much faster as if it is but a single word. *Keenkawn, keenkawn.*" The used VHS machine they purchased for five dollars at a local charity store seems just about to stop working completely,
but it does not need to last very long. Ngugi had to cut several wires
in order to make it play through the ancient black and white television set in the crummy hotel. Now it barely runs. But that is enough.

He rewinds the video again and plays the scene from Rudy Ray
Moore's *Dol-o-mite in Harlem* several more times. Together Msoto and
Ngugi repeat, "I got a *dawwwnng* as *lawwnnnng* as *keenkawn,* I got
a *dawwwnng* as *lawwnnnng* as *keenkawn.*"

Msoto pauses the tape. "Are you quite certain this is the correct
way American blacks speak? It seems not altogether realistic," he says.

Ngugi replies, "Don't worry. The tapes were sold to us by a fellow black man who assured us they would help us speak like Americans. Don't you know that in America all black men are brothers?"

Msoto and Ngugi break up in fits of derisive laughter. The only people Msoto finds more offensive than Kikuyu like Ngugi who have sold out to the whites and adopted their ways, and the only people Ngugi finds more ridiculous than backwards Masai like Msoto who refuse to accept the modern world, are American blacks who think that everyone with dark skin ought to be their brother.

Suddenly the Interociter springs to life, its triangular antenna glowing blue with unearthly power. Ngugi and Msoto turn away from the TV. The Interociter's oblong screen, suspended on a stalk-like projection from the dull metal control box, pulsates and forms into abstract shapes, which soon coalesce into the image of a man with a head the size of a medicine ball. Huge veins pulsate on his giant bald cranium. He wears a pair of black wrap-around sunglasses with a single lens.

The medicine-ball-head man speaks. "Thaw pap hens," he says.

Together Ngugi and Msoto reply, "We do hynie."

Msoto adjusts the round plastic dials on the front of the machine. The medicine-ball-head man fizzles out again. Ngugi smacks Msoto on the back of the head.

*   *   *

Wilma Fierson whistles a cheerful hymn as she shakes the pack of powdered real cheese food flavoring onto the mixture of Kraft Macaroni & Cheese, one-half stick of Parkay margarine and one-quarter cup of Reiter's brand farm fresh milk warming on the little pea-green electric range in her tiny apartment. A picture of Jesus the Lord smiles down upon her from the wall calendar as she cooks.

Today she's making a real American meal for Kim Yong Lee. He's back in the living room, drawing comics for Reverend Goodman. Wilma knew she had found someone special when he got so excited about being able to draw his comics for the riches and glory of God's Heavenly Kingdom, rather than for poorer Earthly rewards which moth and lice doth corrupt.

Wait, is it really "lice"? That sounds wrong somehow, she thinks. As she stirs the golden-yellow mixture to an even, creamy consistency she makes a mental note to look that one up later. Did they even have lice in Biblical times? And how can lice corrupt things? Or moths, for that matter? She picks out two pale blue plastic bowls decorated with flowers from the pea-green Formica cabinet above the range and pours the macaroni into them.

Kim Yong must love American food, Wilma thinks as she places two steaming bowls of macaroni and cheese down on her pea-green kitchen table and sits down to wait for him. It's got to be such a treat after eating only rice and pickled cabbage all your life. A simple bowl of Kraft Macaroni & Cheese must seem such a delicacy to someone from a poor and downtrodden land far, far away. That's a miracle. That's God's infinite grace. The Lord has lifted him up and brought him to the land of the free, the place where dreams can come true if only you believe. I'm so fortunate to be a part of that, she thinks.

What's keeping him so long? "Kim Yong! Come on out of there and have some lunch!" she screeches.

*   *   *

Once I got home, I sat down at the Warped Formica Table in the Kitchen of the Forever Damned and stared for a while at all the mannequin heads, old plastic toys and moldering Akron Beacon Journals piled on top of it. What was this thing Steve had for mannequin heads, anyway? People were always giving them to him. His whole room was full of the damned things, carved into ashtrays, used as lamp stands, painted with weird faces - the entire make-up era KISS line-up including Vinnie "Wiz" Vincent and Eric "The Fox" Carr were represented.

Whatever. I figured I'd better prioritize what I needed to do, so I got a pen and some old punk rock flyers and tried to think.

By now you think I'm crazy. If you don't, you should. If you're the kind of person who can accept a story like the one I've been telling you without questioning it and concluding that anyone who believes such nonsense is crazy, then you're not someone I want to associate with. Anyone who readily accepts the unbelievable isn't just crazy, he's dangerous. It's like all the people who believed what Hitler said without ever examining it. This is exactly why I did not resent Charmaine, or anybody else for that matter who didn't accept my stories of what was truly going on. If anything, I respected them more for not believing. This makes me smarter than most people.

But before you finalize your decision regarding my insanity, let me try to explain it this way. Suppose there's a person who lives in Ravenna, Ohio and thinks he's Napoleon. He's nuts, right? Of course he is. But in his mind he is Napoleon, and his mind is the only mind he will ever know. To him it's the rest of the world that's mistaken. What the majority of people have to say has no bearing whatsoever. His mind is his whole world. He can never know he is crazy unless he changes the very nature of his conscious mind.

The definition of mental illness is when a person has a self image which is so different from what the rest of the world thinks of him that it causes the person great difficulty in adjusting to and dealing with society. But maybe no-one's image of reality matches up with the Truth, meaning the ultimate Truth rather than society's interpretation of things. Maybe society itself is insane. Society would be no better able to judge its own sanity than our "Napoleon" would be able to judge *his* own sanity. It has no outside reference by which to judge.

In that sense we're all crazy. Just because everyone believes something does not make it true. Look at how popular shitty bands like Journey or REO Speedwagon used to be. It didn't make them objectively good.

That's why, even though I am demonstrably crazy, I believe that I am not. And maybe I'm really not, how would you know? Perhaps the things you believe are crazy, and no-one tells you because they believe the same crazy things. If everyone in Ravenna believed that guy was Napoleon, then he really would be Napoleon. If all of human society is, in fact, dead wrong about the nature of reality, then maybe crazy people like me are correct. Human beings can't see outside of their own collective illusions. Well, most of them can't, anyway.

Who cares? All that stuff didn't matter at this point. What mattered now was what I was going to do about the alien invaders. If I was going to get anywhere, I had to have a strategy. What my ultimate goal was, I still did not know. Maybe if I made up a list of things that had to be done, that ultimate goal would present itself. So I found a Magic Marker and an old Zen Luv Assassins flyer and wrote on the back of it:

— Introduce Charmaine to the resistance
— Identify the nefarious "Messrs. Noftsinger, Hoftsinger and Nafzinger"
— Identify the true nature of the organization known as Christ the Crowned King
— Identify all agents of Planet X

That was enough to begin with. I went upstairs to my room and pinned the list to the inside of my door. I put a Dickies tape on the eight-track and laid down on my moldy futon to have a good think about all of this. I only ever listen to eight-track tapes these days. It is the best music storage format available, in spite of what anybody says. Records get scratched and warped, CDs and cassettes are for suckers.

I dozed off somewhere in the middle of *Stuck in a Pagoda with Trisha Toyota*. When I woke up again I took a look at my watch and realized I'd nearly missed my appointment with destiny. I scrambled down the stairs, leaping over The Cat With No Name, who didn't even bother to react, and dashed out the door.

*　　*　　*

Kim Yong Lee had wanted to travel to Japan and draw cartoons for one of the famous manga companies there like Tatsunoko or even Tezuka Productions. He is quite fluent in Japanese. It's relatively easy for Koreans to pick up Japanese since the grammatical structure of both languages is quite similar, while at the same time completely different from the grammatical structure of nearly every other language in the world, save Hungarian and of course Finnish, which is, in itself, a linguistic mystery. The vocabulary of Japanese is altogether different from Korean, but Kim Yong Lee is pretty good at learning new words. He never bothered much with English though, so his English is terrible and he knows it.

However, his father had talked him into going to America instead. The Japanese all hate Koreans, he told him. After the great Tokyo earthquake of 1923, hundreds of Koreans living in the area were burned alive by superstitious Japanese who believed that Korean magic was somehow to blame for the quake. Even today, third and fourth generation Koreans living in Japan, people whose grandparents had been born and raised there, were denied Japanese citizenship. It would break his mother's heart for him to go to Japan, so his father had said.

If he had to leave to seek his fortune, America was better, his father had declared. The opportunities were greater, too. He could be an animator at Disney or Pixar. One just had to be careful, his father said, because everyone in America owns handguns.

His father and mother did not know, nor indeed could they ever know his real reason for needing to leave Korea. Nor did they know about his secret background as the co-star of a series of cheap martial arts movies, the very thing that made it necessary to leave the country.

Akron, Ohio was a shithole. To Kim Yong Lee, America was places like New York City, Hollywood and Dallas, Texas. Akron, Ohio was a dump. He wished he was in Tokyo instead. Even back home in Seoul he'd made a good living inking in animation cells for bizarre American breakfast cereal commercials in which small furry animals and cavemen blew each other up with big sticks of dynamite. What was it with Americans and breakfast cereal anyway? He'd tried some once but could not see the appeal. What's breakfast without kimchee? Sweet breakfast makes no sense at all. And neither does the junk they eat the rest of the day.

He'd been lured to the armpit of America by Reverend Goodman, who he met in Seoul. He should have known there was something shady about the guy. His sermon seemed to consist mainly of rehashed notions from bad science fiction films. And yet there was something compelling about his delivery that made Kim Yong want to stay afterwards. When the reverend heard about his interest in animation and saw some of the portfolio he'd been carrying home from work with him, he made a powerful pitch.

It caught Kim Yong Lee's imagination, and soon he found himself compelled to follow the man. It was almost like a trance now that Kim thinks about it again. But these days the spell was being broken.

As he sits at his drawing board doing pencil work for the latest comic by Reverend Ben Goodman, Kim Yong Lee thinks about his first few nights with Wilma. All those promises she'd made him about riches and glory. What the hell had she been talking about? He'd done six damned comics for Christ the Crowned King Publishing and hadn't been paid yet. Moving in with Wilma had been the biggest mistake of all. She was out there making some more of that horrible pre-packaged processed food she always made him. No doubt she'd expect him to think it was some sort of exotic delicacy.

"Kim Yong," she called. "Lunch is ready. Then we've got to go out!" This is a nightmare, thinks Kim Yong Lee.

He finishes his meal, such as it is, and immediately Wilma whisks him off to that horrible church. What kind of church is constructed from the ruins of an old fast food restaurant anyway? Wilma smiles like a mad woman the entire way there.

I hate my life, thinks Kim Yong Lee as Wilma leads him by the hand through the church's double doors and puts him right beside her in one of the pews. Together they sit facing what had once been the fast food restaurant's order counter, with what had once been the big lit-up menu behind it, now replaced with transparencies of Jesus Christ that Kim Yong Lee himself had drawn. All he knows for certain is that he has to find some way out of this.

*   *   *

I had seen Christ the Crowned King before. It was just down Market Street about halfway between the Clubhouse and Johnny Teagle's HyperMart. It used to be a Red Barn burger restaurant before they all went out of business. Their buildings were all shaped like barns. You still saw them all over Ohio, now transformed into used clothes shops or offices or Chinese restaurants.

When I arrived, disheveled and out of breath, just in time for the Monday service, I started looking around for my contacts. About thirty worshipers were stuffed into four rows of worn-out pews, awkwardly crammed into what had once been the Red Barn's dining area. The pulpit stood where the order counter had been. Above and behind the pulpit the old menu sign had been replaced with plastic panels depicting weirdly psychedelic scenes from the life of Christ, illuminated by fluorescent lights from behind. The pictures could have come straight out of some deranged Japanese manga version of the Bible. I'll have a crucifixion with a side of fries and a strawberry shake, please.

I found Wilma and Kim Yong Lee sitting on a pew near the front. They seemed surprised that I had come. This let me know immediately that we were being observed and that the rest of the parishioners were not to be trusted. There would have been no need for them to continue the act in here if it were a safe place.

"I'm so glad you could make it today," Wilma said, beaming a very passable imitation of a pure and warm smile up at me.

"I got your message and I decided I'd better show up to get the rest of the story," I said, hoping that might let her know I was in on the game.

Maybe I shouldn't have been quite so obvious, because she pretended to be puzzled by that statement for a moment. Then she smiled again and said, "It's a glorious story, too. About the salvation of all mankind by a single great sacrifice."

That was all I needed to hear. There was no doubt about it, these two knew what was going on and were prepared to take a stand against the alien menace. "I'm looking forward to hearing it," I said with a wink as I squeezed in beside her.

"Must forgive my lack of memory, sir," her Asian partner leaned around her and said with a heavy accent - obviously a put-on as part of his clever disguise. "Please restate your name."

My name? Surely he knew my name. They must have been scouting me for a long time before they decided to make contact. I was thrown for a minute. Possibly this was some kind of test. Maybe I was being recorded and they would match my statement of my own name with known recorded samples of my voice.

"You're Mr. Noftsinger. Isn't that right?" Wilma said with a slight look of chastisement at her partner.

Noftsinger again. There had to be some reason. "Nof-*ziger*," I said, emphasizing the last two syllables.

"Oh that's right," Wilma said with a chuckle. "I'm so sorry. My orthodontist when I was a kid was named Noftsinger."

At this point I wasn't sure what they were trying to convey. It had to be something important, but I just wasn't getting it. An orthodontist named Noftsinger? Then I realized that the Asian guy was wearing braces. He had to be at least 25 or 30, too old for braces. She must have been trying to clue me in on something about the braces.

"I see," said the Asian guy. "Noftsinger is same man who is now in process of straightening said teeth." He pointed at his braces. I was right! The braces could have hidden some kind of recording and transmission device. Perhaps whatever I said was being transmitted to this Noftsinger fellow right now. Maybe Noftsinger was the head of the whole operation.

"It's very nice to be here at Christ the Crowned King," I said, being careful to speak up and to enunciate very clearly.

"Crown-*ed* King, Mr. Nofziger," Wilma said. "Not Crown'd King but Crown-*ed* King."

"I see," I said. But I didn't. Obviously this was yet another coded clue. But they were way over my head at this point and I couldn't follow.

"By the way," said Wilma, "the reverend really liked your video. I think he wants to talk to you about it."

Before I could reply, a lady up near the front began to play "Amazing Grace" on a Farfisa Combo Organ through an old Leslie speaker cabinet, the overheated amplifier's vacuum tubes lending a distorted edge to the swirling reedy sound. It sounded like something by The Doors or Iron Butterfly or some other organ-driven band from the psychedelic sixties. The lights dimmed in the pews section. A spotlight came on over the pulpit and a man stepped into the pool of light. I gasped.

The preacher was the legendary Ben I. Goldman himself.

*   *   *

Joe Nofziger's sister Lori is surprised to find that her son Danny and her daughter Skylar both really like Goofy Feet* cereal. Danny is especially impressed by the toy prizes inside, having ripped open all three boxes Lori brought home from Johnny Teagle's HyperMart in order to get at them. Ever since he got the things he's been going on and on about "Dogs on TV." It's like an obsession. Lori's brother used to go through obsessive phases like that when he was a kid, so maybe it's normal. Then again no-one would ever call Joe normal.

Danny now has a collection of Dogs On TV, one blue, one white and one mauve. Lori nearly steps on the mauve one when she walks into the tangled jungle that is Danny's room. Curious, she picks it up and looks through the little lens in the back. In one frame there's a picture of a Great Dane wearing a policeman's hat. She clicks the button on top and there's a photo of an English sheepdog wearing one of those powdered wigs like a British magistrate. Cute. She picks up the blue one next and sees that the pictures are in a different sequence and that there are a few dogs in the blue one that aren't in the mauve one. She checks out the white one next. That one too is a little different from the others.

There must be other dogs I haven't even seen yet, she thinks, I wonder how many colors of TV sets there are in all. Immediately she grabs her car keys off the kitchen counter and heads out the door on her way back to Johnny Teagle's HyperMart.

Collect them all, she thinks, *collect them all, collect them all...*

*   *   *

There was no mistaking it. I'd seen pictures of the famed director on location during the filming of *Gill Women of the Prehistoric Planet.* Thirty years had passed and he had changed: lost his hair, grown a beard, gained some pounds. But there was no doubt it was the legendary Ben I. Goldman.

"It's always delightful to see a healthy crowd here on a Monday evening," he began. "It is especially gratifying to see so many newcomers.

Welcome to Christ the Crown-*ed* King. May the blessings of the Lord be upon each and every one of you." He raised his open palms to bless the crowd in what even I recognized as a Jewish, not a Christian gesture. I suppose the people here would never have spotted such a thing.

The resistance was now being led by Ben I. Goldman, it seemed. Of course, it made perfect sense. Why hadn't I worked it out before?

I turned to Wilma and whispered, "What is the preacher's name?"

"That's Reverend Goodman," she said. "He's a very deep and spiritual man."

Goodman? Of course, he couldn't call himself Goldman if he were trying to pose as a reverend.

At that point one of the worshipers on the other side of the room stood and started babbling nonsense syllables. Wilma elbowed me and whispered, "He's speaking in tongues. Spontaneously witnessing for the Lord in a language he doesn't know. That's the glory and wonder of God's grace."

Whatever language he was speaking it was one which used only the letters B, L and A. All I could make out was a stream of something that sounded like "Baba-la, ba blabab ab bala blaba."

When he was finished someone behind him stood and said, "Go beyond language. Go beyond thought. For therein only dwells the Truth."

"That's the translation," Wilma whispered. "One person spontaneously speaks and the other spontaneously understands. It's so full of glory."

It was all happening too fast. I was not getting it. Something was being conveyed to me, but it just wasn't getting through. I followed the sermon as closely as possible, but I couldn't find any particularly relevant messages. As far as I could tell the theme was something about how God commands us to see beyond form and emptiness to the ground of all being and non-being. Whatever that meant! I never really did get Christianity. Perhaps a public place was not the proper forum to deliver the true message against the alien oppression. Or perhaps the code being used was too clever for me to penetrate. I would have to wait.

After the sermon was over I filed out with the rest of the congregation around what had once been the salad bar, but was now a baptismal font. Ben I. Goldman, in disguise as Reverend Goodman, stood at the door chatting with each of the parishioners as they left, bowing Oriental-style to them rather than shaking hands. When it came my turn I said, "I really enjoyed your sermon."

"It's your first time here, isn't it?" Ben replied.

I wasn't sure what he was driving at so I simply said, "Yes, it is."

Wilma, who stood behind me, said, "This is Mr. Nofziger. Reverend Goodman is interested in making films, Mr. Nofziger, just like you." She was pronouncing my name correctly now. Was that another signal?

Wait. She said I was interested in making films. There was the pivotal clue, smacking me right in the face like a three-day-old fish. "So you're the film maker?" said "Reverend Goodman."

"Yes. Well, um, that is..." I had to be very careful and play the game just right or I might end up blowing the whole thing right in front of the line of overstuffed Christians waiting behind me. "I make, kind of, amateur films. Mostly videos. I've done lots of work with local bands."

"Really?" he said, a cryptic gleam in his eye. "I have an idea you might be interested in, it's sort of a Christian science fiction film."

That was all I needed to hear. I smiled and said, "Yes, let's talk about that." I gave him a broad wink. He pretended to be puzzled by that.

Wilma said to the reverend, "We'll show Mr. Nofziger around the place." Then she turned to me and said, "We can come back when the reverend is a little less busy." We bowed together and went outside.

She showed me around the empty back of the church where teenagers had once deep-fried potatoes and chicken nuggets for the poor and hungry of Akron. Churches always gave me the chills. It was like antiseptic minds were at work in them. Like there was a big stink somewhere and they were spraying on as much Lysol as possible to cover it, but you could still smell the stink underneath.

Wilma and her Asian friend, who I learned was named Kim Yong Lee, led me around to the back of the building. I seemed to recall the name Kim Yong Lee from somewhere, maybe from one of those Korean martial arts movies Mark always got in at the video store. Could he be one of those actors, slumming in Akron, Ohio, waiting for his big break in America?

I was ushered in to Ben I. Goldman's, i.e. Reverend Goodman's, little office behind the pulpit. It had probably once been the manager's office when the place was a Red Barn. Wilma closed the door behind me. The office had a small banged-up wooden desk at which Goldman sat. The rest of the space was crammed full of outdated film-editing equipment. Goldman didn't waste any time on pleasantries: as soon as I sat down in the folding chair in front of his desk he got straight to the point.

"My film will be called *Jesus vs. Mecha Jesus*," he said. "Just imagine it. A 200-foot tall mechanical Jesus Christ stomping through downtown Akron. He pulverizes the EJ Thomas Hall with one mighty blow from his titanium alloy fist. He demolishes the Civic Theater with his gigantic chromium-plated boots. He atomizes the entire University of Akron physics building in seconds with a ray beam shot from his eyes. Tanks can't stop Him! Rockets can't stop Him! Even guided missiles cannot slow down this megalithic mastodon of destruction. Who can battle this marauding mechanical menace, this psychopathic savior sent by Satan himself?"

I was on the edge of my folding chair. The great Ben I. Goldman was letting me in on his latest project and it was pure genius. With a grand sweeping gesture Goldman said, "Jesus Christ, the Lord, that's who. Suddenly a gigantic Jesus Christ appears in the center of Canal Park Stadium, brought to life by the prayers of the devoted. He towers over the spectators, as big as a skyscraper. Mecha Jesus turns. The robot smashes his way into the stadium and a mammoth battle - colossus against mighty colossus - breaks out right there in center field. The battle moves outward to a breathtaking climax atop Akron's tallest building, the 21-story WAKR Tower."

Goodman stopped, his eyes twinkling at me. I took a deep breath. "*Jesus vs. Mecha Jesus*," I said.

"Yeah," said Goodman, taking a deep breath and lowering his voice by several decibels. "Just like the Japs do all the time with all their Whozits vs. Mecha Whozits movies. I watched a whole marathon of those stupid things one day on cable TV. They even had a robot King Kong in one of them. Anyway, I figured what a great way to take the Book of Revelation and put it into a form that'll grab people by the throat and never let 'em go. This idea's got blockbuster written all over it, kiddo. Believe you me. There's no way this one can fail. Every other religious film is just a boring piece of white bread crap. Nobody but converts and Jesus groupies like Wilma and her crew will even look at them. But not this baby. No way."

"Amazing," I said. At that moment there was no doubt. This was him. This was the mysterious Ben I. Goldman, director of *Gill Women of the Prehistoric Planet*. I was in the presence of one of the true giants of modern cinema.

"I saw your special effects stuff," Goodman said. "The giant iguana thing. I believe if you had a real budget to work with you could do something truly wonderful. We'll make it just like one of those Jap pictures. Rubber costumes, balsa wood buildings. I think you're the man for the job. What do you say?"

What could I say? I took the job.

*　　*　　*

"Come on, Mr. Walters, we are not so stupid," says Milena, the co-inventor and patent holder of the Dogs On TV toy. She crosses her long shapely legs and notices the supermarket manager trying to take a peek at her panties under her black patent leather miniskirt during the moment her legs part. Blurry photos of the window display advertising "Goffy Foot™ with Dogs On TV now availible in specially marked boxes" are spread out across Carl's cheap prefabricated desk next to the cross-promotion contract she and Ljes have drafted.

"You make a lots of money from our Dogs On TV." Ljes, perched beside her on one of two shoddy vinyl-covered chairs in the dingy little office, concurs. He can barely fit his muscular frame in such a chair, his barrel chest is barely contained within his blue suit. Milena finds this exciting.

"Look," says Carl, shifting distractedly in his seat, adjusting his silly-looking striped tie. "I have no idea what you are going on about. I bought the cereal from American Mills. Those toys of yours were already inside. It's my prerogative how I want to advertise it."

"You are trading on the goodwill engendered by Dogs On TV to bring customers into your store," says Milena pronouncing the word "engendered" in four syllables. "This is a clear example of using a licensed product for cross-promotion purposes." She smiles at her own cleverness.

"Let me get this straight," says Carl. "I advertise your product with a lousy hand-drawn poster in my window and now you're asking me to sign a contract and pay you a 20% royalty? On everything I sell in the store?"

"That is exactly what we are asking," says Ljes. They have got the supermarket manager over the barrels now.

"You're crazy," Carl replies. "I deal with some of the biggest distributors in the United States. Nobody has ever asked me to pay a royalty on advertising. My god, they *pay me* to place their products in our display ads and TV commercials. They *pay me* to put their stuff on certain shelves or near the check-out counter. I'm the one who should be asking for money, not you. How long have you been in this business anyway?"

"Dogs On TV is a premium item," Milena says, dismissing his nonsensical arguments with a wave of her hand. "Dogs On TV is bigger than anything you have got in this store of yours."

"Premium item my ass," says Carl. "I'll tell you what I'm going to do. I'm going to tear down that stupid poster and take all references to Dogs On TV out of my advertising. Let's see how your premium item does then." Carl stands, walks to the door, opens it and waits there.

Milena and Ljes get up and walk to the door. "We have the evidence," Milena says, gathering up her photos of the window display and waving them in his face. "You have not heard the end of this."

"Not the end of this," says Ljes. Together they stomp out of the supermarket manager's pathetic little office, heads held high.

*   *   *

Nicole arrives at Soon Park's house on Burlingame Avenue for her weekly Tae Kwon Do lesson. Tiny jackhammers batter away at the insides of her skull. Nuclear war, she thinks, maybe they'll declare nuclear war today. That would at least get things over with quickly. Or maybe religious fanatics will drop canisters of nerve gas from the sky. She scans the sky. No such luck. It's just a rare sunny day in Akron with no religious fanatics in sight. She's going to have to live through it, apparently.

The door is blurry. She rings the bell. Soon Park grunts at her obvious condition but lets her in anyway.

After Nicole runs through a few Tae Kwon Do routines, some basic kicks and punches, Soon Park comments that she seems distracted. Nicole collapses onto the couch and sobs uncontrollably. Nicole knows Soon Park almost never accepts women as students. He's probably even more regretful than usual for breaking that rule, she thinks. And this makes her cry even harder.

Rocking on the couch, her legs folded in front of her, Nicole is just about to tell Soon Park all about Charmaine and what happened last night. She's not sure how they feel about homosexuality in Korea. She's heard that Oriental cultures are more open to it. She read once somewhere that they don't have the concept of a sexual sin over there. Anyhow, she figures, Soon has suffered enough intolerance as a minority member and should be able to relate.

The doorbell rings. "Hold on a moment," says Soon Park and goes over to get the door.

*   *   *

It's so wonderful to bring the word of the Lord to people, thinks Wilma Fierson as she takes Kim Yong Lee by the hand and leads him out to do a little bit of witnessing on a rare sunny afternoon in Akron.

"This looks like a nice place," says Wilma as they step up onto the porch of a cozy little brick house just off of Burlingame Avenue. "The sign on the door says 'Mr. S. Park.' Can you read that, Kim Yong? Park is a British name. Mr. Park's family must have come to America a long time ago to escape the religious intolerance of Great Britain. Did you know that in Britain the government tells you what religion to believe in? They don't have freedom there like we do in America. They believe their Queen is given power by God. They even believed Princess Diana was given power by God. Isn't that so silly? Princess Diana never rose from the dead! See?" She points to the nameplate on the mailbox at the end of the walkway to the house, "P-A-R-K, that spells Park."

*   *   *

Of course I know how to read your language, thinks Kim Yong Lee, as he walks up yet another lousy concrete path set into another obscenely wasteful front yard. I was forced to learn it when I was a little kid. You probably wouldn't even recognize the Korean language if you saw it. Of course he doesn't have enough vocabulary in English to express any of this properly, and anyway he's too angry to try.

Americans, he grumbles silently to himself. They really do think they own the whole world, these morons. If only everybody everywhere could learn to think and act like them, then everything would be just perfect. That's what they really believe. You could see it in their beady little blue eyes. The more Americans he saw, the more he hated the entire species.

And all that Christian nonsense they swallowed. Although his own countrymen were just as caught up in it as the Americans were. It was like the whole nation - both nations - were hypnotized by some make-believe dream of a paradise after they died, because the way they lived was so lousy. All this in spite of the fact that Americans, and most South Koreans too, for that matter, had pretty much everything money could buy.

But it wasn't just the lousiness of Americans that was making him mad, and he knew it. He had allowed himself to get suckered into this position. His own stupidity and ambition had brought him here. If you're going to be ambitious, he thought to himself, at least you have to be smart about it. He had believed getting to America was enough, that once he was anywhere in the country he would be free to move about as he pleased. But it was turning out to be a lot more difficult than he had ever expected.

This thought just made him angrier. Angry at America, angry at Christianity, angry at the ridiculous fat woman who insisted on being with him at all times wherever he went. Only one thing could possibly have made Kim Yong Lee any angrier, and that would be the presence of his most hated nemesis, Soon Park.

* * *

When I got back home I found a note from Steve thumbtacked among the flyers on my door, saying I should call Charmaine. I tried calling Nicole's place since that's where she was living now as far as I knew, but nobody was home. As soon as I put the phone down again, it rang. "Where *were* you?" Charmaine said as soon as I said hello.

"Where were *you*?" I asked.

"Whatever," she said. "I'll be there in ten minutes."

I sat in the Kitchen of the Forever Damned, waiting for Charmaine to show up. Had someone rearranged the Star Trek Colorforms stuck to the Atomic War Board Game box on top of Steve's Shelf of the Weird? I tried to discern a pattern. The rubber iguanodon skeleton was pointed at an odd angle relative to the King Kong model. Why? The doorbell rang.

I stepped over all the stuff in the Living Room and opened the door. "Do you want to come in?" I asked.

Charmaine laughed. "I don't think I'm welcome at The Clubhouse.""Nobody else is here," I said. But I knew she wouldn't come in. The rumor that Charmaine had slept with everyone who lived in the Clubhouse was something Charmaine herself had gone to great lengths to propagate. It wasn't entirely true, but there wasn't much about Charmaine that wasn't an exaggeration. Still, Charmaine acted like the house itself was tainted, so I went outside onto the porch. "We can take a walk," I said.

We walked around the block, in the direction of Christ the Crowned King, where I intended to introduce her to Ben I. Goldman, though I did not mention we were going to a church. She doesn't like churches.

Whatever she wanted to talk to me about, she wasn't saying it. We just walked in silence. Just before we got there I told Charmaine that I wanted to introduce her to the Reverend Goodman who in reality was Ben I. Goldman, the famed director of *Gill Women of the Prehistoric Planet,* one of the great lost classics of science fiction cinema. She sighed deeply, but said nothing.

We were greeted at the back door by two men who appeared to be in their forties. One was a chubby guy in a T-shirt and jeans with a bushy mustache, the other wore a blue suit with a yellow and orange tie, his black hair plastered back against his head. "Is Reverend Goodman around?" I could feel Charmaine's cold stare.

"Oh yes," the man with the mustache said, "Please come in." He opened the door. "It's nice of you to come here," he said as he led us inside.

"My name's Joe Nofziger. I'm a friend of Reverend Goodman. This is my friend Charmaine Poole."

"Oh yes," he said. "He mentioned you might stop by. I'll go and get him. You wait here, all right?"

Charmaine and I sat on one of the pews in the empty church for a while, not speaking. Charmaine seemed surprisingly unwilling to talk, in spite of having called this meeting herself. She was so antsy I figured she might bolt out the door at any moment. Presently the reverend arrived, carrying his portly form with the ease of a much younger and lighter man. "Hello, Joe," he said. "I'm glad you stopped by."

"Thank you, Reverend," I said, standing and shaking his hand. "This is my friend Charmaine."

"Nice to meet you," the reverend said, shaking her hand. "My name's Ben Goodman."

Charmaine stood and shook his hand, but said nothing. The reverend shrugged and said, "Have a seat. So what's up?"

"I've been thinking about that movie we talked about," I said. "Would you mind telling Charmaine a little bit about it?"

The reverend smiled and said, "*Jesus...*" he paused for effect then said, "*Versus Mecha Jesus.*"

After hearing the outline of the plot Charmaine said, "You have to be kidding."

"Never more serious in my life," said Reverend Goodman.

"Why would a mad scientist build a 200-foot tall mechanical look-alike of Jesus Christ?" Charmaine asked, suddenly talkative again. "What's the point?"

"He's not just any old mad scientist," Reverend Goodman said. "He's the Anti-Christ!"

"Good lord," said Charmaine.

"It's brilliant," I said. "Don't you think that's just pure genius?"

"And looking at you gives me further inspiration," said the reverend. "How would you like to play the role of Mary Magdalene? A beautiful Nubian Mary Magdalene. It would be incredible."

"A black Mary Magdalene? And a white Jesus Christ, I'm sure." Goldman nodded. "This is deranged," Charmaine said and abruptly leaped out of the pew and headed for the door.

"Excuse me," I said to the reverend and went chasing down the street after her.

"He's nuts," Charmaine said, marching along the sidewalk in huge agitated strides.

"He's not nuts," I said, running to keep up with her. "He's an original. The man is a cinematic genius."

"Right," she replied without looking at me. "Anyway, someone like you should be an expert on crazy."

We continued down the weedy sidewalks of East Cuyahoga Falls Avenue without speaking. When we got to the corner of Burlingame, Charmaine suddenly stopped and turned. "I'm sorry. It's just too weird."

A couple of white guys in a pick-up truck honked as they drove past us and shouted something with the word "nigger" in it. I flinched, then went on. "That was him. I'm certain of it. Reverend Goodman is actually Ben I. Goldman, director of *Gill Women of the Prehistoric Planet*. He is the key to ridding the world of the domination it suffers under."

Charmaine sighed. "Listen, Joe, you know what I think of all that already. There's no point in going over it anymore." She looked me in the eye and said, "Look. I care about you, I really do. You're a terrific person when you're not being bat-shit crazy. I know I can be a little crazy-pants myself, but at least I don't think aliens control the world."

"You're involved in this too," I said.

She smiled at me, probably the first time she'd smiled at me since we split up. "Because I know too much?" I nodded. She sighed. We kept walking towards my place. There was some kind of a fight going on about a block away, crazy people screaming in some foreign language. I picked up the pace. Charmaine rolled her eyes at me, like I was being paranoid or something. Crazy foreign people fighting and I'm paranoid. Right.

"Here's what I came to tell you," Charmaine said without stopping or turning to me, "I'm staying at the Clubhouse tonight." I couldn't reply so I didn't. "I'd stay just about anywhere else, but I can't go back to Nicole's and I'm not going to stay with my parents, they don't approve of me. I'd try someone else, but I don't need anyone to know what's going on. As nuts as you are, Joe, you're my best hope." She turned and flashed me a strange smile, then went back to looking straight ahead.

"What's Nicole going to think?" I asked, not looking back at the crazy people shouting. I hoped they weren't the same guys from the truck, now coming after us to beat the shit out of the "nigger lover" and rape Charmaine afterwards.

"I don't care. She doesn't own me," she said, "no-one owns me."

*   *   *

"Bastard!" shouts Soon Park in Korean as he throws open the door and leaps at Kim Yong Lee. "I will kill you! I will tear your heart out of your chest!"

*   *   *

Wilma gasps as an Oriental madman leaps out of the door of this cozy-looking little brick house and shouts something in a strange and foreign language. He is attacking Kim Yong!

*   *   *

"It is you who shall die!" shouts Kim Yong Lee in Korean. "You shall get what you deserve and be reborn in the hell of black metal, reserved for the most wicked!" He assumes the sawhorse position, ready for battle.

*   *   *

Nicole dashes to the door to see what's going on. She is shocked to see Soon Park facing an Asian man she has never seen before. From their stance she can tell that neither man intends to let the other walk away from this battle alive.

*   *   *

"Stop this fighting!" shouts Wilma. "In America we do not solve our differences by fighting each other. We resolve matters peacefully in a court of law!" Just then she sees a woman with very short hair emerge from the door. She's white, so maybe it's her whose name is Park. At that moment she realizes what the situation is. And she feels a strange sense of camaraderie with another woman who has found she has a taste for yellow-skinned men.

*   *   *

"Hey!" Nicole shouts. "What's going on with you two? Stop this!"

Startled, Soon Park turns to her. "You never speak to your teacher that way. Do you understand?"

"Then you stop trying to kill people who ring your doorbell!" Momentarily distracted, Soon Park does not see Kim Yong Lee is about to deliver a jump spin heel kick.

But Nicole does. She counters with a powerful front leg sweep, knocking the stranger off balance.

*   *   *

Wilma catches Kim Yong in her arms as he staggers back. "I said stop this you two! Stop it right now!" she shouts. She hopes Kim Yong can feel the way her breasts are rubbing against his firm back.

*   *   *

Kim Yong Lee wrenches himself out of Wilma's grasp. "This is between you and me, Soon Park. This woman is not involved!" he says in Korean, pointing at the woman with the short red hair.

"You can talk about involvement with women," Soon counters, with a nod in Wilma's direction.

*   *   *

Wilma turns to the short-haired woman, Miss Park she assumes, and says, "Do you understand what they're saying, Miss Park?" The short-haired woman shakes her head. Wilma turns back to Kim Yong Lee and the Oriental man who was in Miss Park's house and says, "Listen you two, you are in America now and in America we speak the American language. That is so that all of us can live together in harmony though we are of many different lands. Now speak in American!"

*   *   *

Soon Park spits on the ground. In Korean he says, "Leave this place and take your fat woman with you!"

Kim Yong Lee says, "This is not finished." Then turns and walks away.

*   *   *

"I am so sorry, Miss Park," Wilma says to the short-haired woman on the porch after her Oriental friend stomps back into her house slamming the door behind him. "I really don't understand all of this." She rummages in her purse, pulls out one of the "What Happens When

You Die?" tracts and hands it to her. "Peace be with you," she says, then leads Kim Yong Lee brusquely off the porch. "What do you think you were doing?" she says to him angrily. "This is America! We do not behave this way in America!"

"I killed his wife!" Kim Yong Lee shouts back and storms off.

*   *   *

Miss Park? wonders Nicole. She stuffs the comic in her pocket and follows Soon inside. "What was that all about?" she asks.

"It is not a matter for discussion with outsiders," Soon answers sternly.

He sits down in a chair and stares at the floor.

After a few moments of gloomy silence, Nicole picks up her backpack, quietly leaves the house, gets in her car and drives off.

*   *   *

"Oh god," Charmaine said and turned away from the street, hiding her face with her hand.

"What?" I said. Then I saw her too.

I couldn't tell if Nicole noticed us or not. She drove right past without so much as a glance to acknowledge our presence.

That night Charmaine and I ordered pizza from Rizzi's. As usual it was incredibly greasy and fantastically cheap. There was a call on the Clubhouse answering machine saying that I would not be needed back at Johnny Teagle's HyperMart tomorrow. Big surprise. It also said that Mr. Manning from Vector Temp's Summit County Bureau wanted to speak with me. I suppose it was meant to impress or even scare me. Sorry, Mr. Manning, I thought. Guys like you just don't bother me anymore.

We switched on the TV in the Living Room but hardly paid any attention to it. We talked a little, but strictly about topics of little or no importance. Charmaine didn't bring up seeing Nicole in the street, so neither did I. I could tell that this was not the time for that. Anything I did to try and force any issues would drive her away. We finished off the six-pack of Red White and Blue she'd bought earlier and started on some of Mark and Lesa's beer. Big deal. They'd stolen plenty of mine. When the terrible twosome did show up about nine they just rolled their eyes at the two of us and slinked upstairs to their rooms.

After the Big Chuck and Little John's Midnight Movie was over - the movie was *Gamera vs. Monster X* - I said to her, "I don't know where you plan to sleep tonight..."

"In your room, you idiot," she said, suddenly grabbing me around the arm. She nibbled at my ear and said, "I thought you'd never ask." She was drunk. So was I.

Charmaine knew very well that ear nibbling is my fatal weakness. I took her by the hand and led her up to my room. The Cat With No Name stared up at us as we passed. He knew what a mistake I was making, even if I did not. But he was wrong. I knew exactly what kind of mistake I was making. I just didn't care.

I closed the door and pushed Charmaine down on my futon. I turned off the lights. It was never very dark in my room, even with the skull and crossbones curtains closed, what with Larry and Bob's Chevron station next door and all the streetlights from East Cuyahoga Falls Avenue. I swooped down on top of her and began unbuttoning her shirt. She smiled and giggled. I opened it up and undid the white bra she had on, exposing those magnificent chocolate-brown breasts of hers.

She worked her way out of her jeans. Her legs were like a gazelle's. Long and taut. I ran my tongue down her flat stomach and soon I had those amazing legs wrapped around my neck.

I had to rummage around in the closet for a while before I managed to find the last box of Trojans I'd bought when Charmaine and I had been together. There were three little red envelopes left inside. We fucked. I came much too soon. It had been a long time. If she minded she didn't show it. I decided not to apologize.

As we lay there afterwards staring at the glow-in-the-dark stars and planets I'd gotten from a box of Trix and pasted on my ceiling, Charmaine said, "It's different having a cock inside you. I'd forgotten how good it felt."

Like I really needed to hear this. She rolled over and, resting her hand across my chest, looked in my eyes and said, "Do you mind me talking about this? I can't talk to anyone else about this."

"I don't mind," I lied. She seemed like she really needed to get it out. I suppose I had to be the designated victim.

"I mean, the first time Nicole seduced me, it was like nothing else that had ever happened in my life. It was like she knew exactly where to touch me. My body was completely hers. Her tongue was so soft and so rough on my tits. And god, when she went down on me I couldn't believe it. Her tongue was like a cock. She just drove it right down deep inside me. She licked me everywhere. She licked my asshole even. I would've thought I wouldn't like that, but it sent chills through me. I was shaking."

Her eyes weren't even on me as she spoke. I didn't know how to feel, hearing this. In spite of myself I was getting hard again. "When I went down on her, I thought I wouldn't like licking another woman down there. But her cunt was sweet, I mean really sweet. I don't know why. Maybe it was something she ate. Who knows? The scent was light and it made me high. She bucked her hips against my mouth when she came and she held my head against her. I could feel her coming against my tongue, jerking, like a man. I didn't know women did that." Actually the only woman I'd ever had that particular experience with had been Charmaine, but I didn't think she'd want to hear that.

I was rock hard at this point. And I am not a guy who can usually go two times in one night. In fact I never have before. Charmaine reached down and grabbed my cock, then said, "but there's nothing like a stiff, hard cock inside you." And with that she reached over beside the futon, unwrapped another Trojan, slipped it on, then rolled over on top of me and slid my cock back inside her. This time I did not come too quickly.

*   *   *

Early the next morning Ben I. Goldman sits in the basement of Christ the Crowned King pondering what happened the previous day, tormented by the decision he must make. He wonders if this is a stroke of luck beyond his wildest dreams, or if it's the beginning of the end. Has he found the one man who can help him to finally rip through the veil of secrecy that has shrouded the truth for far too long? The one who can attack the puppet people who pretend to rule over us and expose the real forces behind the scenes? Or is this the start of a chain of events that will destroy him once and for all?

Gill Women of the Prehistoric Planet was a failure. Discovered by the powers that be before its message could be delivered, the film had mysteriously disappeared from every cinema it had been shipped to. Now every last print was gone. And the world had hardly taken notice. To the few people who were even aware of the film's existence its commercial failure and subsequent disappearance seemed like nothing more than what had happened to a hundred other low budget science fiction movies of that era.

But there were a few out there who wondered why this one film, among all the other "cult classics" and "drive-in favorites" that had been revived since the advent of video, was nowhere to be found. They could hardly suspect the real reason. You'd have to be clinically insane to believe that a movie with a title like *Gill Women of the Prehistoric Planet* actually contained secrets that could bring down the entire shadow government that had ruled the whole world for more than a century.

Joe Nofziger, Goldman suspected, knew the truth. But this Joe Nofziger fellow was quite clearly clinically insane.

But there's something Goldman knows that Joe Nofziger does not. Oh, Joe knows who "Revered Goodman" really is. The disguise is not that difficult to penetrate. After all, Goldman himself had designed it this way hoping that one day he would be discovered by someone like Joe Nofziger. He had had no need to hide from the powers that be. They knew precisely where he was at all times. They'd let him live this long, Goldman assumed, because his untimely death would only draw attention to the very thing that could bring them down.

No, this Nofziger fellow didn't have to be smart to figure out who Goldman was. But until Joe Nofziger knew who Joe Nofziger was, Ben

I. Goldman's work could not be completed. This would not be an easy task to accomplish.

*   *   *

Charmaine shook me awake at dawn the next morning. "I'm going home now," she said.

I squinted one eye up at her. She was blurry. Her hair was frizzed out. She looked like a big brown lollipop with an afro. "What time is it?"

"It's six o'clock. I'm going home," she repeated, getting up and pulling on her pants.

I sat up and brought her into focus. She was beautiful when she was disheveled. Her natural scent was enough to drive me to distraction. "You want coffee or something?"

"No," she said sharply and continued dressing. Obviously at this point I was supposed to do or say something specific, and only Charmaine knew what that could possibly be. This is how our entire relationship had worked. It was like a play in which I'd forgotten my lines. Or perhaps I was never even given a script, just thrown onto the stage without even knowing which character I was supposed to be. Maybe I was supposed to get up with her? I decided to try that out. I got up and managed to find a pair of pants to pull on.

That must have been in the script because suddenly she said, very quietly, "I'm sorry."

"Sorry? Don't be sorry. I had a good time."

I knew immediately I'd flubbed my line by the sour expression on her face. "Just don't let's talk about it. OK?"

"OK," I said. Now what?

"I'm going to go now," she said. But she didn't go. I desperately looked offstage for someone to feed me my next piece of dialogue, but there was nobody there.

I tried, "Let's have breakfast somewhere?"

"I'm leaving," she said and walked out the door. What I really need in life is a prompter.

70

*   *   *

Milena shakes Ljes awake in the Anthony Wayne Hotel and shoves the Akron Beacon Journal into his face. His eyes still bleary, Ljes struggles to make out the headline. Milena helps him out by shouting it at the top of her lungs. "Toy Sensation Sweeps Akron!"

Below the headline is a picture of a line of people outside Johnny Teagle's HyperMart in Cuyahoga Falls. And below that is a large photograph of a white Dogs On TV.

"No copyright notice!" Milena shouts at Ljes, her huge breasts straining against the sheer fabric of her nightgown. Ljes rubs his eyes and tries to focus. "No trademark notice! No mention of Dogs On TV Corporation of America! They have misrepresented us by saying one of the photographs shows a poodle in a fireman's outfit, when in actuality it is a sheepdog! They say we are 'unavailable for comment,' an outrageous lie! Are you going to let them get away with this? Are you?"

Ljes bolts up in bed, the rusting springs shrieking in protest. "I shall stand for no more of this!"

"This newspaper company is cheating us out of what is rightfully ours!" says Milena. "They sell their papers on the backs of our difficult labors and give us no compensation!"

"We should ask for 8 percent!" Ljes shouts and leaps out of bed, completely naked, his rippling muscles gleaming in the gray Akron sunshine filtering through the grimy windows of the hotel.

"Fool!" Milena shouts back, pushing his chest. "They have injured us! We shall sue them for damages! Millions and millions of dollars, Ljes, we shall earn!" She looks down to see that his gherkin-sized member is fully erect. She tears off her nightgown, revealing her pendulous, melon-sized breasts and wide accommodating hips. "Make love to me now and then we shall take on these thieves!"

*   *   *

In room 224 of the Anthony Wayne Hotel in downtown Akron, Ohio, Ngugi and Msoto have worked all night to get the Interociter to some semblance of working order. Through a misty haze of static the Controller of Planet X speaks. "Is this thing on now? Have you finally managed to follow the simple instructions I gave you?"

The two men nod in unison. The Interociter coughs and sputters, sparks bursting from its antenna, its aluminum casing visibly overheating, but at least it's working. "Good. As you know - or should I say as you're supposed to know - the Interociter beam, the plasmatic energy wave that carries these transmissions creates temporary convergences between parallel dimensions within ten-dimensional space-time. It must be treated very carefully. Do not bang on it!" Though his eyes are invisible behind the single lens of his wrap-around sunglasses, it is clear that the Controller is looking at Ngugi and Msoto in turn. The two men exchange furtive glances. They have been beating the machine senseless all night. "Now that we understand each other, let me try and explain this to you very, very clearly." The thick green blood vessels in his bulbous brown head pulsate in staccato rhythm.

The image on the Interociter screen wavers slightly, then comes into focus again. "We are trying to invade this planet," says the Controller, light from some unseen source glinting off his single-lensed wrap-around sunglasses. "We want to take it over, enslave its people, plunder its resources, the whole ball of wax. This is not some kind of vacation for you two, some sight-seeing excursion to the wilds of Akron, Ohio to soak up the local color, sample the native cuisine, and check out the ruins along North Main Street. You are here on business! A mission of conquest! Have you ever taken part in a planetary invasion before? Well, have you?"

Ngugi and Msoto shake their heads, eyes cast to the floor.

"Then what makes you think you can devise your own plans for the invasion of this one? Come on, answer me." Ngugi and Msoto do not reply.

There are grunts and groans coming from a couple having sex in the next room. They strain to hear the Controller of Planet X over the noise. The Controller says, "Now, just whose idea was it to dress up like Americans and attack Joe Nofziger on the street? I don't seem to recall that being in the manual we gave you. You were told where he was likely to be and that you were to stop him and question him. Was there some specific reason you chose to interpret that order as 'dress up like bad rap singers, chase the man down and beat him senseless'? Is there a section here on reinterpretation of orders?" He picks up his own copy of *To Serve Man: A Cookbook* and flips through it theatrically. "No, not here. Not in the chapter on methods of subjugation. Not in the chapter on native resources. Is it in the chapter on psychological profiles of the intelligent species. I don't think so..."

"It was the notion of this Masai fool," says Ngugi, pointing at Msoto.

"It most certainly was not," says Msoto. "It was this Kikuyu dog who insisted on buying Nike Air Pumps and who purchased the pair of baggy..."

"Shut up both of you!" says the Controller of Planet X, the veins in his forehead pumping even more forcefully now. "You are neither Masai nor Kikuyu. Both of you were picked for this job because you are of pure Dogon extraction. It is only an accident of fate that over the course of generations your families were displaced. Do you know what it means that you are Dogon people? Come on, speak up!"

Hesitantly Msoto says, "Our ancestors were seeded on this planet hundreds of thousands of years ago by the people of Planet X. We are not native to this world. Our true tribe, the Dogon people, worship the star Zeta Reticuli, annually performing a ritual which depicts the transit of Planet X around its sun to a precision unattainable by a people who never invented a system of complex astronomy."

"And..." says the Controller of Planet X.

After a moment Ngugi picks up where Msoto left off. "We are superior to these Earth beings both mentally and physically." His voice rises at the end as if he is asking a question. He wonders if the Controller can hear all that noise in the background."Supposedly you're superior," says the Controller of Planet X. A large brown cockroach scurries up the wall behind the Interociter and disappears into a hole in the wall near the ceiling. "We have been secretly visiting your planet since the 1940s. However during that time a few accidents have occurred. One of these accidents allowed a very sensitive piece of Planet X-ian technology to fall into the hands of the Earth people. They do not know how to use it. But the object possessed by the man you tried to beat the snot out of the other night could tip the scales. We cannot allow this to happen. Should it happen it has the potential to ruin our entire plan for this world."

The Controller of Planet X pauses, rubbing the veins in his forehead agitatedly, then adjusting the stiff, high collar of his patent leather uniform. "You know, there is a specific setting on the Interociter that can sometimes make it act up. When the orange wire at the back is connected to the blue socket..." Ngugi and Msoto exchange looks. "You did read the instruction manual thoroughly before attempting to assemble the Interociter, didn't you?"

"Oh yes!" says Ngugi.

"Absolutely!" says Msoto.

The walls rattle from a large thump from the room next door and the grunting and groaning abruptly stops.

"Good," says the Controller of Planet X. "It's a very complex piece of machinery. Expensive," says the Controller of Planet X.

"We understand," says Ngugi. Msoto nods. Some flakes of paint from the wall float gently to the ground.

"No more interpreting direct orders on your own?"

"No sir."

"Good. Now carry on. Thaw pap hens," the Controller of Planet X says giving the secret salute, showing the backs of both hands with only the pinkies raised then rapidly turning them around.

"We do hynie," Ngugi and Msoto reply in unison, returning the salute.

*   *   *

Ben I. Goldman tries to calm down Wilma Fierson, who has called him far too early in the morning and is blubbering inarticulately about that Korean guy she got to draw all the comic books for him for free.

There was something about a fight on the street and something about a short-haired woman named Mrs. Park. None of it made much sense. Goldman rubs his eyes. His temples ache from the weight of the prosthesis he has been wearing on his head for the last few hours.

"Kim Yong told me he killed his wife!" Wilma sobs.

"Then you're better off that he's gone," Goldman says distractedly.

"I wanted to find out what had happened. How this had come about. But I drove him away!" she shouts. "I'm wrong, wrong, I'm always wrong. I woke up this morning and went down to his room and he was gone!" She breaks down into sobs and incoherent syllables.

What was the deal with those two anyway? Could the Korean have guessed something about what was actually in those comic books? Could Wilma? No. Put that out of your mind, Goldman says to himself.

As Wilma babbles on, Goldman gets an idea. "You need something to take your mind off of this for a while," he says. "How would you like to help me with a project I'm working on?"

*   *   *

I sat there for a while on the Couch of Doom pondering what had happened with Charmaine. The phone rang. I looked at my watch: ten in the morning. I'd sat there for four hours. I went into the kitchen and picked up the phone. Are we the only people in the world who still have a rotary dial?

"The Reverend Goodman was very enthusiastic about you," the voice on the phone said. It was Wilma, the chubby girl from the church. "He thinks that the church needs more people with artistic talents."

Was this some clandestine way for Goldman to make contact with me? Or maybe Wilma was a double agent, working for Goldman and, at the same time, also working for this mysterious Noftsinger person who everyone kept mistaking me for, not to mention Hoftsinger and Nafzinger. "The reverend wants to make a movie," she said. I knew that, of course, and had assumed she knew that I knew. Maybe she did. Maybe that was part of the code.

"It's an interesting idea," I said. "Let's talk." Why did I say that? I didn't want to talk to anyone right now.

"Oh yes," she replied in a breathy voice. "I'll tell the reverend and we can make an appointment for you to come by his office and speak to him."

At that moment I had a flash of inspiration. If I took advantage of the situation properly I could discover what was really going on. "Yes. Let's do that," I said. "But that's not exactly what I had in mind."

"Oh?"

"What I had in mind was that perhaps you and I could discuss this further before I talk to Reverend Gold...Goodman." There was a pause.

"Well, the next sermon isn't until Sunday morning," she said after a time.

I pressed on with the attack. "I'd rather get together sooner. Could you come over here?"

"C-come over there?" she said.

"Sure," I said. This just might work. "You know where I live. You've been here. Are you very busy?"

"Right now?" There was a tremble in her voice. Good.

"Why not?"

She said she'd be right over. What the hell did I think I was doing?

I went upstairs and put on some decent clothes - the red shirt that Charmaine had once said looked sexy on me, and some tight black jeans. I looked in the mirror and realized immediately that looking in mirrors was not the best thing to do if I wanted to boost my self-confidence. I tried telling myself that maybe some girls liked sallow-faced guys with bags under their eyes. Yeah, right. This whole idea was stupid. I found an old flannel shirt and some Dockers and started taking off the red shirt and black jeans.

The doorbell rang. She was quick. I re-buttoned my shirt and pulled the black jeans back on then sprinted downstairs, narrowly avoiding squashing The Cat With No Name, who nonetheless made no move to get out of the way. Egomaniac.

Wilma stood at the door wearing a white T-shirt with red roses on it and a pair of "stone wash" blue jeans. Do they still make those? If they do, the factory should be shut down forever. "You got here very fast," I said.

"I live nearby," she replied, still catching her breath, "just a few houses away from the church."

"Come in," I said.

Bad idea. Leave her outside, part of me said.

Be quiet, she's already in, the other part replied.

As soon as she stepped through the door her eyes went wide. I could tell she'd never seen a place quite like the Clubhouse before. There was a plastic mannequin in the Living Room with a top hat on its head. There were moldering punk rock flyers all over the walls. There was a big "We're Shooting For Zero Defects" poster on the wall by the stairs - it was a Firestone Rubber safety poster, the joke was that Steve used to be in a band called Zero Defex. There were plastic and Styrofoam heads all over the dining room table. The whole gestalt was having a pronounced and visible psychological effect on her. I figured it would be best to maneuver her into the Kitchen of the Forever Damned, which was the least bizarre room in the house. "Would you like to have a drink or something," I said, leading her towards the back where the kitchen was.

"Have you got Coca-Cola?" Wilma asked.

"I think we've got some Valu-Time Cola. It's pretty much the same, but thirty cents cheaper. Would that be all right?"

"Sure," she said. I sat her down at the table, facing away from Steve's Shelf of the Bizarre. I rummaged through the fridge looking for some cola.

This is a stupid idea, I said to myself. Stop right now. Yet I pressed on.

"Don't Breed They Say Then Scats," Wilma said.

"Huh?"

"The note stuck to the side of the refrigerator. It says, 'Don't Breed They Say Then Scats.'"

"Oh yeah," I said. "It used to say 'Don't Feed The Cats.' One of the guys who used to live here had a cat that had to have special food or something. After he left we kept the sign and started adding on extra letters. It's kind of an in-joke. There used to be a punk band in town called They Say Then. It's not really funny enough to bother explaining. Anyway we're all out of colas, but I found some Golden Seal Ginger Ale." I held up a lime green can for her to see.

"Okay," she said. I went over and put two cans on the table then sat down. "Don't you have any glasses?"

"Sure," I got up again and went to the Cupboard of a Thousand Bloody Nightmares for some glasses. There weren't any, but there were a few coffee cups. I dug around hoping to come up with one that wasn't shaped like an alligator head or a smiley face and didn't have some stupid slogan on it. I especially avoided the set of Barberton High Purple Devils mugs with the face of Satan, or was it Ghoulardi, on the side.

Suddenly I heard Wilma gasp. I looked back to see that she had turned around and was staring at Steve's Shelf of the Bizarre. "Good lord," she said.

I sprinted back to the table, plunked down two Ravenna Fire Dept. coffee mugs in the shape of fireman's hats—the least abnormal things I could find—and poured ginger ale into each one. "That stuff on the shelf belongs to Steve who lives upstairs. He's very interested in, you know, pop culture and kitsch." I could hardly imagine how Steve's collection of old plastic dinosaurs, weird beer cans, bizarre toys and other assorted oddities looked to someone like Wilma.

"Kish?" She said the word as if it were the name of a poisonous snake someone had told her was just about to strike, not taking her eyes off the shelf.

"Kitsch," I said. "Camp. Stuff that's so bad it's good, so out it's in."

"I see," she said, calming a little. "Is that King Kong up on top?"

"The very one," I said. "An Aurora plastic model from the mid-sixties. They don't make those anymore. See the head and hands, and the girl he's holding? They glow in the dark."

"Ugh," she said.

"Here, have some ginger ale."

She drank a little, turning away from the shelf, which relieved me greatly. "A very unusual place," she said. "But I suppose that's the way you creative types like to have it. You don't want to live in a place that's just like everyone else's."

"I guess so," I said. I'd never really thought about it.

"I know! You're a slacker, aren't you?" she said, like she'd just figured out some great deep mystery. "I read an article about slackers in Newsweek."

"Don't ever call me that," I said to Wilma bitterly. "The term 'slacker' implies that people like me live this way by choice. As if 12 years of Republican despotism permanently disabling the economy and making it impossible for anyone to get a decent job has nothing to do with it. Like anybody would want to do temp work and live in a rat's nest just because they thought it was cool. As if the fact that even if you get a job with a real company, they write up the paperwork to make it seem like you're not a full-time worker even if you slave away at the place 40 hours a week for ten fu--," I caught myself short. Obscenity is a sin, I think. "For ten gosh-darned years, has nothing whatsoever to do with anything. 'Slackers.' Ha!"

"You don't like it here?" she said.

It was at that point I heard someone moving around upstairs. Steve, maybe. I never knew when that guy was home and when he wasn't since he lived up in the attic and never opened his door. I'd forgotten about the hole in the kitchen ceiling where you could see up into the bathroom. "Let's go to the other room," I said, standing up suddenly. "There's an eight-track player in there. We can listen to some music." I took her by one fleshy arm and led her into the Living Room.

I sat Wilma down on the Couch of Doom and said, "I'll get a tape. Just wait here a minute." I sprinted upstairs, again avoiding The Cat With No Name, who at least made the effort to acknowledge my presence this time by staring at me like I was a complete and utter idiot. Condescending bastard.

I went through my eight-track tape collection looking for something suitable. The KISS albums were no good, neither was Alfred Hitchcock's *Music to be Murdered by,* and anything from my George Harrison collection was risky, since he might start singing about Krishna at any given moment. There were a bunch of old "Trucker's Music" tapes which I'd never listened to. Iffy. The Beatles might have been okay, but then again church people burn Beatles albums I think. Or was that just Rolling Stones albums? Finally I grabbed an Esquivel tape, *Other Worlds Other Sounds* in quadraphonic sound. That would do. I ran back downstairs. The Cat With No Name had apparently gotten fed up with being leaped over and had gone somewhere else.

When I got back to the living room, Wilma was gone. "Wilma?" I said. "Are you still around?"

"Over here," I heard her voice from outside the kitchen door.

I found her back by the garage cleaning out the litter box. "I couldn't stand the smell. It looks like this box hasn't been cleaned out in months. Don't you know your cat could get sick? Not to mention the people in the house."

"It's not my cat." She glared at me and went on scraping the gunk off the sides with the plastic scooper thing and shaking the stuff out on a dead patch on the Lawn That Will Live in Infamy. Actually the Lawn That Will Live in Infamy was mostly dead patches and over-grown weeds strewn with beer cans, cigarette butts and the remains of plastic models blown up with firecrackers.

"Do you have any more Kitty Litter? I want to refill this."

"I think we do. Somewhere," I said and went back into the Terrifying Garage. There was a big bag of potting soil in the back. "Will this do?" I said, presenting it to her.

She sighed. "I guess so. But you're going to have to go out and get some real Kitty Litter right away. Tomorrow. Promise?"

"I promise." She smiled at me and poured the potting soil into the litter box. She was pretty when she smiled. Tubby, but somehow pretty. Underneath that layer of chubbiness was a cute blonde with a sweet smile. I felt terrible about what I needed to do, yet at the same time, not so bad since at least she was kind of cute in her own way.

"There. That's much better," she said and went back to the Living Room and put the litter box back. "I found some Lysol under the sink. The can was half empty, but I managed to cover up the smell a little bit."

"It is better now," I said. And it was better. Lysol-y, but better. She went off to the kitchen and washed her hands, then shouted at me to wash my hands too, since I'd touched the litter box. So I did. After that we both went back and sat down on the couch.

"All right," she said. "Now let's listen to some music."

I put on the Esquivel tape. It wasn't too wobbly. But since the Stereo That Can Never Die isn't set up for quad sound some of the instruments tended to disappear from the mix occasionally. Wilma didn't seem to notice. "Did you watch any of that video I gave to the reverend?" She nodded. "What did you think?" I asked.

"Interesting," she replied.

"Not really Christian stuff, huh?" I said.

"Well, not really. But that's not bad. See, Reverend Goodman doesn't want to make a regular Christian movie, all clean and pretty and sanitized. He wants to do a movie that will attract a larger audience with the Christian themes embedded into it. In fact, he's interested in science fiction, a lot like you."

Of course he is, I thought. She seemed not to know about Goldman's conversation with me on the subject. Or was that a put on, too? Suddenly she said, "I'd better be going."

"Going?" I said. Think fast. Something clever. "I have some more ginger ale."

"I really have to go," she said, starting to rise.

I grabbed her by the shoulder. "Stay," I said looking her in the eyes.

The look Wilma gave me back was almost fearful. She sat back down and stared at me, silently, her eyes darting back and forth between mine. What next? A sudden impulse. I took her in my arms and kissed her.

Stop this. Stupid move. Stupid move. Danger. Danger. Alert. Alert!

She resisted for a moment, then began aggressively kissing back, her tongue plunging deep into my mouth. What the hell was I doing? Information, I answered myself, trying to get information.

She dug her nails into my back, right through the sexy red shirt. I tried to pull away, but she wouldn't let me go. Her small breasts crushed up against my chest, her paunch, nearly as large as her tits, undulated against my stomach.

She suddenly broke loose, looked away and said, "This is wrong."

"Well, I..." I said. But I was cut off when she grabbed the back of my head and pulled me into another deep kiss. This wasn't working out quite the way I'd had in mind.

We kissed for a long time until I finally broke away. When I looked down she had her blouse unbuttoned all the way down. Don't ask me when she had time to unbutton it. I don't know. Physical impossibility. Does not compute.

She reached between her breasts and unhooked her bra. Her tits were like little round scoops of vanilla with cherries on top. Very pale cherries. She caught my eye when I looked up from her chest and grabbed me again, pulling me close and thrusting her tongue down halfway into my lungs.

I broke off again. "Wilma, I think we'd better go upstairs. There's no telling when someone might walk in."

"I thought you'd never ask," she said, and got up, pulling me up by the arm after her. When we got to the landing she said, "Which room is yours?"

"The one with the Ultra Man poster on the door."

"Ultra Man? What's that? Is it the one at the back with the guy in the silver alien outfit standing in the middle of the toy city?"

"Ultra Man is a cultural icon throughout Asia. He's like Mickey Mouse or something over there. Ultra Man is a very important pop culture..." She had already pushed her way through the door and gone on inside. I shut up and followed.

When I got inside my room Wilma was pushing all the stuff off the top of the futon and onto the floor, absolutely destroying my entire organizational structure. "Hey stop that!" I said, grabbing the last few eight-track tapes and magazines and stacking them in their proper places.

"What? All you did was exactly what I did; take the stuff off the mattress and stick it on the floor."

"No," I corrected her sternly. "I have a system." I started trying to rearrange things a little when she pulled me onto the futon.

"Come here, you," she said, pulling me towards her face. "You're so bohemian, sleeping on a mattress on the floor." By this time she'd dropped her blouse on the floor and was undoing her pants as she kissed me hard on the mouth, and then started hammering her tongue into my ear. In spite of myself I was starting to get a hard-on. She was grabbing at my pants trying to find the fastener when I pushed her away.

I looked down and saw her lying there in just her underpants. They were baby blue with little cartoon Hello Kitties all over them. Not the small kind of panties most girls wear, but big. The kind of underwear your grandma probably wears. Lying down on her back her paunch wasn't so apparent. I reached up and switched off the light.

Discontinue mission. Abort. Abort.

I straddled her, my dick straining against my pants.

I took a deep breath, then said, "Thaw pap hens. We do hynie."

"What?" she said, rubbing my hard-on through my pants with one hand and trying to get the zipper down with the other.

I pushed her hands away. "You heard me. Thaw pap hens. We do hynie."

"Come on, Joe. I'm ready for you. Feel how wet I am." She grabbed my hand and drew it to the spot between her legs. She wasn't just wet, she was soaking.

I pulled my hand away and said, "The wops new pad. Ah yuie."

"I don't understand you." She sounded distressed. My dick got even harder.

"Wahpeshnode! Who is Noftsinger?"

"Nofziger? You're Nofziger. Come on," she whispered, "Let's *fuck*." She giggled at the sound of her own voice pronouncing such a forbidden word.

"There was a message in that tract you gave me. The comic book thing," I said.

"Of course there was a message in it, silly."

She admitted it. I had her now! Then I realized she might just be being cagey with me. Of course there was a message, "All men are brothers" or some such nonsense. "I mean there was a message. A secret hidden message aimed directly at me." I disentangled myself from her and went rummaging through the piles of crap on my floor until I found the little comic book, "What Happens When You Die?" I shoved it in her face. "See? There? Hidden in the letters of the title is the secret message 'Thaw pap hens. We do hynie.' Admit it! Confess!" As I shouted at her I could feel my dick straining so hard I had to pull down my pants just to give it some room. I looked down and Wilma was crying.

"You're scaring me. What do you want?" she said.

At that moment my fully erect dick popped out of my underwear. "This is what I want!" I shouted and threw the comic aside. I ripped off her big blue Hello Kitty panties in a single swift motion, spread her cellulite-encrusted thighs apart, briefly faltered for a moment to dig the last condom I owned out from inside my pillow (the emergency spare) and pull it on, then I slammed my dick into her hard.

Within seconds she had reversed our positions and was on top of me riding my prick like a Merry-Go-Round horse. I had never been ridden so hard in my life. I thought she was going to break my penis right in half. The whole time I kept hearing this weird buzzing noise at regular intervals. I wasn't sure if she had gas or what. She came mightily within minutes, grabbing at my chest with every jerk of her heavy pelvis. I shot my load and we collapsed on the futon.

"That was so wicked," Wilma said after a time. "Wicked and bad and sinful." She said it with relish, but then her tone changed. "I'm so evil. I'm weak. The flesh is weak. I've done wrong. Oh God. Oh please forgive me my sins."

This was just what I needed. She got up and started looking around for her clothes. "Thaw pap hens," I said weakly. "We do hynie."

"Oh shut up and help me find my bra will you?" she said. "The sins of the flesh. The weak and vulnerable flesh."

I got up, pulled my pants back up and helped her look. Downstairs the doorbell buzzed. I then realized it had been buzzing for some time. That was the noise I had heard. "Wait up here. I have to go and get the door."

I went downstairs, pulling on my sexy red shirt inside out as I did. I opened the door. Charmaine stood there, her eyes red. "What took you so long?" she sobbed, pushing her way inside.

"I was...I, uh, didn't hear the door," I said.

She plopped herself down on the Couch of Doom. "Nicole and I had a fight. I can't go back there. Maybe not ever. I need a place to stay."

Oh shit.

*   *   *

The line outside of Johnny Teagle's HyperMart stretches out into the Giraffe Section of the parking lot. Each section is named after a different animal. This is something that previously struck Lori Nofziger-Feinman as ridiculous. Now it seems heartwarming. Everything seems heartwarming today. The giraffe section is way at the back, far from the store.

Dogs On TV have become trendy, she laments. It was that story on WAKR that did it. None other than Cleveland's famed weatherman, Dick Goddard, came all the way down to Akron to file a special report about how the toys were sweeping the city. The phenomenon was unprecedented, he said, and no-one could understand just what the appeal of the little toys was.

Well, of course outsiders couldn't understand. You had to be a true fan to appreciate the nuances of Dogs On TV. Looking at the crowd in front of her Lori thinks she should be depressed. But instead she feels elated. There are so many of us, she says to herself, we are strong, we are one.

Then she counts the number of people ahead of her and estimates that if each of them buys only ten boxes of Goofy Feet', the entire shipment of 500 boxes will be depleted before she even gets inside. She's been here since midnight when the store closed, and it has just re-opened. She has to think of something. The sun is up and it's a beautiful warm fall day.

Lori still needs two more Dogs On TVs for her collection. She doesn't have the mauve one with the dog who looks suspiciously like Benji, or the light blue one with two pictures of the same collie dressed up as a pro wrestler. Among collectors these two are known as a Mauve Benji and a Two Blue Lassie. She could try trading her doubles of the Red Yorkshire Fireman and White Sheepdog with one of the Dogs On TV groups on the internet. But true Dogs On TV collectors need the thrill of buying the cereal, and then the anticipation of digging through the lightly sweetened fruit flavored corn shapes fortified with 8 essential vitamins and minerals to find out if they've gotten the right one this time. And Lori is nothing if not a true Dogs On TV collector.

Waiting in the line of Dogs On TV fans in front of Johnny Teagle's HyperMart, Lori notices that there is a strange, old Black man leaning up against the building. As Lori moves, the old man moves. But he does not appear to be in line. He is not threatening-looking at all. In fact, he seems to exude a kind of calm strength. Still, Lori is suspicious. Nervously she strikes up a conversation with the woman in front of her. She is short and fat and has a streak of silver through the center of her black hair.

"Which colors are you looking for?" Lori asks as the crowd shuffles slowly forward.

"Oh, I'm still missing the Pearloid Daisy and the Red Yorkie Fireman," the woman says in a breezy tone. "I'm online every other hour checking the prices. Right now my brother's at home on the computer."

"Online?" Lori asks as if she does not know.

"Oh yes," says the woman. "Dogs On Line is my favorite. But I also network with On Line Dogs and Cyber Dogs. There's so much in-fighting between the rival fan groups, though. It's really too bad."

"Wow," says Lori. "I didn't even know there were groups like that." She is lying, of course. But she doesn't want to be taken advantage of, so she plays dumb.

"You really need to be online to keep up," says the woman.

"Computers are so expensive," Lori says. "But then again, you only live once."

Suddenly the strange little old black man steps over to Lori and says, "Some folks believe you live many times."

Lori is strangely shaken by what the little old black man has just said. Of course she's heard of reincarnation before. She's quite an expert, having read nearly everything Shirley Maclaine has written on the subject. But for some reason, it doesn't seem that what he said has anything to do with reincarnation. There's something else there. Something Lori can't quite put her finger on.

The little black man snaps his bony fingers with a loud pop. "Quick," he says, "before you heard that sound where was it? After it finished where did it go?"

For a fleeting moment it seems like Lori is on the verge of understanding something which could never be put into words. But before she can respond, the woman in front of her says to the little black man, "Reincarnation is of the devil. In the Bible it clearly states that it is given that each man liveth once and then the judgment. That's the word of God, not the imagination of some Indian guru."

"Yes, ma'am!" the little old back man says with a smile. "I ain't never believed much in no reincarnation anyhow. To me, seems like the only real time is right now and the only real place is right here. My name is Charlie. It was very nice to meet you both. Have yourselves a good time." He laughs and ambles away through the rusting cars in the parking lot.

Lori is dumbstruck. Something just happened here, but she's not quite certain what it was.

*   *   *

"I left the water running upstairs, you just wait here a minute, all right?" I said to Charmaine as she stood there in the Clubhouse's doorway. Not waiting for a reply I ran up the stairs taking them three at a time.

Wilma was still in my room sitting on the futon sobbing. I sat beside her and put my arm over her shoulders. She pushed it away sharply. "Are you OK?" I said.

"Am I OK? What a question to ask. Don't you know anything? Don't you know what a sin is?" She grabbed a handful of blankets and sobbed into them.

Actually I'd never really been able to get my mind round that particular concept. But I figured saying so would only make things worse. "Maybe you should go home," I said.

Wilma turned and looked up at me, sad little reddened eyes in a sad chubby face topped off with disheveled blonde hair. "You don't want me around?"

"It's not that. It's just that I think maybe you'd like to be alone right now." There was no telling when Charmaine might suddenly decide to come upstairs. The way she felt about Mark and especially about Lesa, I knew she wouldn't want to risk meeting them in the Living Room. She had no way of knowing they weren't home.

"You hate me," Wilma said. "I made you hate me. I came on like some kind of whore of Babylon and now I'm cheap."

"No, no," I said, listening closely for the sound of footsteps on the stairs. What was I going to do if Charmaine did come up? Shove Wilma out the window? It might work, but then again I might end up killing her. And if I killed her it would be even more difficult to explain things.

I was no closer to knowing the truth about the conspiracy than I had been before. My entire plan was stupid. Now there was no way Wilma could get out of the house except by going down the stairs that led directly to the Living Room, and by extension directly to Charmaine. That meant I would have to explain Wilma's presence to Charmaine in some way that would satisfy both of them and not raise any suspicions. Although I am a genius with talents in many diverse areas, this, I knew, would prove difficult even for me.

"I've failed," Wilma said, starting to sob again. "I've failed not only myself. I have failed in my duties to the church. My mission was to bring you to God and set an example of Christianity to you. Some example."

"No. You didn't fail. I'm convinced," I said.

"You are?" She looked up at me with a mixture of confusion and hope.

"Sure I am," I said. Oh boy, I thought, and set about to improvise. "Your devotion to the church is so strong that you will go to any length to bring someone new into the fold. I can sense that. The only reason you did what you did was because you hoped that by doing something like that you could..." I made vague gestures in the air, trying to come up with something. "You hoped that by acting in a very radical way you would make me see the error of such immoral behavior through a concrete example."

"I did?" she said. My life had turned into an episode of Three's Company written by someone on a very bad and very heavy acid trip.

"Yes. And I, uh, well, I believe. By seeing the remorse in your eyes, I have come to understand the error in acting in an immoral way. By acting immorally you have taught a powerful lesson of morality." It had sort of a Zen ring to it. I still didn't hear anyone coming up the steps, but it was only a matter of time. Would my window even be wide enough for Wilma to fit through?

"And you have faith now?" she asked.

"Oh yes. Faith. Lots of faith. Busloads of faith. Praise be to the Lord my God," I said.

"I'm so glad," she said, again with that smile of hers. She had a knock-out smile, I'll say that for her.

"So now do you feel like you can go home?"

"Yes," she said, standing up. "Will I see you at church?"

"Of course," I said. Now what? If I went downstairs with her that was obviously no good. If I went down first I'd be there on the couch with Charmaine and she'd probably want to say good-bye to me and then, then it'd be a disaster. The only solution was to have her go down first and let herself out, and pray that she didn't say anything to Charmaine. Maybe Charmaine would assume Wilma was a friend of Steve's or someone else in the house. People come in and out all the time. It wasn't a good plan, but it was all I had. Actually, maybe praying she didn't say anything wasn't such a good idea. Any credit I might have had with God was gone for good by now.

"I have to straighten things up in here. Can you let yourself out?" I said.

She looked confused, hurt. "All right," she said in a small voice. "I'll see you later?"

"Of course you will. I said so, didn't I?" I said. She smiled a little fake smile and turned and left. I stood there in my room petrified, hoping that this was going to work. I tried to come up with some explanation, some sort of spin to put on the story if I went down stairs in five minutes to find the two of them chatting away in the Living Room. Nothing came. My genius had deserted me.

I looked down at the futon. There were little spots of blood on the sheets. Did we really go at it that hard? The whole room smelled of sex. I got rid of the spent condom and then lit a few sticks of incense. I went around the room trying to remove any traces of fornication. I straightened the sheets on the futon, reorganized the eight-track tapes, picked up some of the books and magazines. Then it looked too neat. Like I was covering something up, which I was. So I went around and messed up the sheets, re-scattered the eight-track tapes and tossed the books and magazines I'd picked up back on the floor. Then it looked too much like it was an organized pattern trying to appear random. It would never work. And anyway women can sense these things. It's useless trying to hide them.

After about three minutes I opened the door. I could hear Charmaine and Wilma talking downstairs. I was doomed.

The more I let them talk unsupervised, the more trouble I'd be in. I had to get down there and intervene as quickly as possible. It might already be too late. If the wrong things had been said, I was sunk for sure. I felt like I was a soldier with no choice but to head into an ambush and hope I had enough firepower on me to survive it.

The Cat With No Name was sitting on the landing again, looking up at me as if he would have known better than to get himself into a situation like this. Sure you would, smart ass.

When I reached the bottom of the stairs and stepped into the Living Room both of them suddenly stopped talking. After a protracted moment of awkward silence, Charmaine said, "Your friend was telling me all about her church." Her voice was laced with battery acid.

"She was?" I said.

"Oh yes," Wilma said. "I was telling her about how I had been ministering to you."

"Ministering to me," I echoed.

"*Ministering* to you," Charmaine said, arms crossed over her chest.

"About God's plan," Wilma said.

"God's plan," I said.

"His *plan*," Charmaine said, head cocked sideways, eyes narrowed.

More silence followed. Finally I said, "Well I'm glad to hear that. Anyway, Wilma was just about to leave..."

"Were you?" Charmaine said. "And just as I was getting interested."

"You're interested in hearing about Christ?" Wilma said.

"Charmaine..." I said.

"Oh yes," Charmaine said, with a withering look in my direction. "I'm very troubled, you see."

"Oh really?" Wilma said with guileless sincerity.

"Yes," I broke in, "well maybe we can get together later, some other time."

"But I'm troubled right now," Charmaine said, glaring at me. "I just had a fight with my lover. I don't think we'll ever get back together again."

Wilma looked relieved and shot me a brief smile. You should not have done that, I thought, but it was too late. "I'm sure your boyfriend still loves you," Wilma said to Charmaine.

"Actually she was my girlfriend," Charmaine said, her voice smug and condescending.

Wilma's smile fell. Her face turned red. "Oh."

"Charmaine..." I said.

"Yes. She was my girlfriend. We're lesbians." Charmaine's voice went from just being laced with battery acid to pure hydrochloric. "She didn't like the way I sucked pussy so she threw me out."

"Charmaine..." I said. Wilma turned to stone.

"I tried to suck her pussy good. But she didn't like it. Maybe I didn't stick my tongue in deep enough. Maybe I should have shoved more fingers up inside her." She wiggled her fingers in Wilma's face to demonstrate. Wilma shrank back. "Maybe you can show me how to suck pussy. Do you know how to suck pussy good? Can you give me pussy-sucking lessons? Do my fingers smell fishy? I hate it when my fingers come out smelling all fishy."

Wilma was shaking. "Charmaine..." I said. My life had turned from Three's Company into a Peter Bagge comic, and there was nothing I could do.

"Or maybe I can practice sucking pussy on you. Will you let me suck your pussy? I bet you have a nice pussy. A nice pink pussy like nice blonde white girls like you always have. Pink with pretty blonde hair all around it. My pussy's brown, you know. Ever seen a brown pussy? Honey you ain't never tasted nothin' till you licked up some of that fiiiine brown sugar. Taste jest like ol' gran' daddy's molasses."

"Charmaine..." I said.

"What?" she snapped back at me. "This is girl talk. Ain't none of yo' business what us girls want to talk about." She rocked her head horizontally on her neck, her eyes fixed on mine. She turned back to Wilma. "Is it, honey pie?"

"I think I'd better go now," Wilma said and darted for the door.

"Come on over and see me some time," Charmaine shouted after her. "We'll have a real good time together!" I could hear Wilma's flat feet slapping down on the pavement outside and quickly fading into the distance.

"Well, that's that, I suppose," I said.

"That's what?"

"Christ, Charmaine. You didn't have to do that to her."

"Who was she anyway?" Charmaine said. "Did you fuck her? You're so pathetic. You'd fuck anything. You fucked me, didn't you? That proves you've got no taste whatsoever."

"Be quiet," I said.

"Oh, now *The Man* be tellin' me to keep quiet! I got news for you Massa Joe, I ain't gonna be quiet for you no more!" she shouted. "Did you fuck her? Did you? Were you just up there fucking that fat little Christian girl?"

"Charmaine I..."

"I knew it! I could smell it on you the minute you opened the door. I knew you'd been fucking somebody. But someone like her? What are you, totally and utterly desperate?"

"Charmaine, calm down!" I snapped. She went quiet. "It was you that broke up with me. You that wanted out of our relationship, not me. What I do now is none of your business."

Very softly, without looking back up at me, she said, "I know."

I paused for a bit. Then I said, "She had... information." Charmaine looked up at me with raised eyebrows. "About the conspiracy," I said.

"Oh, Jesus Christ on a Stick. You are completely out of your mind," she said.

I tsk-ed. "It's no use talking to you."

"No, no it's not. And it's no use me talking to you either. What a fool I was to believe we were still friends. To believe that what happened last night meant anything to you. I'm just another one of your conquests, aren't I? Just another bimbo on your fuckable bimbos list. Me and that fat little Jesus freak and whoever else you've got." She turned and stomped out the door slamming it behind her.

I stood there for a second or two, trying to decide whether to go out after her or not. Then I heard something crash against the concrete driveway. Then another crash. Then a door slamming and her Nova peeling out of the driveway onto West Main street. Someone honked.

I went outside. On the driveway were the remains of my toaster, which I'd given Charmaine. Beside that were several Lou Reed eight tracks. She'd tossed them on the driveway then run over them on her way out. My Japanese double tape import of *Metal Machine Music* was in ten thousand pieces. *Berlin* and *Rock and Roll Animal* were in similar shape.

"Thanks for giving my stuff back!" I shouted down the street. "I really appreciate that!"

All in all a fine and very productive day.

*   *   *

Ljes and Milena enter the spacious marble floored lobby of the WAKR building and stride up to the receptionist who sits in the center of a huge round desk near the back. The grand flamboyance of the lobby is undercut by the cobwebs clinging to the unwashed marble pillars, and the thick coats of dust covering the ornate bronze wall clocks. There are cracks here and there in the elegant marble. This was once a place of luxury, but now it seems that no-one cares anymore. "We wish to speak with the President and CEO of this company," says Milena.

"Do you have an appointment?" the receptionist asks, peering over her glasses. She is perhaps old enough to remember when this place used to be something spectacular. But her beauty has faded just like that of the building.

Ljes leans towards her and says, "We do not need the appointment. We are here on an urgent business."

"I'm afraid you will need an appointment," says the receptionist.

Milena says, "This is not a decision for you to take, you are in no position to make the judgment that we cannot talk to your President and CEO without such an appointment. You call him up and tell him that representatives from the Dogs On TV Corporation of America are here and wish to speak to him about copyright infringement."

"Hold on," says the receptionist with a sigh. "Let me see what I can do."

"See?" Milena says to Ljes. "You have to know how to handle these people. This one is just the peon. We need to talk to the top person."

The receptionist calls WAKR's building security.

In moments a man in a black suit arrives in the lobby. Ljes asks, "Are you the President and CEO?"

Milena laughs and elbows Ljes aside. "Of course my partner here is just making the joke. We know that the President and CEO would not come down to the lobby personally. Is very good joke, Ljes." She slaps Ljes hard on the back. Confused, Ljes forces a single laugh that ends up sounding more like a stifled sneeze. "You are the assistant to the President, no?"

"Listen, folks," says the man in the black suit. "The president of WAKR-TV is a very busy man. Trudy here tells me you don't have an appointment. So just what is it you wish to talk to him about?"

"Our rights have been infringed!" bellows Ljes. "We have been wrongfully damaged and we demand compensation!"

"Woah, woah," says the man in the black suit. "Just hold your horses there a minute, big guy." He gives a nod to the receptionist and she pushes the button on her phone that automatically calls for assistance.

Milena pushes Ljes out of the way. "My partner, he is very emotional. I must apologize. He is businessman who takes his work very seriously. Essentially, what he says is correct." Milena's pronunciation of the word "says" rhymes with "weighs."

"So am I to take it that you want to see the president about some kind of a legal matter?" says the man in the black suit.

"You are right," says Milena smiling at him and licking her lips suggestively. "And so very perceptive. Now, may we be shown to his office?"

Two other men in black suits appear behind the first.

The first man in a black suit says to Milena, "If you folks want to, you can make an appointment to talk to one of our legal department. I think Trudy here could even get you in to talk to one of them before the week is out. Right, Trudy?" The receptionist nods.

Milena is furious. "If I wanted to talk to your legal department I would have sent someone from our legal department!" she yells. "We have teams of lawyers working around a clock on this case. We will not be treated as if we are the foolish people to be taken so lightly to cleaners!"

"Around a clock!" Ljes says, pounding his fist into his hand.

"You best watch it with that kind of behavior, sir," says the man in the black suit. The other men in black suits step forward.

"We will not be trifled with!" says Milena. "Our lawyers will contact you. You will be shut down! Out of the business! We are an international firm and we can crush such a feeble company as yours! Crush you!"

She stalks off out of the building. Taken by surprise, Ljes hesitates for a moment, then follows.

*   *   *

Wilma arrives back at her apartment. Tears fill her eyes. And, to make things worse, Kim Yong has returned and is back in the spare room, drawing. No matter what he said he did to that man's wife, she has to tell him what happened with Joe. There's no way she can hide. Even if she could hide her sin from Kim Yong, there is no way to hide it from the Lord, who can see directly into her heart.

"Kim Yong!" she shouts, stumbling to her green vinyl couch. Her legs ache and she still has a warm and sinfully-pleasing tingle between them. The tingle extends its blissful way deep into her body. Cast such thoughts aside, she tells herself! Into the Pit of Fire with such wicked imaginings! She tries but it's no use. "Kim Yong!" she shouts again.

He comes into the room, looking tired. "What wrong? What happen?" he says.

"Sit down," Wilma says, taking him by the hand and pulling him down to the couch. She looks him deep in the eyes. He has such sad little monkey-like eyes. The sad dignified eyes of a man who has known suffering and degradation in a poor and desolate country, who came to this Christian land longing for freedom and an end to poverty and strife. Longing for the love of a pure white maiden. And now she has tarnished those dreams forever. She breaks down and cries on his shoulder.

"What happen? What wrong?" he says again. Even his voice is so beautiful. So free from the materialism of a jaded Westerner. His brave attempt to conquer a new language, it's so touching. Wilma loosens her embrace and holds him by the shoulders, looking into those soulful eyes again.

"I am tarnished," she says. "A man has had his way with me. I have sinned against you." She breaks down and begins to weep heavily into his shoulder.

"What? Some man?" Kim Yong Lee says. "Some man do something to you?"

*   *   *

"Now just calm down here a minute," Larry Barnes, the Akron Beacon Journal's city features editor says to Ljes and Milena, who have been in his small but well-appointed office for the last seventeen minutes delivering a tirade about copyright infringement.

The newspaperman's kindly smile does not fool Milena for one moment. "Don't you see?" the editor says finally, "this newspaper article is like advertising for you. Do you know how much it would cost if you asked us to place a picture of your product on our front page?"

Ljes considers this. Milena glowers at him, then says to the man from the newspaper, "You are selling more of your papers by placing this photograph on the front."

"It was a very slow news day," says Larry. "There wasn't anything interesting to put there. It was between that and the idiot who calls us up all the time claiming aliens have taken over a supermarket up in Cuyahoga Falls. Frankly, it was a tough choice." The newspaper man chuckles.

"Maybe it will help us sell some more products," Ljes says quietly.

"Shut up, you fool!" says Milena. "We must present a united front! No arguments between us in front of the third party!"

"I am sorry," says Ljes, bowing his head sheepishly.

"Your partner's right," says the newspaperman. "Think of how many more people are aware of your toys now."

"He is not correct!" shouts Milena. "You must compensate us for damages! You have to pay!" She waves a contract in his face.

*   *   *

Kim Yong Lee finally manages to figure out what happened to Wilma. It takes him forever to even get her to say anything sensible at all. Even when she does, he has to ask her to repeat herself again and again because his English is bad, and it's hard to understand whenever she starts saying religious stuff, which she does so often it's a wonder he can understand anything she says at all.

Kim Yong Lee figures out that she had gone around to the house of one of the church members, that strange little man who makes movies. She went over there to talk to him about the church and then he dragged her inside his smelly old house and raped her.

Kim Yong Lee is outraged. Maybe this kind of thing is common in America. Maybe they rape each other all the time. He wouldn't be surprised. The whole country is on drugs and everybody always seems to be fighting with everybody else. But he doesn't care. He cannot stand by and allow such a thing to go unpunished.

Even if Wilma is not his woman, she has been kind to him and allowed him to share her apartment until that bastard preacher decides to come through and pay him for the work he's been doing. No-one, woman or man, deserves such treatment.

He stands and shouts the word "Vengeance!" in Korean. He does not know the word in English and hopes that she will understand from the situation and the tone of his voice. He marches out the door and off to the house of the strange little man who makes movies.

*   *   *

"You were weak!" Milena shouts at Ljes as they leave the offices of the Akron Beacon Journal. "You showed to the enemy our hand. It is like we are playing the poker game and you display to our opponent which cards we have gotten."

"I displayed nothing!" Ljes shouts back. "Maybe he is right, Milena. Maybe this appearance of Dogs On TV in his newspaper will promote the product, and if the product becomes more well-known then we make the more money because of the more selling product!"

"You're a fool and a Cretan to that!" Milena says. She turns and stalks off.

Ljes stands in the center of the graffiti-covered ruins of Cascade Plaza, in the center of Akron's dead downtown. The broken concrete fountain behind him drips quietly, its waters long blocked off since no-one comes to see it anymore. Ljes paces through the silent courtyard, empty save for a few homeless men shuffling about looking for places to sleep. Ljes is a man alone in a strange foreign city.

*   *   *

Wilma sits on her couch and sobs. He called me a slut, she thinks. Or a whore of Babylon, or some other unspeakable thing. I confessed to him that I made love to Joe Nofziger and that it had been my own doing. My own lust and desire for passion. I could not lie, she thinks.

"Don't blame him," she had said. "Lay the blame on me. For it is I who have betrayed you." She had told him over and over the story of how she went to the house to speak about the Lord. To witness to someone as yet unforgiven. To spread the teachings, the light of the world. She told him how, possessed by passion, possessed by low and vile passion, she went for him with wild abandon. "Oh, forgive me," she cried. "Forgive my horrible sin!"

But he did not understand. Poor lost lamb, the very idea of sin unknown in his native land across the sea. No sin and no forgiveness. Oh how empty, how utterly empty and sad their poor lives must be.

Kim Yong had been so good. In all the weeks he had lived in her apartment he had made no move to touch her. That long, lean, tanned and taut body of his had never made contact with her flesh. She had watched him day after day. Those animal legs. Those animal eyes. Waiting. Longing. Until the passion had welled up inside her and could no longer be contained by prayer. Betrayal was the result. Betrayal of one so innocent.

God forgive me, she prays. I have driven him from the fold. I tried so hard to save him, and yet through passion and lust I have driven him from You.

*   *   *

I stood there for a long while looking at all my broken stuff on the driveway. Finally I sighed and gathered up the toaster and as many fragments of ruptured eight track tape as I could and took it all inside. I dumped the lot of it on the Couch of Doom. Nobody would complain about the mess on the couch because nobody ever went in the Living Room. I suppose it didn't smell like cat shit anymore. But it would be a while before the others noticed. The Cat With No Name, now seated at one end of the couch cleaning itself, looked up at me with a smug, self-satisfied expression. I shrugged. The cat went back to cleaning itself. Helpful.

I went back up in my room and sat there thinking: Well, at least that's over with. Like vomiting, it was one of those horrible things that makes you feel so much better when it's done. Downstairs the doorbell buzzed. Maybe Charmaine had come back to apologize. I went down to answer it. Things couldn't get any weirder than they already were.

At the door was that Asian guy who was with Wilma when she came over the first time. He was mad as hell about something. That much was for certain. "Can I help you?" I said.

He screamed something in a foreign language then punched me hard in the stomach.

Pure pain. I went down, the air knocked completely out of me. I regained a semblance of a standing posture and attempted to retreat back inside.

He grabbed me by the collar and pulled my face up to his. "I see you around her again I kill you!" he shouted.

"No problem," I sputtered. It was still hard to breathe. Around who? Around Wilma? And then it dawned on me. The two of them were probably married. She must have told him what happened. Christ, that was quick.

He let go of my collar, then made a move like he was going to punch me again. I flinched. He shouted something else at me in a foreign language then walked down the porch steps laughing.

*   *   *

Milena knows that the task of making Dogs On TV a success in America is too big for one person. If Ljes will not help her, then others must be recruited to the cause. Milena goes to Kinko's Copy Center, rents a computer and prepares a flyer. It says:

CHANGE TO YOUR LIFE!
BE INVOLVED IN MOST EXCITING
THE NEW ENTERPRISE
IN WORLD OF TODAY!
GROW TO RICHNESS AND SUCCESSFUL!

On the bottom she puts the number of her mobile telephone. She has 200 copies made and gets to work pasting them to walls and stapling them to telephone poles and trees all over Akron and Cuyahoga Falls.

*   *   *

Even with agents of the Planet X, Oriental Kung Fu assassins and toaster-wielding ex-girlfriends in hot pursuit, I still managed to work on *Jesus vs. Mecha Jesus*. This is a good example of my near miraculous ability to be creative in the face of overwhelming adversity. I should be given an award of some kind, really.

Ben I. Goldman, sorry, Reverend Goodman, gave me an old 16mm camera, some editing equipment and enough cash out of Christ the Crowned King's donation box to buy plenty of film stock. I called Vector Temps to say I'd be unavailable and devoted all of my time to making *Jesus vs. Mecha Jesus* the masterpiece it deserved to be.

Logan agreed to grow a forked beard for the part of Jesus Christ. Mark got to work constructing the Mecha Jesus costume. I stole a bunch of cardboard boxes from behind Johnny Teagle's HyperMart and started building downtown Akron, Ohio in 1:25 scale. I felt like Eiji Tsuburaya himself. I hope I don't need to explain who Eiji Tsuburaya, Japan's God of Special Effects, is. He was just the special effects director for all of Toho's best-known monster movies of the 1960s. Only someone especially dense would not have known that.

Mark and Logan's band, The Zen Luv Assassins, said they would write the theme song and play live at the movie's world premiere party. A party that would, in Logan's words, "Kick Akron's collective ass all the way to Brimfield", and feature the not just the Zen Luvs, but Logan in full Jesus garb battling Mark as the evil Mecha Jesus in person.

I placed an ad in Scene magazine for crew people. A man with a foreign accent whose first name was Ljes and whose last name was made up entirely of consonants answered. He had a blond crew-cut, muscles like the Incredible Hulk and he needed a place to stay. I hired him and placed him on a "deferred payment schedule." That meant he would get paid plenty once the film was a massive hit. Once *Jesus vs. Mecha Jesus* hit the theaters we'd all have more money than we'd know what to do with anyway. For the time being his payment was free lodging in the Living Room and all the beer and Macaroni and Cheese he could eat.

When we got to the scenes where Jesus and Mecha Jesus were to have their fight in downtown Akron, smashing the Civic Theatre and the Canal Park Stadium in the process, we had a problem Even though Logan looked Christ-like enough and Mark's samurai warrior-inspired robot Jesus costume, made of cardboard, bits of old ducts and Salvation Army television sets, was stunning.

But when we started rehearsing the fight scenes it became readily apparent why it would not work. Both Mark and Logan fought like girls. We needed someone to teach them how to do it right. I could only think of one person, but I wasn't sure she would help me.

I had to bring the tape with me in case I needed to prove that what I was telling her was true. I rummaged through my sock drawer, pulled it out and put it in my jacket pocket. Then I went out on a mission doomed to failure.

*   *   *

Ljes can do without Milena. Already he has gotten a job on the crew of a major motion picture. America is the home of the motion picture industry. Maybe he will become a famous actor one day. In the meantime he rented a room in a very artistically decorated house that the people who live in it have nicknamed, "The Clubhouse." It is dirty. But artistic people are not so clean. The movie is sure to be a big hit, after that he will be able to buy and sell the likes of Milena as he pleases.

In the meantime, he continues looking for work as a helicopter pilot. His experience flying for the People's Republican Liberation Army should impress any potential airline. He is having a hard time finding any airlines with offices in Akron, Ohio. But he will find them. Of this he is absolutely certain. Things are looking up.

*   *   *

Ben I. Goldman calls in some favors owed him by various members of Christ the Crowned King and manages to arrange for the world premiere of *Jesus vs. Mecha Jesus* to be at the Civic Theater in downtown Akron. Built in the 1920s, when Akron was a city that seemed destined for greatness, the theater's Moorish garden-themed interior is set under a ceiling inlayed with twinkling stars and drifting clouds projected from a special system located just below the second balcony. A gigantic crystal chandelier hangs in the center of a palatial three-story lobby. Lately, though, talk of razing the building and turning it into a parking facility has begun again. The managers hope that the world premiere of a locally-made film will boost their image in the community. The title of the film will not be announced until the day of the premiere.

Goldman's office is full of editing equipment, as well as props and costumes for his movie.

Abruptly Wilma enters and says, "I have sinned against our Lord and Savior."

Ben I. Goldman has a lot on his mind at the moment, having decided to finish his grand epic movie in the face of powerful forces who would stop at nothing to see that the truth is never known to the public at large. What's more, the new plot twist he has introduced is proving to be harder to work into the story than he had anticipated. "What have you done?" he says, hoping it's something simple and easily forgivable. He is really getting fed up with this kind of thing. She and the others know him only as the Reverend Goodman and he still has to play that role.

"I have committed an act of adultery," Wilma says, tears streaming down her chubby, reddened face.

"Oh," says Goldman, going back to typing the scene where the fake Christ snaps under the weight of his own efforts to hide who He truly is. "No problem. Do you repent?"

"Oh, yes," Wilma says, sniffing. "Oh, Lord, oh, yes. I repent. Truly, I do."

"Fine, fine," says Goldman, trying to think of what Reverend Goodman might say at a time like this. "Absolved," he says and continues typing. If the fake Jesus is actually the real Jesus, then who is the supposedly real Jesus?

"Absolved?" says Wilma to the man she believes is Reverend Goodman. "How can I be absolved? I have sinned. I have transgressed against the Lord my God." She bursts into sobs.

"Look," says Goldman, still typing furiously, not wanting to lose his train of thought and be forced to start the entire rewrite over from scratch, "it's in the past. There's nothing you can do about your past. You've got to look at just this moment. Like you were just dropped into this situation. Sink or swim. Start here and now and do what is right. The mind of the past is ungraspable. I think Jesus must have said that somewhere."

Wilma sobs even harder. "How do I know what is right? Oh, I'm so confused!" she wails.

"Life doesn't have a rule book, you know," says the Goldman. "It's not like traffic laws. Who did you sin against?"

Wilma sniffs and says, "I told you! Kim Yong Lee!" Then she breaks down sobbing again. "I whored myself to another man," says Wilma. "And I drove Kim Yong away from the Lord."

"All right," says Goldman, realizing he won't get out of this easily, and finally looking up from his typewriter, "you made a mistake. Everybody makes mistakes. It's what you do from now on that counts. You can't change what's already happened. Right?"

"Right," sniffs Wilma.

"Good," says Reverend Goodman. "I've got to get back to this now," he indicates his typewriter. "Will you be okay?"

"I suppose so," says Wilma. She stands up for a moment and then leaves the office. Ben I. Goldman continues his typing.

*   *   *

Kim Yong Lee leaves Wilma's apartment for good and rents a room in the Anthony Wayne hotel downtown. Cut off from Wilma and from the church, he needs to find himself a job. After being turned down by Vector Temporary Services for lack of a proper working visa, he spots a "help wanted" sign outside the Jade Palace restaurant, a combination Chinese/Japanese restaurant in Cuyahoga Falls.

It is a horrid place, the remains of a fish and chips chain called Arthur Treacher's. Kim Yong can still read the name on the marquee, even though it is covered over with the words Jade Palace. It has now been converted into what barely passes for a proper sit-down restaurant.

The Jade Palace, he learns, is owned and operated by a family of Korean immigrants. The "Chinese" or "Japanese" food they serve is actually Korean, but no-one in Akron seems to notice. Kim Yong Lee is hired on the spot.

*   *   *

Carl arrives at The Jade Palace restaurant on Main Street in Cuyahoga Falls for his meeting with the representative from Marutani Foods Corporation. The restaurant is divided into two. One side is Chinese and one side is Japanese. Carl hopes that the side where you have to sit on the floor is the Chinese side because he'd rather sit at a table. An Oriental man in a black suit enters the restaurant. Carl can't be sure, but the man looks vaguely familiar.

*   *   *

It takes Soon Park a while to find the Jade Palace restaurant, where he is to impersonate a Japanese representative of Marutani Foods Corporation. He doesn't like earning money this way, but it seemed harmless enough and business has been bad for him as a Tae Kwon Do instructor.

He doesn't go up to Cuyahoga Falls much, even though it's just across the bridge from Akron. There's not much reason to go up to Cuyahoga Falls. As far as Soon is concerned, Cuyahoga Falls is just a slightly smaller, slightly more upscale version of Akron. "Caucasian Falls" the natives call it, proudly. It doesn't exactly endear the place to him.

The Jade Palace is a Japanese restaurant on one side and a Chinese restaurant on the other. Typical American invention. Soon hopes the Japanese side isn't one of those places where you have to sit on the floor. He hates sitting on the floor. He goes inside and is disappointed to see that all of the tables on the right side of the restaurant are the typical low Japanese-style ones surrounded by thin cushions. A man is standing near the register. He has an enormous behind and fat legs. Soon has seen him somewhere before.

*   *   *

Carl asks, "Are you Mr. Ken Suzuki?" The man hesitates for a moment then says he is. "Glad to meet you," Carl says. "*Ohio!*" Then bows like Sean Connery did in *Rising Sun*.

*   *   *

Soon is caught off guard. Then he remembers that *Ohio* is Japanese for good morning. *"Ohio,"* he replies, even though it is not morning. Hopefully this indicates that the supermarket manager knows even less Japanese than he does. He had no idea the man would be able to speak Japanese at all. He'll be in real trouble if the guy tries to test him. The manager even bows to him. Soon bows back, hoping he has the angle right. Koreans bow too. But they're not crazy about the custom like Japanese people are and there aren't so many rules about how low you have to bow according to what social position you hold.

*   *   *

Carl fishes his business card out of his jacket inside pocket. He makes sure to hold it at the edges with both hands, displaying the side on which he has written out his name in Japanese characters he copied from the book in the library. Actually the characters he's written would be pronounced *Ku-rari Wa-ru-ta* and carry the meaning "I hate Walter." *"Origato,"* he says.

*   *   *

Soon's eyes widen seeing that Carl has passed him a business card with handwritten Chinese characters on one side. He cannot read them, at least not pronounced in the way a Japanese person would, but hopes they are just the man's name. *"Origato,"* he replies. The supermarket manager smiles. Soon bows again and passes the guy one of the business cards sent to him by Marutani Specialty Foods, making sure to hold it with both hands just like the supermarket manager did. This fellow really knows about Japanese culture, Soon thinks, I'd better be careful.

A waitress appears and shows them to a table in the Japanese section.

*   *   *

Kim Yong Lee picks up two menus and takes them out to the Japanese section. He is shocked to see Soon Park sitting there. He passes Soon the menu, staring at him with eyes full of hatred.

*   *   *

Soon looks up to see that their waiter is none other than that dog Kim Yong Lee himself. He accepts the menu from him and stares back at him with eyes full of contempt.

*   *   *

Carl notices that the waiter at the Jade Palace seems to know Ken Suzuki. Maybe all the Japanese people in town know each other. There can't be many Japanese living in Cuyahoga Falls. After all, they do call the place "Caucasian Falls", even though it's a hell of a lot less Caucasian these days than it used to be when Carl moved here. Nothing good can last long, after all. He's not sure if the look Ken Suzuki and the waiter are exchanging is friendly or not. The ways of Oriental peoples are inscrutable indeed.

*   *   *

"You are a traitor and a cur," Kim Yong Lee says to Soon quietly in Korean in an even tone so that the White with the fat legs sitting uncomfortably across from Soon will not understand. "If this were not a public meeting place I would tear your heart out of your chest while it was still beating."

*   *   *

Soon Park replies evenly in Korean, "You have neither the will nor the power to make good such a threat."

*   *   *

Carl sees that the waiter and Ken Suzuki definitely do know each other. They seem to be exchanging pleasantries in Japanese. He does not hear the word *ohio* or the word *origato* so he can't follow the conversation at all. Maybe they were childhood pals and moved out to Cuyahoga Falls from Japan at the same time. Maybe they both belong to the Japanese version of the Elks Club or something. The waiter bows and leaves the table, his eyes never leaving Ken Suzuki's. They must be very good friends.

"You know him?" Carl asks Suzuki after the waiter leaves.

"An old acquaintance."

Carl nods, then says, "I suppose you know Japanese food better than I ever will. Why don't you do the honors?" Carl closes his menu.

*　　　*　　　*

Soon Park pores over the menu for a while. He's always hated Japanese food. Avoided the stuff like the plague. He wishes they'd chosen the Chinese side instead. Then he looks at the pictures of some of the food and realizes that in spite of the Japanese names written in the text, the food itself is all Korean.

With Kim Yong Lee back behind the counter he wonders if it's even safe to eat here. The man is a dog and a traitor, but would even he stoop so low as to poison someone? Park does not know, but it is not worth the risk. "The food here is not so tasty," he says. "Would you like to try another place?"

*　　　*　　　*

Carl is puzzled by Ken Suzuki's sudden request to go someplace else. Maybe Suzuki left Japan because he didn't like Japanese food and wanted to try cheeseburgers and deep-fried onion rings, delicacies the East does not have to offer. "Sure," Carl says. "Let's go somewhere else." He's glad to get up off the floor. His legs were starting to get cramped.

*　　　*　　　*

Kim Yong Lee notices that the pig Soon Park is retreating. Typical behavior for a coward such as he. He rushes out and says quietly and evenly to Soon, "You always were a fearful mutt, a servant in a poor man's house."

* * *

The waiter certainly seems concerned about us leaving, Carl thinks. He practically ran the whole way from the kitchen up to the front, and seems to be asking Ken Suzuki if he has offended him. In some ways their culture is very beautiful.

* * *

In Korean, Soon says quietly and evenly to Kim Yong Lee, "I feared a traitorous hound such as you would poison a man's food."

Kim Yong Lee shouts back, "I have had enough from you! Face me as a man faces his enemy!" He assumes the traditional guard stance of a Tae Kwon Do master.

* * *

What the hell is going on? Carl thinks. It looks like the waiter wants to attack Ken Suzuki. Carl backs away to the door. The waiter is shouting in Japanese and now Ken Suzuki is shouting back at him in Japanese. Both men are crouching slightly, their hands doing slow stiff circles in front of them. The man behind the register yells something in Japanese at the waiter. The waiter ignores him and continues his tirade at Ken Suzuki.

* * *

"Now you will die!" Soon screams at Kim Yong Lee, tearing off his tie and coat. He leaps at Kim Yong Lee and the two of them go crashing into the cheap plaster Chinese-style fountain in the restaurant lobby.

Water, pennies and tiny goldfish go flying across the room. A green dragon's head snaps off and shatters on the floor. Kim Yong Lee grabs Soon by the throat. Soon delivers a swift kick to the man's midriff.

*   *   *

"Someone stop them!" shouts Carl. The man at the register is already phoning the police. The entire restaurant is in disarray. The lovely Chinese fountain, probably a valuable antique, has been wrecked. Patrons and workers alike have gathered around as Ken Suzuki and the waiter continue punching and kicking each other.

*   *   *

Within minutes the police arrive. They handcuff both the waiter and Ken Suzuki and read them their rights under American law. Carl wonders if suspected criminals are given such fair treatment in Japan. Ken Suzuki turns to Carl and apologizes. Carl is not sure how best to respond to that and simply says, "*Origato.*"

For some reason the waiter shouts, "He not even Japanese, you foolish fat man!"

"As far as I am concerned you are not part of this," Carl says firmly to the waiter who is now handcuffed and in police custody. He turns back to Ken Suzuki and bows. Ever dignified even in his torn suit, bruises and bloody scratches all over his body, Ken Suzuki bows back. Carl vows to learn more about the unfathomable ways of the mystic East.

Ken Suzuki and the waiter are led away by the police.

Carl gets into his car and drives back to the Cuyahoga Falls Johnny Teagle HyperMart, a deep sense of Oriental peace and serenity filling his body and mind.

*   *   *

Behind the fountain in the center of Cascade Plaza, near where someone has spray-painted the words "Zepplen 4-Ever," Milena assembles her portable Interociter. The fountain is running today and the noise it makes, a kind of pinched-off squeal mixed with the intermittent white noise of rushing water, should make it impossible for others to eavesdrop on her conversation. The portable Interociter looks something like the miniature battery-powered TV sets people take with them to soccer matches, but with a screen shaped like an upside down triangle.

Ljes is a fool. He has no idea about how to be successful in the merchandising business. Nor does he realize the true importance of Dogs On TV. She has never told him about her secret communications with the people of Planet X in the Zeta Reticuli star system, some 33.7 light years from Earth.

A face forms on the three-inch screen. It is a pale skinned man, thick green veins throbbing on his oversized bald head. This is the Controller of Planet X, supreme leader of the planetary government. "Why have you contacted me?" he says in a voice that sounds like a 33 r.p.m. record being played at 45.

"My partner has left the organization," Milena whispers.

"What?" says the Controller of Planet X. "I can't hear what you're saying. There is noise in the background." Milena repeats what she has just said louder so it can be heard over the noise of the fountain. "I see," says the Controller of Planet X. "You must carry on the mission. Propagate the devices throughout the planet according to the instructions you have received."

"I am following the plan precisely," Milena says. Actually she is not. She knows much more about how to propagate devices that will eventually enslave human civilization than these aliens do. Besides that, the way she is doing it will make more money. "Thaw pap hens," Milena says.

"We do hynie," replies the Controller of Planet X.

* * *

At home Lori opens another box of Goofy Feet˚ cereal and dumps the contents into a large pink mixing bowl. The crunchy, multicolored, foot-shaped corn nuggets enriched with 8 essential vitamins and minerals clatter together as she pours, sounding like pieces of broken porcelain being thrown into a marble vase.

Finally, at the bottom, she finds an ivory-colored Dogs On TV toy. She snatches it up and looks through the little viewfinder at the back. Breathlessly she clicks through the pictures. There's the German Shepherd dressed like a policeman, there's the poodle with ribbons tied round its ears and there...my God, there it is. She puts the toy down for a moment and grips the edge of the table, catching her breath.

After ten deep breaths, she picks up the Dogs On TV again and looks through. Yes! She wasn't imagining things. There, right before her eyes is the sheepdog with the cowboy hat. Lori has finally managed to get that most rare prize of all Dogs On TV collectors, an ivory fuzzy John Wayne—or Ivory Fuzz, as serious collectors have shortened it to.

*   *   *

I stood at Nicole's door for a few minutes trying to work out what I was going to say. It was eerie being here. I'd lived in this house when Charmaine and I first started going out. I moved into the Clubhouse after she dumped me. That's when Nicole moved in with Charmaine, supposedly to "help out with the rent." I didn't want to think about what happened after that. I knocked on the door.

It was a nondescript two-story house with pale brown aluminum siding in one of Akron's less reputable neighborhoods. The house was set back from the street and another house stood on what had probably once been the front lawn of this one. The upstairs of the place always seemed to be occupied by weirdos. Charmaine once said she found a bullet hole in her bathroom ceiling. Apparently the guy upstairs had been messing around with a pistol up there. Thank God neither Charmaine nor Nicole had been home at the time. The guy upstairs wasn't really violent, just deeply stupid. Stuff like that was why I moved into the Clubhouse.

I saw Nicole peer through the blinds on the little window beside the door. There was a brief pause, as if she was deciding whether to try and pretend she wasn't home, or call 9-1-1 or something. Then she opened up. "You?" she said. "You've got a lot of nerve showing up here." She opened the door wide and said, "Come on in."

I stepped inside Nicole's apartment. They'd changed some furniture since I left, but it was still the same place. "Have a seat," Nicole said, motioning towards the blue vinyl couch, the one Charmaine and I had picked up at Goodwill for seven dollars. She went off to the kitchen, "Want some coffee? I'd offer you some toast, but we haven't got a toaster anymore now thanks to you," she shouted.

"Thanks to me?" I said. "That was my toaster to begin with. I brought it with me from my parents' house."

She came back into the living room with two mugs of coffee, one with the words "Men are good for two things...Three if you count cooking" printed on it and one in the shape of Oscar the Grouch. Oscar had belonged to Charmaine's father. "Thanks to our mutual friend then," she said, setting the cups down on the coffee table, then sitting across from me on the black Naugahide recliner I had personally fished out of a dumpster behind Silver Meadows apartments in Kent and spent half a week cleaning and repairing. "How come you aren't at church? I hear you're quite the regular church-goer these days." She lit a cigar and began to smoke. It was foul, but there wasn't much I could say. It was her house now.

"Listening to that smug tone of yours a person might almost think you knew what you were talking about," I said to Nicole. I took a sip of coffee, chocolate-mint flavor, expensive stuff. "Not that you deserve any kind of explanation, but I'm still working with the church in a different capacity. That's what I came here to talk to you about."

"About me and the church?" Nicole said. "I don't know how much you know about me, darling. But I don't think the church likes my sort of person."

"It doesn't matter if they do or they don't," I said. "I'm in charge of making a movie for them. The head of the church used to be a very famous science fiction film director. The movie is called *Jesus vs. Mecha Jesus*."

Nicole laughed. "Okay. Now I'm intrigued."

I told Nicole the basic plot and then explained to her about the Kung Fu scenes at the end. "I need someone to coach Logan in some karate moves. You study Kung Fu, don't you?"

"Tae Kwon Do," she said.

"Whatever," I said. "No-one will know the difference."

She thought about it for a minute. Then she said, "Okay. I can do it."

"There's just one thing," I said. "Charmaine is playing the part of Mary Magdalene," I said. It felt weird to say her name out loud like that. "She's supposed to be, anyway. I can't find her. Maybe you know where she is?"

"I don't know where she is or when or even *if* she's ever coming back again." She took another long sip of coffee. Her hands were shaking.

I have no idea why, but I suddenly blurted out, "Do you love her?"

There was a long silence. Nicole did not look at me, she just stared into her cup. I sat there stiff, wondering why the hell I had asked such a thing and waiting to see what her answer would be. She stubbed her cigar out in an ashtray on the arm of her chair.

She looked up from her cup. "Do I...? Do I, what? Jesus H. Christ on a Stick, you have a hell of a nerve, don't you?"

I paused, then quietly asked, "Do you?"

She turned, stared out the window blankly, chewing on the side of her left index finger. Then she said, "Yes, I love her."

I sighed hard. I guess that wasn't what I had wanted to hear. Maybe I'd wanted her to say no, or to get confused and flustered. I don't know, I had no agenda. But hearing Nicole say she loved Charmaine made me wonder what my answer would have been to the same question from her. I hoped she wouldn't ask.

"I thought she felt the same," Nicole went on. "But after what happened between you and her the other night I just don't know. Maybe I'm not enough for her."

"It didn't mean anything to her," I said.

Nicole looked up and gave little half-laugh through her nose.

"Let's find her," I said.

"You don't think I've tried already? You don't think I've called everyone she knows, gone everywhere she used to go, chased down everyone who might possibly know anything at all?"

"What about her parents?" I said.

"I called them, but I didn't want to upset them. I talked to her dad. I don't know, they might have been covering for her for all I know. But I thought if I pushed too hard they'd think something was wrong."

"You never asked me," I said.

"I knew better," Nicole said.

"Did you?"

"All right, smart boy. Where do you think Charmaine is?" She rested her elbows on the table, her chin cradled in her hands and stared up at me with cold green eyes.

"I think she's in trouble," I said. "I think a man called Noftsinger or possibly Hoftsinger or even Nafzinger has her. I'm not sure who this Noftsinger or whatever he calls himself is, but he may not be human."

"You have gone totally off the deep end," Nicole said, leaning back and shaking her head at the ceiling. "Charmaine told me about you and your alien invasion obsessions. I suppose this guy Noftsinger is a Martian disguised as a human being or some such crap."

I had warned Charmaine never to reveal my secrets. I should have figured she couldn't keep a secret. I went on. "The aliens can't disguise themselves as human. Their physiology is very different from ours, although they are probably genetically related. They don't morph, they don't shape shift, they don't control people's minds through implants under the skin or erase people's memories. It's all much more subtle than that."

"Subtle..." she said.

I said to Nicole, "Did the Nazis need to implant control devices in people's necks to get them to stuff human beings into gigantic ovens? Did they need to erase people's memories to get major corporations to manufacture Zyklon-B gas, build the gas chambers and then create advertising campaigns to market the stuff to the government? Do totalitarian leaders in Asia have to shape-shift into Caucasians in order to buy weapons of mass destruction from fine upstanding family men in America? The creatures of Planet X have much more effective ways of operating. They use our greed against us. Anyway, that's not the point. When I say that Noftsinger may not be human, I simply mean that the name Noftsinger may be nothing more than a cover for an alien operative who works behind the scenes, trying to recover an item which could put a stop to their plans for world conquest."

"Look," Nicole said, abruptly standing up, pulling another thin cigar out of a pack in her green T-shirt sleeve pocket and lighting it up. "I am very, very upset as it is. Someone who I love is missing. Possibly in trouble. I don't need you coming over here and handing me a lot of half-baked science fiction bullshit. I only listened to you because I thought maybe, just maybe, you'd want to do something to try and find her. Something real. Now I see that all you care about is spinning your cheap little fantasies and playing, I don't know, Astronaut Joe or something. I don't need this. Nobody needs this."

"Look, look," I said, "Just let me show you something." Before she could make a move to stop me, I got up, pulled the VHS tape I'd carried to her house out of my jacket pocket, put it in her VCR and switched on the TV. The image of a flying saucer hovering over a lake faded into view on the screen. "I've never shown this to anyone before," I said.

"So what?" Nicole said. "It's special effects from some cheap movie. You can even see the wires holding up the toy flying saucer!"

"They're not wires! They're..."

At that moment the doorbell rang. "Jesus H. Christ, what now?" Nicole said, and stamped over to answer it.

I looked through the blinds. "Men in black," I said to Nicole. Though I couldn't see their faces, their style of dress was classic men in black. Hollywood may have tried to make the men in black into a joke, but they were very real. They were here because I knew too much about Planet X. Were they on the government's side or the aliens' side? Was there any difference?

"No matter what they ask, I can't speak to them," I said to Nicole. She shrugged and opened the door. I switched off the TV and hid behind the couch.

*   *   *

Ngugi and Msoto are walking along Chalker Street looking for Joe Nofziger's house. According to the information provided to them by the Controller of Planet X, he shares a house on this street with a woman named Charmaine Poole. Charmaine is an African American.

Ngugi and Msoto are dressed in matching black suits with inch-wide black ties in accordance with instructions from Planet X.

After some searching they arrive at the proper address. It is behind another house, which explains why it was so difficult to locate. According to their information, Joe Nofziger lives on the bottom floor.

Msoto rings the doorbell. A woman with very short hair, like a man's, answers. She is smoking a cigar. "Is this the home of Mr. Joseph Nofziger?" Ngugi asks.

"Not anymore," says the woman with the short hair. "But you're in luck. He just happens to be here. Let me get him." She closes the door.

Msoto says to Ngugi, "These black suits are foolish. We look nothing like film buyers. And if he does not agree to sell us the film we will have given ourselves away completely."

"He is a poor man," says Ngugi. "Just witness how he lives. He will surely agree."

"Then what is taking him so long to respond?"

The woman with the short hair appears at the door again. "May I ask what you gentlemen wish to speak with Mr. Nofziger about?"

Ngugi says, "We want to make a purchase. We are film collectors from Brunei and we understand he has some very rare and valuable items."

"Hold on," says the woman with short hair exasperatedly and disappears inside again.

*   *   *

"Good God Almighty, Joe," Nicole said to me when she got back from the door. "They look like church people. Maybe you gave the church your old address or something."

"They're not church people," I said. "They're men in black!"

"What is wrong with you? Since when are you afraid of black men? Have you gone KKK all of a sudden or something?"

"Not black men, men in black!" I peeked through the blinds again. "Oh, my God, they *are* black."

"As a matter of fact..."

"Black men in black. What does that mean? Is that double jeopardy? Go and ask them what they want." I pushed Nicole toward the door. She shot me back a dirty look. She went outside, spoke to them for a moment and came back again.

"They want to buy some movies from you," Nicole said. "They're film collectors from Brunei."

"Brunei? What the hell is Brunei?" I said. "Why do they want films? None of my films have ever been shown in Brunei! None of my films have been shown outside Akron! What is Brunei? Is that a country? I never heard of a country called Brunei! There's no such place as Brunei! Where the hell would you put a country with a name like Brunei?"

"Would you please calm down?"

"I am perfectly calm!" I whisper-shouted. I took a deep breath, tried to think. Nothing. Then I realized what they were after. "We've got to get away from here."

"Why?" said Nicole.

"Why? You ask me why? Can't you see? It's so goddamned obvious!" I could clearly hear the men in black were shuffling around nervously on the front porch. I knew who they were now. "That's them. Those are the guys that attacked us on the street." Everyone in town had heard about the attack by now. I knew Charmaine must have told Nicole.

"Now I know you're crazy," Nicole said. "What would the two high school punks who attacked you on the street be doing showing up here with suits on acting like film buyers from Brunei? It's completely absurd."

"Brunei my ass!" I said. "They are alien operatives and they want what I've got! Noftsinger or Hoffsinger or whatever he calls himself is at the bottom of this. Him and the whole organization behind him. They're holed up in Cuyahoga Falls at Johnny Teagle's HyperMart."

"Oh, good lord. The supermarket?"

"Out the back way," I said to Nicole, not waiting for her reply, as I slid quietly out the back door. I circled around the house next door and out onto Chalker Street, then slipped into the Wheezing Dragon and headed for the Cuyahoga Falls Johnny Teagle's HyperMart, a.k.a. Alien Operation: Earth Headquarters.

*   *   *

The woman with short hair comes to the door again. "I'm sorry, guys. Joe Nofziger has just left the building."

Ngugi and Msoto exchange panicked looks. They turn and run for their bicycles. The situation is critical and they have their instructions. They hop on their bikes and head northward, towards the supermarket in Cuyahoga Falls. The Controller of Planet X said they should rendezvous there should a major disaster like this occur.

Nicole stands at the door in utter amazement at what has just transpired. She goes back inside and sits down on the couch for a few minutes and tries to get her mind together again. Failing that utterly, she decides to go after Joe. She gets in her car and heads for Cuyahoga Falls.

*   *   *

Two cars and two Black men in suits on bicycles whiz past Wilma as she walks the streets of North Hill. Even the reverend could not help her with her deep and scarring sin. She has nowhere to go. She walks along the lonely streets, not bothering to look up at the trees or hear the laughter of the children playing. She wishes she were dead. But not even death could save her, for the Lord would surely punish her for her sins with eternal torment.

Then she sees something on the sidewalk, a Xeroxed sheet. She picks it up. It says:

CHANGE TO YOUR LIFE!
BE INVOLVED IN MOST EXCITING
THE NEW ENTERPRISE
IN WORLD OF TODAY!

GROW TO RICHNESS AND SUCCESSFUL!

There is a telephone number at the bottom. Wilma decides to call.

*   *   *

Ljes is finding there is not much call for qualified helicopter pilots in and around Akron, Ohio. He only manages to find one small firm in a town called Ravenna. They have a fleet of five black helicopters purchased from the US Secret Services. They rent these out to various people for sightseeing, though there isn't much call for that around here. The two pilots they have on staff are more than enough, Ljes is told. But they take his number and promise to call if there is any need for extra pilots in the future.

Ljes does not despair. Work on the motion picture is continuing. He likes working in film. He is learning so much. He had no idea, for example, that the miniature sets depicting American cities in major productions were made out of old cardboard boxes. After a quick meal of instant mashed potatoes and Macaroni and Cheese, he goes back out to the garage and continues painting an old Frigidaire box to look like the University of Akron's Physics Department building.

*   *   *

Milena is deeply disappointed. Only three people have shown up for the first Dogs On TV Sell-abration Workshop held in what used to be the ladies' dresses section of the now defunct O'Neil's department store in downtown Akron, just up Main Street from the Anthony Wayne Hotel.

The drafty old building smells of dust and wood rot. The display floors have been divided up with cheap panels to make conference rooms, and the entire building re-named the Akron City International Convention Center. This is a joke. Who would want to present themselves and their business in a place like this? Milena has only done so because she can't afford anything better. High windows coated with a greasy gray film, the result of decades of tire factory smog, overlook Main Street, though the view is little more than a discolored blur. It is just as well you can't see the decaying city outside.

Milena turns to inspect her students. One is a sad-looking chubby woman with blonde hair, wearing a flowered dress, probably the same woman who called her up just fifteen minutes before, asking for directions. No-one knows where the Convention Center is until you tell them it's in the old O'Neil's building. Behind the chubby woman is a wiry little old Black man with a vacant smile, who looks like he might have wandered in, thinking he could pick up a free sandwich or some spare change to buy whiskey. Milena's third student is a grinning brunette in her twenties wearing a pink T-shirt on which she has written "I J for Dogs On TV!" with a felt tip marker. Milena has no idea what this could possibly mean. No matter. She decides that she will make something of this motley assortment.

"Okay," Milena says, "today you are about to be introduced to the most exciting and wondrous trend item developed in the past decade. How many of you are familiar with Dogs On TV?"

The brunette in the pink T-shirt's eyes light up and her hand shoots into the air. Milena rolls her eyes and asks, "What's your name, dear?"

"My name is Lori Nofziger-Feinman and...Oh my God! Oh my God! I love Dogs On TV! I'm a Dogs On TV collector! Oh my God! I have every one of them! I can't tell you how cool they are! Oh my God! Oh my God!"

Nut case, thinks Milena. "Very good," she says. "How about the rest of you?"

The wiry little old black man beams that big smile of his up at her like he hasn't got a care in the world, the moron. The sad-looking chubby blonde woman in the flowered dress shrugs her shoulders and continues to look like she's on the brink of tears. This is going to be wonderful, thinks Milena, because I will make it wonderful.

"All right, people!" she shouts. "Let's learn all about how to sell this product. Though, I should warn you, Dogs On TV is a product so hot it sells itself. All you do is just sit back and reap the profits!"

"Oh my God, that is so cool!" squeaks the brunette in pink. The little black man nods. The woman in the flowered dress begins weeping softly.

Milena says, "Dogs On TV is the fastest-selling trend item on the market today." She switches on the overhead projector she rented from

Kinko's Copy Center near the University of Akron the previous day. It's really not necessary. She could just as easily pass the transparency around for everyone to look at. But that wouldn't be professional.

On the fly-spotted gray stucco back wall the Potential Sales Growth chart for Dogs On TV is projected seven feet tall and eight feet wide. The figures on the graph are purely Milena's own invention. "By the mid 21st Century, according to this chart, every household in the Western world will own a complete collection of Dogs On TV, if current trends continue," she says. "Wouldn't you like to be a part of an enterprise with such world-shaking growth potential?"

"Oh yes! Oh my God! Oh yes, please!" says the brunette in pink, sounding as if she is on the verge of orgasm, and perhaps she is. The little black man chuckles. The sad woman in the flowered dress stares at the image on the wall with an expression so blank her eyes seem to be carved out of candle wax.

*   *   *

After tossing their bicycles aside, Ngugi and Msoto amble into the Cuyahoga Falls Johnny Teagle's HyperMart as casually as possible. In fact, their poor attempts at looking inconspicuous only serve to make them stand out more. They do not understand much about the task they have been given, only that they have been told to do this if they are unable to purchase the film from Joe Nofziger.

Both men are having serious second thoughts about having accepted what seemed like a glamorous offer of travel to an exciting foreign land. They are starting to wonder if they have been cheated, if the whole thing about them being descendants of a lost race of space people might, in fact, be a lie. But they are each far too stubborn to admit this to the other.

They make their way to the seafood section, looking this way and that to make certain they have not been observed. Msoto glances briefly at the crumpled fax in his pocket showing a poor photograph of the animal they are seeking and explaining how to disable its water filtration system.

Page 122

"Let us leave this place and return at another time," says Msoto shoving the paper back in his jacket pocket and looking around nervously.

"You are a coward," Ngugi counters, although in reality he is in complete agreement with Msoto. "Our instructions are quite clear."

A large man wearing a red and white striped blazer comes upon them from behind. "May I help you?" he says. Ngugi and Msoto nearly jump out of their own skins.

"We were just observing the sea foods selection," says Msoto.

"If you gentlemen are looking for some specific item I would be very glad to help," says the man whose nametag, Ngugi observes, identifies him as Bob, the head of security. There is more than a hint of menace in his voice.

"We just be lookin' around. Ain't no harm in that," says Ngugi, his attempts at imitating the local accent becoming even worse as he gets more nervous.

"Well, all right then," says Bob. "We're looking too." He points out the TV cameras above each aisle and at strategic observation points around the store. "Have a nice day, gentlemen." He walks off swinging his massive shoulders as he goes.

"We must abort the mission at once," Ngugi says.

"As I had advised earlier," Msoto replies with utter smugness. "But what shall we tell the Controller?"

"We will decide that later. Let's go."

*   *   *

"Where's the manager? I want to see him," I demanded to the check-out girl at register four of the Cuyahoga Falls Johnny Teagle's HyperMart. Her name was Wendy, or so her nametag said. She was shocked to see me again after my firing the week before, I could see it in her eyes. The store was bright, neat, antiseptic. Just the way *they* like things to be.

"Please go to customer service. They'll have him paged," she said and went back to her customer, a pathetic young hipster businessman in a sports coat and Converse high tops buying several bottles of rum. A mobile phone displayed in his breast pocket let me know they'd got to him too. Portable phones send out a continuous signal that makes critical thought impossible and renders the user more susceptible to subliminal messages hidden in advertisements.

Obeying the instructions given to me by a dupe of the invaders from space, I went over to the counter marked Customer Service. They'll get you to follow their orders even as you're bringing them down, I thought, as I stood in line behind an old woman getting some film developed - bargain basement prices and convenient free censorship of compromising images - and someone complaining about a cabbage she'd purchased only two days ago which had developed a strange fungus. Genetically encoded to do just that, no doubt.

Nicole appeared from out of nowhere and came rushing up to me. "What do you think you're doing here?"

"What do you think *you're* doing here?" I replied. "This is dangerous."

"Dangerous? What dangerous? This is Johnny Teagle's. What are you trying to prove?" She grabbed me by the arm and started pulling me out of the line.

I pulled my arm away. "I'm not leaving until I get some answers."

The old lady in front of me in line at the so-called "Service Counter" turned in her roll of film and obediently gave them her name, address, telephone number and a list of numbers which were no doubt codes clueing the organization in on the movements and whereabouts of potential troublemakers. "I want those enlarged. Only those, you understand?"

"Oh, yes," the pimply-faced boy behind the counter, whom I recognized as another of my former fellow Vector Temp employees, replied. He read back the list of numbers to her and she confirmed them.

"Last time I got the wrong ones back. I don't want the wrong ones again or I'm talking directly to your manager."

"Yes, ma'am," the kid said. He had 'Dave' written on his nametag, his true identity was spelled out in the bar code below. The old woman huffed and went about her business.

Nicole said, "Let's go." The cabbage lady was giving 'Dave' hell about her vegetable purchase.

"Not until I've seen the manager," I said. "You should care about this more than me, you know."

The cabbage lady left and I stepped up to the counter. 'Dave' smiled at me and acted all friendly, like we knew each other. "How've you been? I haven't seen you around much. They hired me on full time here, you know."

I forced myself to smile back. "Very nice. I need to see the manager."

His smile froze, then fell. "All right. May I ask what this is about?" he said, very business-like now.

"It's a confidential matter. Between he and I alone," I said.

'Dave' clenched his teeth and said, "Okay then. May I have your name and address?"

"Tell him Noftsinger wants a word with him," I said. "That's N-O-F-*T*-*S*-I-*N*-G-E-R. I think he'll want to talk then."

"Joe, come on. This is not the way to deal with things," Nicole said softly.

"Be quiet," I snapped back.

'Dave' picked up the telephone hidden under the counter, out of view of the ordinary population, pressed a secret button on the handset and said, "Manager to Customer Service, please. Manager to Customer Service." He turned to me and said, "Please wait. He'll be here shortly." I obeyed. I wouldn't be obeying much longer.

"Look, Joe, I don't know what you have in mind," Nicole said.

"Then why did you follow me here?" I said. "I work alone. I do not need any help from you or from anyone else."

"I'm here because I'm worried about you. I know we're not close. We're not really what anyone would call 'friends,' but we're both very stressed out about Charmaine."

"And I am about to speak to the very man who knows where she is. The chief of all alien operations in this sector."

"The manager of the Cuyahoga Falls Johnny Teagle's HyperMart is the head of an invading force from beyond the Solar System?" Nicole asked blithely.

"Just in this sector," I said, evenly, not caring if she believed me or not. "They've divided up the Earth into administrative sectors the same way the Europeans divided Africa up into phony 'nations' that had nothing to do with the cultures that existed there."

The manager of the Cuyahoga Falls Johnny Teagle's HyperMart came waddling around the pain reliever counter looking quite surprised to see me. No doubt he thought I'd already been gotten out of the way. He went up to the counter and 'Dave'passed him the card on which he had written the name I'd given him. I knew full well that other secret coded information was also on the card, but it didn't matter at this point. "So, Mr. Noftsinger," the manager said. "What can I do for you?"

"I think you know what you can do for me," I said, looking him right in his reptilian little eyes.

He tsk-ed. "I have already spoken to Vector Temporary Employment Services. They have apologized on your behalf for what happened the other day and they assured me you would not be sent to this store again."

"And you thought that was the end of it, did you?" I said.

"Mr. Noftsinger, I am a very busy man. I have an entire retail grocery operation to run. What is the point?"

Nicole stepped in between us and said, "I'm very sorry. My friend here is under a lot of stress."

"You stay out of this," I growled at her.

"We're sorry to have taken up your time," Nicole said to the manager. She grabbed me by the arm again and pulled hard. I went with her. But only because my work here was finished. I had made my presence known and that was all that was necessary for now. When we got to the door Nicole said, "What the hell do you think you're doing?"

"I've accomplished what I came here to do," I said. "I've let the organization know that I have not been silenced. That should send a message to them."

Then it suddenly hit me. The weird creature I'd seen in the lobster tank. Why hadn't I figured it out before?

I'd been staring at it the last time I was here and it never occurred to me. I ran back to the seafood department. Nicole scrambled to catch up, but I ignored her.

There it was, right there in the tank, pretending to be a helpless captive, when all along it was the one in charge of the whole sordid affair. The aliens themselves are humanoid, their heads are larger than ours and they are hairless. Otherwise there is little discernible difference between them and us. But this is just the dominant species of the planet. Like Earth, Planet X is home to many other species of life. The aliens have established a kind of symbiosis with a number of these lifeforms and use them to do things for them. It's a lot like the way we have domesticated horses to do physical labor for us. Only the Planet X-ians have domesticated certain types of native crustaceans to act as sort of living computers, bio-organic information processors.

Was there any other explanation why this one decidedly weird-looking striped lobster was in its own special tank kept apart from all the others? I didn't think so.

I stared at it for a moment while it waved its antennae around, processing vast amounts of information on behalf of it masters, its claws taped shut so people wouldn't realize the true menace this denizen of the deep posed. It crawled over and stood at the edge of the tank, looking at me and waving its forelegs in a strange and complex pattern. "How much for that one?" I shouted to the skinny man behind the counter.

"Twenty-nine dollars," he replied.

"Joe," Nicole said.

I rummaged through my wallet. Ten dollars even. "Nicole. Lend me nineteen dollars."

"What?"

"Nineteen dollars. I have to buy this lobster."

"You're a vegetarian. Even I know that, you're such a prick about it. What do you want with a lobster?" she said.

"Quick," I said, "before somebody else buys it." Then I said to the man behind the counter, "I'll take it."

He went under the counter to get a little paper box, which he proceeded to take his time folding into the proper configuration. "Hurry!"

I said. He gave me a strange look then pulled on a big rubber glove, reached into the tank and pulled the lobster out. I wondered for a moment why he was willing to comply with my request. Communication between the human operatives was not very good, I assumed. In fact, the lower level operatives probably did not even know who they were working for. He put the lobster in the little box and folded up the carrying handles on top. "Keep it in water until you're ready to cook it. You should eat it today."

"Yes, yes," I said impatiently.

He stuck a bar coded sticker on the bottom of the box and handed it to me. "Pay at the front register."

"You're going to buy that lobster?" Nicole said, following me towards the front.

"Can I have that nineteen dollars now?" I said. The lobster's antennae stuck out through the top of the box, waving around and around. "I'll pay you back on Friday, all right? I've still got one more check coming from Vector Temps. This is important."

Nicole reached into her purse, dug out a twenty and handed it to me. "Take it. It's a gift. Anything to get you out of this store."

"Can you give me about 75 cents in case there's tax?"

"Jesus Christ," she said, and dug out another dollar.

"Thanks." The lobster scraped at the sides of the box.

Just to let them know I was not going to be stopped, I deliberately went through register four and let the so-called 'Wendy' ring up my lobster. She ran the box over the scanner once, and it didn't beep. So she ran it over again. Still no beep. What were they playing at here? Maybe there was information encrypted on the bar code, whatever information had been stored up by the lobster up till that time. Maybe it was so detailed that it took several passes over the scanner to input.

The check-out girl ran the lobster over the scanner once more. It beeped this time. But the bottom of the box gave out and the lobster plopped onto the register. It started crawling towards the conveyor belt, clicking its pincers and waving its antennae around. The check out girl jumped back and screamed. "Tom! Tom!!!"

"Another one trying to escape!" said a beefy high school drop-out type in a red and white striped Johnny Teagle's HyperMart vest as he stomped manfully over to the register. He grabbed the lobster and held it up. Its legs and antennae waved around in the air.

"Be careful with him!" I shouted.

The beefy drop-out grunted. 'Wendy' handed him a new box from underneath the register. Interesting how they were prepared for just this particular contingency. He wrangled my lobster into the box and handed it over to me. I grabbed it away from him. Moron.

I paid my money, tucked my lobster under my arm and walked out the door. Nicole followed. As soon as I stepped outside I sneezed twice. This happens to roughly 75% of the American population. When they leave an artificially lit environment and step into natural sunlight they sneeze. It is a documented scientific fact. You can look it up. Someone behind me said, "Excuse me sir, may I speak with you for a moment?"

I turned around to see another guy with football player build, wearing a red and white striped vest. A gold nametag reading "Johnny Teagle's HyperMart Security Chief, Bob" glinted on his left lapel. They were onto me. "Run!" I shouted to Nicole and took off into the parking lot.

The security agent gave chase. I zigzagged through the parking lot, dodging stray shopping carts, knowing there was no way I could get away on speed alone, clutching the lobster tight against my chest.

The security guard closed in on me in the Kangaroo Section. I hurled a shopping cart at him. The cart went clattering about two feet in his general direction when one of the wheels stuck and it toppled over. He stepped around the cart and continued to bear down on me.

I came to an old VW microbus painted up with Grateful Dead inspired colors, giant rust holes all over the body. Still clutching the lobster, I climbed up onto the roof. The security guard stopped at the back of the van and laughed. "Come on down from there, buddy. Where are you going to go?"

I held the lobster up over my head. "You come near me and the lobster gets it!"

The security guard laughed even harder. Of course. When they'd scanned the bar code they'd already gotten their precious information.

What more did they need the lobster for? I hugged the lobster tight to my chest and slumped down to sit on the roof of the VW microbus. Below me the security guard called for assistance on his walkie-talkie. "This is 0-19, need backup in K section," he said in that phony police-man voice all security guards affect. Then he shouted, "You might as well come down. We're not going to let you leave."

There was no escape. They had me. As Philip K. Dick once said, "If they want you, they've already got you. All they need is the paperwork." No doubt the paperwork was being prepared even now.

A couple other beefy guys in red and white striped vests trotted out to the van, but I was already climbing down. The main security guard, Bob, grabbed my lobster away from me. I put my hands up. "Put your hands down. This isn't an arrest. We aren't the police. We just want to talk with you, that's all."

Right, I thought, and as soon as I lower my hands you're going to pull out a gun and shoot me, and then say you did it in self-defense. Nothing doing. I kept my hands clasped tightly on top of my head. "Suit yourself," the security guard said. "Let's go back in the office where we can have some privacy." Already a small crowd of housewives and other assorted shoppers had gathered around to watch.

"You're next!" I shouted at them. "Don't think they're going to stop with just me! They won't give in until they've got total control!" A few people chuckled. Funny. Sure. Funny now, but give them time to com-plete their insidious plans and then see how funny you think it is.

*   *   *

At the end of the seminar Milena has signed all three of her stu-dents on as Dogs On TV regional representatives. She hands out or-der forms, contracts and sign-up sheets and encourages them to get out there and sell. The brunette in pink runs out the door and into the street, ready to sell a dozen to the first person she sees. The little black man looks over the contract, still smiling. Milena waits for him to ask for a hand-out, but he just walks out the door chuckling to himself like an idiot. The woman in the flowered dress takes the papers without looking up at Milena and shuffles out the door, shoulders hunched, sobbing quietly.

*   *   *

Ngugi and Msoto arrive back at the Anthony Wayne Hotel, thoroughly out of breath. It's a long way from Cuyahoga Falls to downtown Akron by bicycle. No sooner have they entered their room when the Interociter begins to hum. An image forms on the screen.

"You have the film?" asks the Controller of Planet X, the green veins in his bulbous brown head throbbing.

"We have had a setback to our plans," says Msoto.

"Setback?" says the Controller. "What you are saying is that you did not get the film."

Msoto and Ngugi exchange worried glances. "Essentially, yes," says Ngugi.

"Fools!" the Controller of Planet X shouts at Ngugi and Msoto. They recoil from the screen. "I have given you detailed instructions. A perfect cover story. And you botch the entire operation. You of Earth are idiots!"

"Now, hold on a moment," says Ngugi.

"No, you hold on!" the Controller of Planet X shouts back. "You have no idea what sort of forces you are meddling with! First was your toy balloon. A harmless game. Then came the hot air balloon, a man could be sent into the sky itself. Then there was your glider and your airplane. Men flew higher and higher. Finally came your rocket ship. Men could be launched to the moon and to the other planets of your solar system and finally into the Galaxy itself." Ngugi and Msoto have no idea what the Controller is going on about.

"Now you of Earth have captured a piece of our technology," says the Controller of Planet X, green veins pulsating in his cocoa-colored head. "Technology so far advanced, beyond the current state of your pitiful planet's primitive science, that it is as if baboons in the jungle have been given access to a gigantic Univac Computer. This technology could propel you into space, farther than you ever dreamed possible. Or it could destroy your entire world. You fools would rather destroy yourselves than explore the vast frontiers of new scientific vistas. Fools! Idiots! Imbeciles!"

Ngugi picks at his fingernails with an Anthony Wayne Hotel matchbook. Msoto sits on the bed thumbing through the TV Guide.

The Controller of Planet X sighs. "Of course you have enacted the back-up plan and retrieved the creature," he says.

"Huh?" says Ngugi noticing that the Controller has asked him a question.

"The creature," the Controller growls.

Msoto puts down the TV Guide and says, "Oh yes. We have it. Of course." He shoots Ngugi a cautioning look.

"Very well," says the Controller. "Await further instructions. Thaw pap hens."

"We do hynie!" Ngugi and Msoto reply in unison. The Interociter screen goes blank.

*   *   *

Still dressed in her pink "I J for Dogs On TV!" T-shirt, Lori Nofziger-Feinman memorizes the Dogs On TV sales pitch. It is important that the precise words be used in order to create Maximum Selling Effect and to instill in the customer the Desire Of Total Purchase, a mystical state in which the customer becomes one with the concrete action of buying the product and participates in the Absolute Purchase Experience which can be likened, the pamphlet she got at the meeting says, to the "dropping away of both body and mind experienced by mystics down through the ages of eternity." Milena, Lori knows, is a woman of strength and integrity. She would never lead anyone astray.

Lori decides to try her selling technique out on her brother Joe. He's into weird collectible stuff, all those old movies and toys and things he's always buying. That whole dirty old house he lives in is stuffed with odd little knickknacks. They can't feed themselves properly, but they still buy toys. Maybe everybody at the house will buy a whole set of Dogs On TV. When she knocks on the door, a man she has never seen before answers. He is rather short, with blond hair, muscles like Arnold Schwarzenegger and an accent to match. "Joe is not home right now. Can I give to him the message?"

Lori smiles. She has a better idea. "Actually, I'd like to speak to you about something very important. What's your name?"

"Ljes," the muscle man says. What a weird name, Lori thinks.

She reaches into her satchel and pulls out a Dogs On TV. "Well, La-yes, have you ever seen such the cuteness of dog life before?" Lori says, hoping she is pronouncing the man's name correctly. She hands him one of the Dogs On TV samples. "Look through the back and enter to the wonderful magic world in which cute dogs romp and play in many colorfule costumes down through the ages of eternity." Why color*fule* and not color*ful,* she wonders briefly. But Milena emphasized the importance of using these exact words. Milena understands.

Lori sees the man with the muscles' eyes go wide as she speaks. Great, she thinks, the sales pitch is working. "Yes, Dogs On TV is in the tradition of such many great the animal stars as Rin Tin Tin, Lassie and Cutie of the TV series Selo gori, a baba se češlja. Delight to the lively and happiness of it!"

The muscle man grunts, "I'll buy them all," he says abruptly.

This is something Lori never expected. It's almost too good to be true. Right away, on her first call the customer has experienced Supreme Acquisition Fervor, the highest state of Desire Of Total Purchase, in which the customer wishes to merge himself with the product as fully as possible by acquiring as much of the product as is available. Many Seekers of Pure Trading work their entire lives to participate in such an experience.

Unable to believe her luck, Lori quickly calculates the price and the muscle man accepts without question. She digs out all the required documents for him to sign and passes them to him.

Lori is ecstatic as she takes back the contracts and the cash and hands over all of her Dogs On TV samples. "Thank you so much for your the business!" she says, quoting the proper Purchase Closure Salutation.

She rushes off to find a convenience store with a fax machine so she can send her contracts in to the home office as quickly as possible.

She finds a Dairy Mart with a fax machine. A woman rushes out the automatic doors. Lori recognizes her from the flowered dress she is wearing. It's the other woman that attended the Dogs On TV Sell-abration Workshop. "Hello," Lori says.

"Oh, hello," says the woman in the flowered dress. "I'm sorry I can't talk now. I have to go."

"Okay," says Lori. "See you."

She goes inside and faxes her signed contracts to Milena.

*   *   *

After the Dogs On TV Sell-abration Workshop, Wilma drives her little 1985 Honda Accord northward, not paying much attention to where she is. She wanders around Cuyahoga Falls at random. Her mind replays a mix of random memories; Kim Yong Lee calling her a slut, the commanding stiffness of Joe Nofziger's beautiful manly cock penetrating her most secret feminine places, Reverend Goodman's casual attitude towards her sin, Miss Park, the woman with the short red hair who, like Wilma, lusted in her heart for lithe, almond-eyed, copper-skinned boys. She begins to re-imagine her lustful encounter with Joe Nofziger, substituting Kim Yong Lee for Joe. In her mind Kim Yong Lee's penis is bright red with thick purple and green veins throbbing, engorged with hot blood and semen, forcing its way deeper and deeper, tearing into her with the fury and anger of the Lord when He smote the people of Sodom.

She pulls her car off to the side of a street, which, as she sees by the sign, is called Herbruck Avenue. She closes her eyes for a moment, willing the visions of lust to cease. They do not. She has to do something to keep this carnality at bay. She tears the Dogs on TV samples and paperwork out of her purse, gets out of her car and walks to the nearest house. Briefly she looks at her sales pitch again, then puts it back into her pocket. She takes a deep breath and rings the doorbell.

"Have you ever seen such cuteness of dog life before?" Wilma says, her left hand holding one of the Dogs On TV samples out to the man with the large behind who has just answered the door, her right hand holding the Approved Sales Pitch so she can read it. "Look through the back and enter to the wonderful magic world in which cute dogs romp and play in many colorfule costumes." Is color*fule* different from color*ful,* Wilma wonders briefly. Milena had said the pitch must be given exactly as written. She clears her throat and finishes, "down through the ages of eternity."

The man at the door scowls at her. "Let me see that," he says, taking the Dogs On TV from her hand. He inspects it carefully.

Suddenly Wilma realizes she's seen him before, "Say, you work at the supermarket, don't you?"

The man grunts, "I manage the foul place," he says. "Where'd you get these?"

Wilma tells him about Milena and the Dogs On TV Sell-abration meetings. The man grunts some more. "How much for everything? I want your whole stock."

Wilma does some calculations and names the price for her entire supply of Dogs On TV's. The man with the big rear end waddles back inside and returns shortly with the cash. She sells him the entire stock, making sure that the man signs the Pre-Purchase Deal Memo, the Purchaser's Contract, the Non Re-sale of Product Agreement and the Proper Use of Purchased Item Pact. He signs without even bothering to read any of the documents.

Sitting back in her car after the sale Wilma feels just like she did when she had her Born Again Experience. The fog of lust and confusion that had threatened to engulf her completely has vanished in the twinkling of an eye to be replaced by joy incomparable. She has been touched by a greater power. Quickly she leafs through the Xeroxed manual provided by the Dogs On TV Corporation of America. She finds that what she is experiencing now is called the Supreme Elation of the Pure Trading Experience. According to the manual, this is a state of pure oneness with the selling of a product. Joy washes over her in great torrents. Her body feels as if it is glowing with a power and purity that reaches from the center of her womanhood and fills her entire body with hot, solid, pulsating might.

Suddenly Wilma realizes that this state of purest joy will not last. She will need to repeat the experience again and again, eventually to dwell in this purity forevermore. She drives off toward Howe Road to go and look for a telephone. She needs more Dogs On TV. She finds one in the Dairy Mart, makes her call, then rushes out of the shop to the pick-up point, brushing past one of her fellow Dogs On TV sellers as she does. But there is no time for chatting now.

* * *

Charmaine can't stand it anymore. For the past week she has been hiding out at her parents' house in Copley, not answering the phone, refusing contact with any of her friends. Only her brother Mark knows where she is. No-one is allowed to say anything to anyone, most especially not to Joe or Nicole.

Mark calls her up to say that the Zen Luv Assassins will be playing at The Grind tonight. Johnny Phlegm's band the V-Nervz are opening. After mulling it over for a long, long time, Charmaine decides she's had enough of hiding. There are only so many mind-numbing daytime talk shows a person can watch before going completely insane. The show starts in a few minutes. She gets in her car and in a couple of minutes arrives at The Grind.

Where is everybody, Charmaine wonders, as she walks across the dance floor. The crowd is pretty thin. That's to be expected on a Thursday night at The Grind, especially when the show starts at eight o'clock. The idea of starting weekday shows early to try and attract the "I gotta be at work tomorrow" crowd hasn't really paid off. This may have something to do with the fact that no-one in Akron, Ohio has a job anymore.

Charmaine at least expected Joe to show up: he shows up at every Zen Luv Assassins gig. There's no sign of Nicole either. Charmaine's whole Return to Public Life plan is beginning to look like a complete waste of time.

* * *

Ljes cannot believe what he is hearing from the lady at the door. This is the very sales pitch he wrote for Dogs On TV. Milena is up to something. What does she think she's playing at?

"Very interesting," says Ljes, fingering one of the Dogs On TVs. Milena is bold, he will give her that. But she will not get away with this, he decides. Not while he is still around to stop her. "How much for the entire stock of them?"

Ljes takes the contracts. He is surprised that door-to-door purchasers of Dogs On TV are only required to sign a Pre-Purchase Deal Memo, a Purchaser's Contract, a Non Re-sale of Product Agreement and a Proper Use of Purchased Item Pact. Milena must be slipping, he thinks. There is not nearly enough paperwork here to cement a full and complete understanding between Client and Sales Person. He signs all of the agreements and hands them back to the sales woman. It hardly matters what he has signed. The Dogs On TV Corporation of America, at least Milena's version of it, will be utterly destroyed.

*　　　*　　　*

The doorbell rings. Carl gets out of his easy chair where he has been sitting reading a copy of *Zen and the Art of Creative Management* he picked up at the HyperMart Book Center before going home. He looks out the peephole and sees a chubby blonde girl in a flowered dress standing there, her eyes glazed over like she has been mainlining pot or something. He thinks about ignoring her, but she might be one of his wife's weirdo Mah Jong club friends. He opens the door, but before he can say anything she says, "I'd like to speak to you about something very important..."

After hearing her pitch, Carl thinks, Dogs On TV door-to-door salespeople? Since when? Immediately he realizes that this will have profound repercussions on Johnny Teagle's HyperMart's sales of Goofy Feet* cereal. If people can just buy the damned things from door-to-door salespeople why buy that stupid cereal? This could be the end of the whole thing.

Not waiting for the chubby girl to finish Carl says, "How much for the lot of them?" He has to sign about a thousand papers, but it hardly matters. He'll put these people out of business anyway.

Carl goes back inside, puts his sack full of Dogs On TVs down on the kitchen table and roots around through his briefcase for Abe Kidman's phone number.

Carl calls up Abe Kidman at American Mills and tells him about the Dogs On TV door-to-door salespeople.

"I know," says Abe, "I heard from my assistant, Charlie. He attended one of their Dogs On TV Sell-abration Workshops."

"What are we going to do about it?" Carl shouts.

"Do about it?" says Abe. "This is life. What do you do about life?"

"Life? This is not life! It's bullshit!" Carl yells into the phone at Abe Kidman. "This is going to kill the whole thing! We're sitting on top of a gold mine with this Dogs On TV craze! My God, you and I could make a fortune on these stupid things. But not if we let these idiots keep selling them door-to-door!"

"I don't know," says Abe. "Have you got something in mind?"

"No," says Carl, "not exactly. Let me work on this and I'll call you back." He slams down the phone and paces his kitchen floor.

*   *   *

After putting down the telephone, Abe Kidman goes out to the main floor of American Mills' packing plant and finds Charlie mopping up behind the number two flour grinder. He tells him about his conversation with Carl. "You talked to me about accepting reality as it is. Shouldn't I just accept this?"

"Well, sir," says Charlie, "I don't think you quite caught what I was intending to say. It's like this. The whole world, the whole entire Universe even, is one living intelligent thing. But even that ain't quite right. Talking like that gives people too many ideas in they heads. And ideas in people's heads ain't what it's all about. Too small. But get this, you are part of all that is. Right here and right now. This is where you have to make your efforts. Ain't like you gotta forget about yesterday and not care about tomorrow. Stuff like that's just more ideas in your head. You accept this world by facing it. You do what you have to do. Do what must be done in this moment. Cause ain't nowhere else you can ever be."

"Then what should I do?" Abe asks Charlie.

"Can't answer that one for you, boss. You got to work that out on your own. Me, I'm walking right into the fire, because that's my place. But you got your business to think about. Lots of folks depending on you for their livelihood."

*   *   *

The phone rings and Milena picks up. It takes her a moment to realize that she is speaking to the sad woman in the flowered dress. Only the woman is not so sad now.

The woman rants on and on about power and purity and glowing bodies and being born again and joy incomparable, quoting liberally from the words Ljes used in his pamphlet about selling things. Ljes' philosophy is pure nonsense, Milena has always thought so. Only idiots make buying and selling into mysticism. Foolish, but it works on the gullible. There are only two worthwhile goals in life: money and power.

At any rate, she does not have time to talk to this silly person. After the woman slows down a bit, Milena interjects that she will send over some more samples right away. "Thank you! Thank you!" says the formerly sad woman - probably still in the same flowered dress, she thinks. "You don't know how much this means. Such purity. Such utter and profound truth."

"Yes, yes," says Milena impatiently. "Fax me the signed forms. I will speak with you later." She hangs up the phone as quickly as possible. She hates dealing with the peons.

Then Milena smiles to herself. In spite of its foolishness, Ljes' motivational strategy has worked out after all. Of course, it only worked because she put it into practice in the proper way. She does some quick calculations. Once she motivates 75 more people to this degree she will reach her first monetary goal. Then she will motivate 50 new people per week and the cash flow will become continuous.

Her fax machine beeps. Milena tears the contract out. Her first direct marketing motivational sale. She wonders where she can go to have this framed. Eventually this contract will hang behind her giant oaken desk in Dogs On TV Corporate Headquarters in the Bahamas where Milena plans to run her worldwide Dogs On TV empire.

She looks over the contact and it is then that she notices the name of the purchaser at the bottom.

Carl Walters. The man from Johnny Teagle's HyperMart.

Milena is in trouble now and she knows it. She did not plan for this. She had figured the Dogs On TV direct marketing motivational campaign would be well under way long before anyone from Johnny Teagle's HyperMart or the American Mills Corporation ever heard about it. Now she needs to make a decisive move, and she needs to do it fast. She needs help and there is only one person left to turn to.

Milena's fax machine beeps again and another set of contracts starts to come through. She tears these out and realizes she's in even bigger trouble than she thought. The signature on the bottom is Ljes Sœiåeffgrußør

*   *   *

Carl has a brilliant idea. He's known one of the guys who runs the Goodyear hangar down on the South side of town since grade school. The man owes him plenty of favors.

Abe calls Carl Walters back. "What do you have in mind?"

Carl says, "Dogs On TV dropping from the skies over Akron!"

He puts the telephone down and makes a call to his friend at the blimp hangar. Then he makes a couple dozen more calls to various members of the city government. Johnny Teagle's HyperMart is one of the few businesses in town that still generates money. Carl has a lot of influence and now is the time to put it all to work. A few hours later he has the whole thing arranged.

*   *   *

Ben I. Goldman gets a call from his contact at the Akron Civic Theater. The world premiere of *Jesus vs. Mecha Jesus* has had to be rescheduled in order to coincide with another big event to be held in downtown Akron. His contact asks him if he can have the film ready in three days.

"Three days?" Goldman shouts. "We've only just started post-production. How can we be ready in three days?"

Goldman is told that he has no choice. Either the film premieres in three days or it doesn't premiere at all. Plans for turning the Civic Theater into a parking complex have already been finalized, after which there will be no more Civic Theater. Don Plusquellic, the mayor of Akron has decided that if the premiere is to happen at all it will have to be at the same time as another event he has just scheduled, for which several blocks of Main Street will be blocked off to traffic.

"Just what is this big-ass important event?" says Goldman, momentarily forgetting that the person he is addressing knows him only as Reverend Goodman of Christ the Crowned King.

"Some nut has rented the Goodyear blimp and plans to drop some kind of toy called Dogs On TV from the sky. It's a big fad of some sort. All the kids are into it these days. It doesn't sound like much to me, to be honest. But they're expecting thousands of people from all over the state, maybe even as far away as Pittsburgh."

Good lord, thinks Goldman, it's worse than I thought. Someone is not acting according to instructions. But who? Could Joe Nofziger be in on this somehow? He has not been able to reach him for two days now. He leafs through this week's Scene magazine and sees that Joe's friends the Zen Luv Assassins, the band who are writing the movie's soundtrack, will be playing tonight at a place called The Grind. Joe will be there, Ben figures. Without the footage that Joe has from *Gill Women of the Prehistoric Planet* the whole plan is sunk. Desperate measures are called for.

Ben I. Goldman gets a call from Kim Yong Lee. He's in jail and needs $350 bail to get out. Ben agrees to put up the money. After all, it is more or less his fault the man got arrested in the first place. Anyway, he may be useful. He drives down to the station and picks him up.

Getting into the Ben's car Kim Yong Lee says, "I so glad you rescue me. Very bad. Do bad against God. Very sad now."

"Shut up, Lee," says Ben, dropping the Reverend Goodman thing. "No more games. No more games from you and no more games from me. Things are very serious now."

He pulls his car off to the side of Howe Road, near Johnny Teagle's HyperMart. He turns to Kim Yong Lee and says, "The church is a scam." Kim Yong Lee looks puzzled. "A lie. The church is not really a church. I am not really a reverend."

Ben sees that Kim Yong Lee cannot follow what he is saying. But he presses on anyway. He tells him the whole Earth is in danger. Then he asks for Kim Yong Lee's help.

Kim Yong Lee agrees to help. Ben knows it probably has more to do with staying out of jail than any real understanding of what's at stake, but it doesn't matter. "I'm so glad you understand," he says. "I'll take you to the church and you can get started. I have to go somewhere else."

Ben Goldman drops off Kim Yong Lee and arrives at The Grind just as one of the bands is finishing. On stage a man in his late 30's with a pink crew cut, wearing only a dog collar and a pair of leather pants, thanks a listless group of about seven young people standing around on the dance floor or leaning against what looks like disused factory equipment. "You're beautiful," the man with pink hair says as the guitarist switches off his amplifier abruptly cutting off cascades of howling feedback.

There is no sign of Joe Nofziger, but at the bar he spots the black girl Joe brought with him to the church before, the one who was supposed to play Mary Magdalene. What was her name? Oh yeah, Charmaine. Like that old song by Bill Haley and his Comets. Another change in plans is called for. Goldman checks his pockets.

*   *   *

I gave up wearing watches. Time is a marketing concept. Did you know there was no such thing as "time" a hundred years ago? It wasn't until railroads started going across the continent and schedules had to be worked out that it became important to synchronize clocks in different cities. Clock and watch manufacturers pushed the concept to the hilt and soon everybody had to know what time it was. I, for one, do not play into it. So I do not know how long, by so-called "Objective Time," I sat alone on the red vinyl cushions of the couch in the interrogation room of the Cuyahoga Falls Johnny Teagle's HyperMart.

They love to keep you waiting. Authority is the ability to make other people wait for you. Over in one corner was one of those vending machines that dispensed paper cups full of rancid coffee or watery cola drinks with too much crushed ice in them. Next to that was one that sold candy and little bags of potato chips and Fritos. Listening devices were implanted in those machines, I'm sure. Cameras too. On the wall was a portrait of the Employee of the Week. I noticed that it had not been changed for six months. At least I know what day it is, if not what time.

Once I saw an ad for a company in England that would sell you, via mail, legal second passports, surveillance equipment, computer viruses to destroy your enemies, equipment to open any type of lock in under seven seconds, all kinds of stuff like that. I should have ordered some. I would have been able to bust my way out of here. But I couldn't afford it and anyway I don't know how much postage to put on a letter to England. You can bet your ass I'm not going to enquire at my post office either. Once I tipped them off that I was going to write to England the whole thing would have been over. They work for the federal government, you know. All overseas mail is monitored closely, especially when you're sending to a former enemy nation like England.

They confiscated my lobster. That was *my* lobster, I have the receipt. I was trying to think of a name for him. I hope he's all right. Actually, they were probably switching the one I picked for another, a lobster who didn't know so much.

If I had some change maybe I could buy some Combos from the machine. But listening devices could easily be embedded in the cheese-product filling.

I looked through some of the magazines lying on the table. All boring crap like Family Circle, Good Housekeeping, and the like. Who buys those things? There was a Newsweek there too. People actually believe what they read in magazines like that. Like any of that stuff really happened.

Bob, my friendly security guard, strutted into the interrogation room in to speak to me. I did not stand when he entered. Bob said, "You seem very agitated, Mr. Nossinger. I only want to ask you some questions. Nobody is being accused of anything here."

"Of course not," I said. Nobody is ever accused. Not officially. They just quietly disappear from view. I did not say this out loud, of course. They knew that I knew. I didn't even want to think who this new character "Nossinger" might be.

"Good," Bob said. "I'm glad you understand that. Now, we run a very large retail operation here. We have a lot of money invested in this supermarket. The livelihood of each and every person who works here at Johnny Teagle's HyperMart depends upon the store being able to show a profit. That's where our wages come from. Shoplifting is one of the major causes of losses at a store like this one. Do you agree that we have the right to be concerned about shoplifting?"

The proper answer was yes, so I said, "Yes." But I maintained my center. This was indoctrination, pure and simple, and they were not going to indoctrinate me that easily.

"Good," Bob said, pacing in front of me as he spoke. That little red and white striped vest must give him such a sense of authority. "I'm glad you agree. Now, we have found that most shoplifters behave in an unusual manner. They know that stealing is wrong and this influences the way they act. Even the best of thieves will always give himself away. Therefore, we are trained to look for people who behave in unusual ways inside the store. Now, Mr. Nossinger, what did you do when you first arrived here at Johnny Teagle's HyperMart today?"

"You tell me," I said. "You seem to have all the answers."

"It would be better if we heard it from you," he said.

I clammed up.

"Okay," Bob said to me after I sat there silently for a time. "If you're not going to tell me your version of what happened, how about if I tell you ours? First you went to one of the registers and demanded to see the manager. You were directed to Customer Service where you made the same demand. Mr. Carl Walters, our manager was paged. When you spoke to the manager you made what seemed to him to be thinly veiled threats, possibly stemming from your dismissal as a temporary worker here. You then went back to the seafood section with a young woman. You had a very agitated discussion with the clerk there and finally purchased a single live lobster. The check-out person who rang you up also reported that you were behaving in an unusual manner. When I stopped you outside to ask you some questions you ran. Why did you run?"

"What gives you the right to ask me questions?" I said.

"I explained to you that we have to be careful about shoplifting," said Bob. "You agreed that we had that right." I had fallen right into their trap.

"I didn't steal anything from you," I said.

"No-one is saying you did. But if you didn't steal anything, why did you run?" said Bob.

Useless. They knew very well why I ran. I ran because I knew the secret of their operation, but if I said so they could label me as "insane." If they wanted to prove I'd stolen from them, all they had to do was produce one object, anything would do. Then all that was needed was for them to say they'd found it on me and that would be that. It would be the word of one defenseless patsy against the accusation of a powerful and respected - read: *feared* - organization.

"Mr. Nossinger?" Bob said.

"Why don't we just get on with this?" I said. "Stop playing games with me and do whatever it is you're going to do."

"And what do you think we want to do to you?" Bob asked.

I narrowed my eyes at him. "I don't know, *Bob*. You're the expert. You're the security person. You tell me."

He chuckled. "I just want the truth, Mr. Nossinger."

"The truth?" I said to Security Chief Bob. "This isn't about the truth. This is about power. You have the power and I do not, and you need to prove it. You're all alike, you know. Whether it's Nazis gassing the Jews or it's the cops harassing punks, or a boss lording it over on his underlings or school principals paddling small children, the impulse is exactly the same. Powerful people disgust me. You're the most repulsive creatures on the planet. You'd sell your own species out for a taste of power."

"Look here," Bob said. "I don't know what that crack about Jews was supposed to mean. My wife is Jewish. I don't like your tone, friend. I will not tolerate racism."

Racism? Me? Was this so-called "Bob" person even listening at all? I tried again. "I didn't steal anything from your store. The reason I do not act like a normal person is because I am not a normal person. I have no wish to be a normal person. I want nothing to do with normal people. Maybe that's a crime. The violation of some unwritten law. Fine. Do whatever you want."

"I'll be honest with you, Mr. Nossinger. I believe you," said Bob. "I don't see any evidence that you stole anything. I talked to your friend. Nicole, is it? I spoke to her outside and she says you don't steal. But help me out, all right? You come into the store, make strange demands and then run away. The manager, my boss, wants to know why."

"Tell your boss that I delivered the message I came to deliver. My business here is finished."

"All right, I'll do that," Bob said. "How's this for your part of the deal? I'll let you leave here. No more questions, no more trouble. In turn you agree not to come back here. Do your shopping elsewhere from now on. Can you do that?"

And they'd keep me under surveillance. They had to. "I have no desire ever to come here again," I said.

"Good," said Bob. "Wait here a moment while I consult with the manager." He left. As if the manager hadn't been watching the whole encounter on closed circuit television and relaying instructions via a miniaturized earphone Bob kept well hidden. They make them so small now you'd never even know they were there. When you see some security person wearing an earphone that you can actually see, you can bet that they're only doing it for effect, to make sure you *know* they are taking orders from someone higher up.

Bob came back in, carrying my lobster. "The manager says you can go," he said, handing me a little blue plastic bucket in which my lobster scratched around listlessly. I stood and reached for it. He pulled the bucket back away from me. "Remember our bargain. From now on you shop elsewhere."

"Fine," I said. He stared at me. "I'll shop elsewhere." He handed me the lobster.

"Good," he said. I brushed past him as I walked through the door and out of the store.

*   *   *

Charmaine goes to the bar and orders a gin and tonic, and then settles in to watch the show. The V-Nervz finish their half hour and the Zen Luvs start setting up. There's nobody but regulars at the bar. She plans to sneak out and go back to her parents' house sometime during the Zen Luv's set. It'd be too much to show up at Nicole's place. "Buy you a drink?" someone behind her says.

Charmaine blinks her eyes twice in surprise. The person offering her a drink is the reverend from that weirdo church Joe dragged her to, the guy they've been making the movie for. "Oh, hi," she says. "What are you doing here?"

"I came here looking for Joe," says the reverend. "Any idea where he is?"

"You're barking up the wrong tree there," Charmaine replies with a sarcastic chuckle.

"Here's your drink," the reverend says, pushing Charmaine's glass over to her.

"Thanks," she replies and takes a sip. Within a few seconds she starts to sway on her stool. She had no idea she could be this drunk after just two drinks.

She excuses herself to go to the ladies room. The reverend follows her and says, "Are you all right? Here let me help you," and takes her by the arm. On stage the Zen Luv Assassins launch into their version of the Velvet Underground's "What Goes On." Charmaine stumbles. The reverend catches her by the arm.

"Are you sure you're okay?" the reverend says to Charmaine.

"I'm fine," Charmaine replies, trying to wriggle out of his grasp. She is too weak. Her legs start to get wobbly. She slips and knocks down one of the bar stools.

"I think you'd better go home now," says the reverend. "I'll take you there."

*   *   *

I drove the Wheezing Dragon back to the Clubhouse, feeling pathetic and useless, but not alone. The lobster was with me, thrashing away inside his little blue plastic bucket on the passenger seat. The Wheezing Dragon's shock absorbers shuffled off this mortal coil sometime around the release of Devo's first single for Stiff Records, and all the bouncing must have been getting to him. What was I going to do with a lobster anyway? During the time they had him he'd probably been memory wiped. Even if he hadn't been, I had no idea how to extract any information from him. It really had been a stupid idea. This whole day had been a really stupid day. My whole entire existence has been a really stupid whole entire existence.

I could at least give my lobster a name. I decided on Space Lobster™. The '™' part was important because I hate it when people steal my ideas. If you put a '™' next to one of your ideas supposedly nobody can steal it. You also need a '©'. So I decided that the lobster's full name would be 'Space Lobster™ © Joe Nofziger All Rights Reserved, Unauthorized Copying is a Violation of Applicable Law.' People could just call him Space Lobster™ for short.

A lot of my ideas have been stolen. One time I read an article in Omni about how you could clone dinosaurs from cells that might be recovered from inside the stomachs of mosquitoes trapped in amber. I wrote a story about how somebody did that and made this big Tyrannosaurus Rex that attacked New York City, and then had to be destroyed by a super-scientific weapon created by a scientist who was afraid his weapon might later fall into the wrong hands and be used against humanity. Omni wouldn't print my story. But obviously they sent a copy to Michael Crichton and Steven Spielberg. They probably attached a note saying "Dear Mike and Steve, Here's some story we received from a pathetic little nobody in Ohio. Please steal it and then give us half the money you make. Love, The Editors of Omni."

I didn't put a '™' or a '©' at the bottom of the story so there's nothing I can do. Well if Steven Spielberg decides to do a movie about a lobster called Space Lobster I've got him dead to rights.

I put Space Lobster™ on the Fascinating Table in the Living Room, put Mark's copy of the three record "Concert For Bangla Desh" set over top of the bucket so he couldn't escape and so The Cat With No Name couldn't eat him, then went upstairs to bed.

*   *   *

Charmaine wakes to find herself handcuffed to a lawn chair next to a washing machine. Morning sunlight streams in through small dusty windows set into gray concrete walls above her. The air is damp. Across from her is a box full of plastic model flying saucers. Lying on the floor next to that is a pile of single-lensed new-wave sunglasses and a number of bulbous rubber costume headpieces with green veins in them. Silver and black jumpsuits hang on a rack to her left, and on her right a huge golden cross leans against the wall. Her head aches, her brain cells are covered in fuzz and glue. What is this place? What is all this stuff?

She tries to bend forward so that the lawn chair will collapse, but finds that the chair is anchored to something heavy behind her. Someone comes down the stairs. "Reverend Goodman!" Charmaine says. "Thank god. Can you get me out of here? I'm handcuffed to this thing."

"I'm very sorry about this, Charmaine," the reverend says stepping over to her and examining her wrists. "You really shouldn't strain so much. You'll only hurt yourself." He fingers a bruise on her arm. She flinches. "In the end you'll see that it was absolutely necessary."

"Necessary? What are you talking about? Where am I?" she says. "This looks like a basement. Is this your church?"

Without making eye contact with her the reverend says, "In 1981 on the nationally syndicated Merv Griffin talk show a respected former astronaut revealed that NASA Intelligence is fully aware of the UFO phenomenon and that he, himself, in fact, was present when a saucer-shaped craft, not of this world, touched down in September of 1952 at Lake Gordon, Nevada in full view of Navy cameramen who filmed the entire event." As he speaks he paces the floor, gesturing for effect.

"The craft," the reverend continues in a slow deliberate tone like he is hosting a documentary program, "had initially been spotted moving at an estimated airspeed exceeding 10,000 miles per hour at a height of approximately 16,000 feet. This information was confirmed by operators of the D.E.W., Distant Early Warning radar system, stationed at nearby Wright-Patterson Air Force base."

Charmaine's head feels like it's been stuffed with cotton. Isn't this reverend supposed to be Joe's friend? What does he want?

"Listen, Reverend Goodman, I..." says Charmaine.

"This is important," The reverend says gently, holding his palm up to quieten her. "You must hear the entire story. You have to understand what is at stake here."

He clears his throat and begins to pace again. "The craft, a metallic disc measuring some 78 feet in diameter, was pursued by Navy helicopters until it reached a point directly above Lake Gordon, hovering at an estimated height of 2,500 feet. Navy cameramen were called to the scene and filmed the craft touching down briefly on the surface of the lake. Aviation experts present at the time have confirmed that the craft was not any type of experimental aircraft then in development by the United States nor any known foreign power."

Charmaine tries to think. She remembers the reverend coming over to her after the Zen Luvs started playing and offering her a drink. Everything after that is rancid cheese.

The reverend goes on. "The film was processed and then sent to the Cambridge Research Laboratory for analysis. Photographic experts at Cambridge concluded that the craft on the film was an unknown type of air vehicle filmed at a distance of some 40 feet from the camera. This confirmation was made possible by the comparison of light refraction from known sources at 28 specific points both on the craft and on the surrounding scenery."

"Look, Reverend Goodman," says Charmaine, "I know you and Joe are real into this UFO stuff, but, honestly, I don't know anything about it. I don't even believe in aliens."

"You don't believe in aliens?" the reverend says calmly. "This is a typical response. Noted scientists such as the late Carl Sagan, who died because he threatened to reveal what he knew, have confirmed the existence of extraterrestrial life forms. JFK, John Lennon, Princess Diana, Mother Theresa, John Denver, Kurt Cobain—all of these people died because they knew too much about the alien presence in our midst."

The man is a lunatic, Charmaine decides. Calm and rational, but completely out of his mind and possibly very dangerous. Swallowing her fear, she says, "OK. Maybe that's so, but what has it got to do with me? What do you want from me?"

"I am getting to what it has to do with you," says the reverend to Charmaine. "It is important for you to know the background".

He goes on. "In actuality, the respected ex-astronaut is not the only one to confirm reports of a filmed UFO landing at Lake Gordon. I saw the film myself and have independently verified its authenticity." The reverend suddenly stops and looks Charmaine in the eye. "Joe has told you about me, right? That I used to be a film director?"

"He did," Charmaine replies. "But I thought he was making it up."

"Scout's honor," says the reverend, "I am the real and very much alive Ben I. Goldman."

*   *   *

I woke up the next morning and went downstairs to get myself a bowl of cereal and some Horrible Instant Coffee. The Cat With No Name sat on the landing and gave me a dirty look, in response, no doubt, to my having so cleverly sealed Space Lobster™ off from him. Greedy bastard.

I peered into the Living Room to check on Ljes. He was not there, but I was startled to see Nicole sitting on the Couch of Doom. "Nobody answered when I rang the bell," she said, standing up. "The door was unlocked so I just came in. You shouldn't leave the door unlocked."

"What about Ljes?" I said.

"Who's Ljes?" Nicole asked.

"He's this guy I've been letting stay on the Couch of Doom. He's Swedish or Russian or something. Or maybe he's from Wisconsin. Anyway he's helping with the movie. He's got this weird accent and he sleeps on the couch."

Nicole shrugged. "I've been here twenty minutes. Nobody else around."

"Maybe he went out this morning. He always forgets to lock the door," I said, lifting up the copy of "Concert for Bangla Desh" and checking on Space Lobster™ who stirred apathetically there in his little blue bucket on The Fascinating Table. "Or maybe they broke into the place to plant listening devices. I've searched the Clubhouse for listening devices before, but they hide them so well you'd never find them. They do perverse things, like putting transceivers inside the speakers of your TV or your radio or CD player. You'd never find them in a million years. This is why I prefer eight-track tapes. It's much harder to hide today's sophisticated observation devices inside such low-tech items as eight-track players."

Nicole rolled her eyes. She still didn't believe. I wondered if they had planted a listening device inside Space Lobster™ when they had it. They could use alien semi-organic technology and disguise the thing as one of Space Lobster™'s internal organs. Nefarious alien bastards. "Why are you here?" I said to Nicole.

"You've still got the lobster," Nicole said, ignoring my question.

"Space Lobster™," I said.

"Is that its name now? Space Lobster?"

"Not Space Lobster, Space Lobster™. You always have to put on the '™' or I could lose my rights."

"You've gone beyond the pale. You know that, don't you?" she said.

I was going around the Living Room at this point seeing if I could spot any obvious wires or hidden microphones. Sometimes they got careless, especially if they were in a hurry. I couldn't find anything, but that didn't mean they weren't there just the same.

"So what if I have 'gone beyond the pale' as you so colorfully put it?" I said. "Did it ever occur to you that maybe the whole world has gone beyond the pale? Did it ever enter your mind that perhaps the entire way of life we've developed is utterly insane?"

"Actually, yes," she said, looking up at me from the Couch of Doom. "Can I smoke in here?"

"Go ahead. Everyone else does." Then she lit up one of those awful herbal cigarettes that only the most pretentious people in the entire known Universe smoke.

"I'm trying to stop smoking cigars," she said. "These are supposed to be healthier for you." As if she expected me to believe that. She coughed loudly then said, "Could you sit down for a minute? You're making me nervous."

"Oh yes, of course," I said, as scathingly as possible. "I'm always happy to follow orders in my own house." I sat down across from her on The Infamous Green Vinyl Easy Chair. Space Lobster™ had settled down a little, but was still scraping around inside his bucket. It smelled like rotten fish.

"You know you're going to have to put that thing in a tank if you want to keep it alive," Nicole said gesturing at Space Lobster™ with her herbal cigarette.

Christ, she was right. I never thought of that. "You also have to give it sea water," she went on. "You'll need to get a filter too. It's very hard to keep salt water fish alive in captivity."

I narrowed my eyes at her. "How do you know so much?"

"There's a guy at work who's a sea fish nut. He's always talking about his fish and his tanks and his filtration system with blue green algae."

Possibly true. I did not really think Nicole was part of the conspiracy. But a cautious policy is always best. "Can you call him up and ask him what I need to do to keep Space Lobster™ alive? It's very important."

"All right," she said. "But listen, I think it's more important right now to concentrate on where Charmaine is. I'm really worried about her."

"I've already told you what I think."

"Just come off it all right," Nicole said. "Charmaine has not been captured by space aliens. She is somewhere real. On this Earth. And we've got to find her."

"Okay," I said with a deep sigh. "I've only ever told Charmaine this. No-one else knows." Nicole nodded. I took a deep breath, then said, "I'm not from this Universe."

"Well that's not hard to believe," Nicole replied.

"I'm completely serious," I said, annoyed, but not surprised. I didn't really expect her to believe me.

"Tell me about it," she said, like a therapist talking to a schizoid patient.

I didn't care what she thought, so I went on. "It started when the Wheezing Dragon, that's my car, broke down, and I was forced to use Akron's amazingly efficient metro bus service." That was sarcasm, as if you didn't know. "I got an assignment from Vector Temps down at Hamburger Station in Cascade Plaza, which was lucky, because Cascade Plaza happens to be one of the four places those buses go. I refused to make the burgers on principle. But they let me keep working making French fries and cleaning tables. After work I was on the bus going home and I sort of nodded off. Before I fell asleep, all of the scenery outside my window had been passing from left to right, but after I woke up it was passing from right to left." I made appropriate hand motions to illustrate, then waited for this to sink in.

"You turned a corner?" Nicole said.

"No! That wouldn't happen if you turned a corner! If you turned a corner all of the scenery would still be passing by in the same direction. Jeez. Turned a corner..."

"The bus was backing up?" she ventured.

"No! It was still going forward." She gave me a puzzled look. She wasn't getting it so I had to explain. "I had passed into another dimension. An alternative Universe."

"Oh..." she said, taking another puff on her herbal cigarette.

"Don't *Oh* me," I said to Nicole. "This is real. I really and truly passed over into another Universe. I assume that my counterpart in this Universe must have crossed over into my world at the same time."

"Like on that Star Trek episode, the one where Mr. Spock has a beard and the Enterprise is evil?" she said.

I tsk-ed and said, "Yeah, kind of."

"Look, Joe," she said. "This kind of thing happens to people. It happens to me sometimes. You get a little sleepy, you nod off, you wake up feeling disoriented and eventually you put things together and move on."

"No, no, no!" I said.

"Okay, okay," Nicole said. "So if you're in a different Universe, then what's different about it? Is this one the evil Universe and that one is good? Did the Nazis win the war in the Universe you came from or something like that?"

"No," I said. "It's much more subtle. When I got back home, I remembered something. I'd hidden something here, in this house, in the basement. Something very, very important. Something that held the key to the survival of the human race. I had no memory of doing that before this happened. It was a new memory. I checked and the item was where I now remembered putting it."

"Uh huh," said Nicole. "Like what? Like some blueprint for a kind of weapon that can defeat invaders from another galaxy or something? The cure for AIDS? What?"

"Nothing like that," I said. "I'll show it to you."

I took Nicole to the basement. I'd spent days constructing the secret hiding place down there and had neither shown nor told anyone what was in there or even that the hiding place existed at all. But for some reason Nicole seemed like a person I could trust. I would never have shown this to Charmaine. Maybe it was because Nicole so obviously despised me that I knew I could count on her.

"There's one more thing," I said, just before I opened the basement door. "In my Universe there are no almond-flavored Snickers bars."

"What?" she said.

"That's right," I said, pausing for effect. "But there are pecan-flavored ones. With green wrappers." I let that sink in as I opened the door and headed down the basement steps.

*   *   *

The image of the Controller of Planet X wavers on the Interociter screen as if he is standing behind a turbulent fish bowl, the green veins in his head enlarged and throbbing, an angry stare reaches out through the single lens of his wrap around shades. He addresses Ngugi and Msoto. "I have been looking over the readings we're getting from the organism and they are very erratic. The last time we spoke, you said that it was in your possession, presumably being handled according to my detailed instructions. Now I am going to ask you this one more time and one more time only, have you got the organism?"

"Alas, we have failed," replies Ngugi. Msoto shoots him a dirty look. Ngugi shrugs.

"I knew it," says the Controller of Planet X. "What was I even thinking sending the two of you on such an assignment? Do you have any idea how much we have invested in this invasion? Have you?"

Ngugi and Msoto shuffle their feet sheepishly and shake their heads.

"A lot," says the Controller of Planet X. "I don't even want to think about it. It makes my head hurt. You know, or you should know, anyway, that the Interociter signal is generated by the organism itself. It is only amplified by the transmission station in Cuyahoga Falls. Now the organism has been moved and it is weakening."

"We shall track down the organism and bring it back to its rightful place," says Ngugi.

"You will do no such thing!" yells the Controller of Planet X. "I have a different assignment for you."

After receiving their orders, Ngugi and Msoto go to the former O'Neil's department store. A sign near the front entrance says that the Second Dogs On TV Sell-abration Workshop will take place on the second floor. Dust scatters through the still air of the empty main floor, caught in the blurred morning sunlight streaming in from cracks in the boards that cover the old display windows out front. Just like America, thinks Msoto, something once splendid crumbling to rubbish from decades of misuse and neglect.

Together they trudge up the dead wooden escalator. Msoto resents that they have been assigned to what is a peripheral operation at best. It is Ngugi's bumbling that has caused this.

The Dogs On TV Sell-abration Workshop is being held in what used to be the ladies' dresses department. Entering the room, Ngugi and

Msoto find several rows of wooden chairs with little writing desks attached to the arms. There are only four people in attendance; two white women with glazed eyes like they've been taking drugs, a blond man with a crew cut and muscles like a Bantu warrior, and an elderly black American man with a goofy-looking grin on his leathery skinned face.

Ngugi and Msoto squeeze themselves into two of the chairs near the back of the room.

*   *   *

"Hasn't anybody ever cleaned this place up?" Nicole said, kicking a mound of rusty, crushed beer cans which slid across the basement floor and hit an old stringless Teisco Del Ray guitar decaying in the corner - spray-painted orange and covered with Minor Threat and SSD Control stickers. "How can you live like this?"

"No-one lives down here," I said. "This is just where the bands rehearse. Wait there a second," I said and squished my way back behind Steve's drum set into the little room over to the right, The Temple of the Ancients. The place was three-feet deep in moldering copies of Trouser Press and Cracked magazines topped with a layer of mangled cymbals, broken drum heads and rusty guitar strings. I'd cleared out a small path along the perimeter over to the corner where I'd hollowed out a little space in the wall. I removed the bricks I'd piled up in front and pulled the film canister out, then emerged from behind the drums and held it up for Nicole to see.

"What's that? A movie?" Nicole said, coughing. "You know the air down here is really foul."

I waded through the debris back to the main part of the basement. Nicole was sitting on Logan's old Vox combo organ case. I showed her the label on the rusting film canister. "*Gill Women of the Prehistoric Planet*," she read. I shushed her.

"What?"

"In 1975, *Gill Women of the Prehistoric Planet* was shown in its entirety one time and one time only," I told her. "It was broadcast on Saturday, July 26th at 11 p.m. Eastern Daylight Time on WKBF channel 61's Nightmare Theatre hosted by Ernie "Ghouldini" Maznik. This was the final broadcast of the legendary channel 61. The next morning the station was off the air. No public announcement was ever made as to the reasons why. Ernie Maznik disappeared from public view, his renowned horror host character 'Ghouldini' was never heard from again. Rumor has it he traveled to California to become a successful announcer at ABC-TV, only to die last summer, a mere 21 years later of causes that have never been fully disclosed. Ben I. Goldman disappeared from public view as well. The public may not have known where he was, but certain people in the government did."

Nicole rolled her eyes. I continued anyway. "This is the only copy of the film in existence," I whispered holding the canister containing *Gill Women of the Prehistoric Planet* where Nicole could see but not touch it. "See the sticker on the can? That's from channel 61. I got this film dirt cheap at Rex's Roadway Express Salvage on South Arlington ten years ago. Nobody even knew what it was. The idiots."

"I'm sorry," Nicole said. "But I don't know what it is either."

"Okay," I said. "Let me explain the complex origins of this little piece of celluloid history. Ben I. Goldman, the producer of such schlock masterpieces as *Earth vs. Count Dracula,* the world's only giant-radio-active-vampire-on-the-loose movie, made this little gem in 1968. The film was built around some special effects footage he bought from the Japanese and the Soviets."

"So?" Nicole said. "Who cares? Unless you're a collector of trashy movies."

"Ah, but there's more to it than that," I said.

"Which is?"

"There are scenes in this film which some very powerful people do not want you to see. Let me show you."

I cleared out some space in the center of the basement, pushing amplifiers out of the way, stacking stray guitars over in one corner, piling up loose microphones on top of the stinking old Ampeg 4 channel mixing board. Then I dragged my ancient 16mm projector out from behind one of the PA speakers and set it up on top of Johnny Phlegm's Marshall half-stack amp. The wall opposite this was off-white and smooth enough to project a film against if you didn't mind seeing the words "Chop off my head! Yeh! Yeh! Yeh!" which someone had scrawled there in Magic Marker. I put the film on, and switched off the lights.

The projector grumbled and finally whirred into action. "Now watch this," I said to Nicole and sat down beside her on the Vox combo organ case. The International Pictures logo came up, the one with the Statue of Liberty behind it and the tinny fanfare. Then a shot of outer space, twinkling stars and paper maché planets, along with somber, slightly out-of-tune Mellotron music and a phlegmatic narrator reading his script like it was a 1950s science film for school children.

"In 1968 the American spacecraft *Mariner 5* flew by the planet Venus and found conclusive proof that it was not the tropical paradise envisioned by science fiction writers of old, but a burning hell of poisonous gases and deadly heat. But was it always so? Who can say, dear viewers, who can say?" The narrator was Ben I. Goldman himself, his voice booming with copious amounts of added electronic echo. The screen showed a plastic model rocket ship suspended by clearly visible wires flying through a cheezy-looking star field trailing smoke. Suddenly the title *Gill Women of the Prehistoric Planet,* written in wavering block capitals rushed up to fill the screen.

The scene dissolved to a panoramic shot of an elaborately sculpted miniature of the plains of Venus, dry ice fog drifting over the cragged, yellow Styrofoam-sculpted rocks. The spaceship Exodus landed in the center, the large Japanese flag painted on its side clearly visible. Another dissolve and the four intrepid Venusian explorers were trudging across the rocky surface of Earth's sister world, portrayed by a cheaply constructed set inside a Japanese movie studio.

The film cut to a close-up of one of the explorers, John Carradine as the unlikely named Dr. Cranberry, exploring alone.

"Cranberry! Look out behind you!" Captain Chaney, played by John Agar, shouted from on top of a high outcrop to Carradine's left.

On the wall of the Clubhouse basement a green iguana with rubber fins stuck to its back leered at John Carradine, its mouth open wide, a lion's roar, heavily echoed and played backwards, emerged from the

2-inch speaker of the whirring 16mm projector. Agar and Carradine fired their laser guns. Pee-tyooo! Pee-tyooo!

The two astronauts ran back inside their spacecraft. "We'll have to use nuclear weapons," Agar, the captain, said with grave concern.

"No!" John Carradine protested. "We must preserve this world for scientific study!"

"We have no choice, Cranberry. We have to save ourselves!" The scene cut to a shot of the rubber-finned iguana flicking its tongue at the model space ship.

"But we have no idea how atomic weapons may react with the Venusian atmosphere. There could be an uncontrolled chain reaction!" Carradine said, colored lights blinking and fat V.U. meters clicking behind him.

Agar pushed him aside shouting, "We have no choice!" He punched a massive red button on one of the instrument panels and the screen cut to the same standard piece of hydrogen bomb test footage that had been used in virtually every science fiction film between 1950 and 1970.

Next the screen switched to a shot of a country landscape. On the screen a title flashed saying "Lake Gordon Air Force Base Two Years Later."

John Agar and John Carradine stood at the edge of the lake. Carradine said, "Now just what is it you brought me out here to witness?" Agar hushed him and pointed into the sky.

At that point the screen went blank. "This portion was what was known to film aficionados as 'The Missing 23 Seconds.'"

Nicole said, "It looks like somebody forgot to develop the film."

"It certainly does, doesn't it?" I said, shutting off the projector and switching on the lights. I opened up the unmarked vial of special fluid I kept in the canister with the film itself, then unwound the film a few feet and swabbed some of the fluid onto it with a cotton ball.

"This is what I tried to show you earlier on the VHS tape, that was my back-up copy..." I re-threaded the projector, switched off the lights and started the film running again.

This time the dark "Missing 23 Seconds" was replaced by a scene showing a flying saucer about 70 feet in diameter settling down over a lake in a remote mountainous region. As the craft lowered, the guide wires seemed to shimmer, then they changed their alignment to horizontal and finally disappeared into the sides of the ship.

"It looks different," Nicole said. "Like this part of the film was spliced in from another movie."

"It was," I said. There was a brief close-up of one of the saucer's portholes. The bulbous head of a human-like creature wearing a pair of single-lensed new-wave style wrap-around sunglasses could be seen. The film then switched to a shot of Carradine and Agar reacting with overstated astonishment to what they had just seen. I shut off the projector and switched the lights back on. "What do you think?"

"What do you expect me to think?" Nicole replied. "It's just a piece of crap science fiction with lousy special effects."

"Mm hmm. Of course it's crap. Everything Ben I. Goldman ever made was total shit," I said. "It also happens to be a very dangerous piece of crap."

Nicole said, "So how come the scene was blank the first time you showed it to me and then we could see it the second time?"

"It's a special film used only by Navy Intelligence," I said. "The film appears completely blank unless it is treated with a special chemical before screening. When you apply this fluid to the film the image becomes visible. But it only remains visible for a period of two hours. After that it fades to blank again."

"So how did you get the special fluid?"

"I'd rather not say." Nicole gave me a nasty look. "All right, I found it inside the film canister when I bought it. That is, when the me in this Universe, whose memories I have access to bought it. It took him, that is me, years to figure out what it was and what it was for."

Nicole rolled her eyes. I went on. "With this film and the fluid," I said, "I have become a very dangerous individual to powerful elements within the military industrial complex."

"The government?" Nicole said.

"Governments don't exist anymore. Giant corporations run everything these days. Backed, of course, by powers from beyond."

"Planet X?" she said. I nodded.

Nicole said to me, "Look, Joe, I'm on your side. We both want the same thing. We want Charmaine back. Right?" I nodded. "So we have to look at this rationally. Right?" I nodded again. "Now is it rational to believe that she has been abducted by aliens from Planet X in the Zeta Reticuli system?" I nodded.

"Don't nod at that!" Nicole yelled. I pulled back from her. "It is *not* logical to believe that. It is totally and utterly *illogical* to believe that. Do you understand?"

I sat there, my eyes wide and my face done up in an expression of fear and total loss. "Now you nod!" she shouted. I nodded. "Good. Now we're getting somewhere!"

I could see I needed an ally. And if Nicole was not yet ready to face the truth of the situation, that our world was slowly being over-run by alien hordes, then I would simply have to work within that framework. I was going to have to play to her delusions before she'd be able to grasp the truth.

Nicole was quiet for a while. Then she said, "Maybe I believe you. Just a little bit. I'm not going to say that everything you say is true. It's just that maybe there's something to it. That's why I came here. You think I'd have even come by if I didn't think there might be something to all of this?"

"If you're going to try and win me over by saying that you might as well give up," I said.

"You're an arrogant son of a bitch, aren't you?" she said. I nodded. She shot me a mean look, then got up and started for the door. "Just forget it then. I don't know why I thought I could talk to you. I'm wasting my time here." She stomped out and slammed the door behind her.

*   *   *

Milena arrives at the Second Dogs On TV Sell-abration Workshop. Ljes is sitting right up front. She has expected this and has steeled herself so that she will be able to ignore his presence. She desperately needs his help. Not to mention the fact that merely seeing him there, sitting in that cramped little chair, the smallness of which only serves to accentuate his hard, powerful muscles, makes her lubricious as a *trømphelßund* on *Økœpzhle's* Day.

Nevertheless, she clears her throat and addresses the group as if he is not there. "It is gratifying to see so many new people here this evening." In fact, it is not very gratifying at all. Besides Ljes, the chubby woman in the flowered dress is back. There are two young black men fidgeting away at the back. Black Americans, Milena knows full well, are more interested in raping white women and playing basketball than they are in selling anything. She's seen enough American magazines and heard enough rap music to know that much.

But they don't look quite right. They remind Milena of the African students she used to sometimes see at home. They would always dress up and try to pretend to be black Americans since they knew black Americans were much more popular with the local girls than Africans were.

The little old black man from last time is back as well, just sitting there at the back smiling like a senile old fool. Probably drunk and homeless. Maybe he lives in this horrid old store.

There is a Chinese man here today too. Chinese people like to sell things, but they also know Kung Fu. If the blacks try to rape her, maybe the Chinese man can stop them with Kung Fu.

*   *   *

Kim Yong Lee is not altogether certain why the Reverend Goodman, or Goldman, as he now insists on being called, has sent him to the Dogs On TV Sell-abration Workshop at the former O'Neil's Department store in downtown Akron to get a sample of the Dogs On TV toys and any literature about them. Does the reverend know that Wilma is here as well? Kim Yong Lee tries to ignore her. The reverend said nothing about Wilma being here. But he did say a lot about spacemen or astronauts or some such thing and dangerous rocket ships. What do dangerous rocket ships have to do with anything?

Maybe this is why Goodman, who is now Goldman, sent me he thinks as he takes a seat.

* * *

Ljes takes a seat right up front at the Dogs On TV Sell-abration Workshop. Cheap, he thinks. He would have gotten a much better place for such an important event. He notes that two of the women here have Xeroxed copies of the *Guide to the Better Sales* which he wrote. He also notes that there are three Negro people here. He did not realize that Negro people would be interested in selling. He has seen plenty of American movies and TV and he knows well the character of American Negro people. They are good at music and sports, but they prefer crime and basketball to selling things.

There is an Oriental there as well. Orientals are smart and polite, but they are dangerous because they know Kung Fu.

Milena's tits look good enough to eat, thinks Ljes. She is wearing a low cut blouse that accentuates their full roundness, like two Christmas *schtrømphëls* in a *klitzenhouffer*. The mini-skirt she's wearing shows off her thick, shapely legs. Highly-muscled and powerful. Ljes is having a hard time concentrating on how he is going to bring about her downfall.

* * *

Milena notices Ljes is staring at her breasts. And while she wants to feel vindictive, his stares only serve to make her inner thighs slipperier. She says, "So let's hear from our current sales people how things have been going so far." She hopes Ljes did not notice the quiver in her voice. Now he is looking at her legs. Milena is not sure how much more of this she can take. She decides to ask people to tell their selling stories.

The girl in the flowered dress raises her hand. Before Milena can even acknowledge her she begins to speak. "I'm Wilma Fierson and Dogs On TV has changed my life. Successful sales have given me an entirely new direction. Before Dogs On TV I was a lamb lost in the woods. But now, having experienced the unfathomable joy of the Supreme Elation of the Pure Trading Experience, it is as if my past has been wiped clean." She turns and addresses herself to the three black men and the Oriental sitting in the back. "Dogs On TV has cleansed me and made me whole."

*　　　*　　　*

Although he is sitting only three seats away from her at the Dogs On TV Sell-abration Workshop, Wilma pretends to ignore Kim Yong Lee. Yet she has something vital to say to him. She has changed now. This is her new life, he was part of her old life. There is no connection, she has left all of that behind.

Wilma addresses herself to Kim Yong Lee. She hopes her words will penetrate his hardened heart and make him see the new light. In addition she hopes the black men will hear her words and turn away from their past misdeeds. It is unfortunate that those of the lower races are so easily drawn into degenerate lives. The poor Orientals spend their days worshiping false idols and smoking opium, while the blacks turn to lives of crime or idly waste their energies on sports. So sad. So pitiful.

A warm powerful feeling courses through her loins. The power of the pure selling experience, she tells herself. In her mind an image of a giant throbbing yellow Dogs On TV lined with thick purple veins forms. She salivates, swallows and continues her speech.

All at once Kim Yong Lee leaps out of his chair, snatches one of the Dogs On TV toys from the display on the table, and runs from the room. "Kim Yong! Kim Yong!" Wilma shouts and follows him.

Ljes and Milena are too engrossed in each other to notice any of this.

*　　　*　　　*

I came up with a plan of action. Typically brilliant. I would not need Nicole, or Ben I. Goldman, or the people from Christ the Crowned King or anybody else to help me carry it out.

There was no ocean anywhere nearby in which to free Space Lobster™, I couldn't afford $800 for a filtration system plus a monthly supply of salt water, and I was not about to eat him. I suppose I could have gone up to Aurora, snuck him into Sea World then dropped him discreetly into one of the saltwater tanks there. But it costs like $15 just to get into Sea World and besides that, how would I know they wouldn't feed Space Lobster™ to Shamoo or something. It was a risk I did not want to take.

My plan was better. There was poetry to it. Natural justice. I wore my long army-issue raincoat because it had the deepest pockets. I knew I was taking a chance walking into the Cuyahoga Falls Johnny Teagle's HyperMart after having been told that I should "do my shopping elsewhere." But really, what were the chances any of those people would even remember my face? Just to be safe I put on a pair of cheap plastic sunglasses and a Cincinnati Reds baseball cap which my dad had given me years ago, when he thought he could make a real man out of me by teaching me to like baseball. Once Space Lobster™ was in place, the rest would follow.

The pets department was in the back on the left. Exactly why Johnny Teagle's HyperMart needed a pet department was anybody's guess. I mean, did they expect shoppers to come in for a loaf of bread, some Macaroni and Cheese, a few boxes of Slim Jims Brand Meat Snacks and, oh yes, while we're here let's pick up something to feed those Slim Jims to. How about a sickly-looking green iguana and a few hamsters? People think I'm weird, but the real sickness is the kind that drives people to put pet departments in supermarkets.

I made it all the way back to the department without attracting suspicion. By now Space Lobster™ was pretty lethargic, so he hardly moved around at all in my pocket. It was a bit difficult to see through the sunglasses, so I kept having to slide them down my nose and look over them. A minor hassle.

The fish section was along the back wall. There were a couple of tarantulas in a terrarium on one side. Apparently they'd sold most of the iguanas, because I only saw one. It was missing some spines on its back and probably wasn't so popular. I know how he felt. I gave him a brief thumbs up, he stuck his tongue out at me in reply. I have a special rapport with reptiles.

There was a man with greasy black hair in one of those late 70's 'feather cuts' wearing one of those stupid red and white striped vests that marked him as one of Johnny Teagle's HyperMart's security staff. He was back in the pet section, doing something with one of those little hand scanners. What sort of information did they store in those little scanners? He looked at me funny when I walked in. I acted casual and said, "I love animals!" in a bright and pleasant voice.

He grunted and went back to scanning the bags of rabbit food or whatever it was over on the other side of the dog and cat toys and grooming items.

The parakeets were making plenty of noise behind me, so I wouldn't have to worry about trying to cover up the plop when I put Space Lobster™ in the tank. Trouble was, how was I going to work out which tanks were salt water and which weren't? There was only one way.

I went around to each tank and stuck my finger in, then tasted the water. They all tasted really, really bad and fishy. There was a lot of debris floating around in each one that I not only could not identify, but I did not want to identify. I thought I would vomit at any moment.

I kept looking behind to see if the fat guy was paying any attention. But he seemed pretty absorbed in whatever he was doing, which I noticed involved pointing his hand scanner at each bag of rabbit pellets and zapping it with a red laser beam which caused a device about the size of a transistor radio attached to his hip to beep at regular intervals. The Planet X-ians must have insatiable curiosity about Earthly life forms to be gathering data on the compositional elements of rabbit food, I thought. Perhaps rabbits were somehow important in their scheme. Who can guess what lurks in the alien mind? Evidently the fat guy had been highly trained by his masters to be an obedient drone and attend only to his assigned task.

Feeling more and more nauseous by the minute, I tasted five more fish tanks and not one was salt water. Fuck.

The seafood section was right next to where they kept the pet fish. Which kind of made sense. I found the live lobster tank. This would be Space Lobster™'s new home. No-one was gonna buy a lobster that cost as much as he did anyway. At least I hoped not.

I reached into my pocket and took a quick look around to see if I was being observed. The fat guy in the striped vest was still absorbed in gathering data for his alien masters. There were no other customers in the area.

With stealth, grace and swiftness of hand I reached into my pocket, drew Space Lobster™ deftly out and plopped him into the tank. I turned to walk casually out of there, just like nothing had happened, but the tubby man in the striped vest blocked my path.

"Excuse me, sir," he said. "But what exactly are you doing?"

*   *   *

Nicole paces around her apartment. This is stupid. Joe Nofziger is a fool and quite possibly clinically insane. On the other hand, what if he is right? Not completely right, of course. But if there is even the smallest chance that Charmaine really is in trouble, that maybe Joe does have something that someone possibly even more misguided than him wants, and that Charmaine has somehow gotten involved in this...

There is only one person who might know what to do about Joe Nofziger. She puts her leather jacket back on and heads out the door. She knows the church where Joe has been hanging out and making his movie, and she hopes that the people at Christ the Crowned King are at least a little bit more sane than Joe.

Nicole drives over to the church. She finds a door near the back with a plaque on it that says "Reverend Ben Goodman." She knocks. She can hear someone shuffling about inside. After a time a stocky man in his fifties, bald with a neatly trimmed beard comes to the door wearing a dark blue Kent State University sweatshirt and a pair of dingy Levi's. So this is Ben I. Goldman, Nicole thinks, or Reverend Goodman, she is still not sure. "I'm here about Joe Nofziger," she blurts out. "He's my, my friend and I'm worried about him. I think he might do something he's going to regret."

"Joe Nofziger?" Goldman says, wide-eyed. "You know where he is?"

"On his way to tJohnny Teagle's HyperMart."

"Good Christ in Heaven," says Goldman. "Johnny Teagle's Hyper-Mart? You have no idea how much danger he's putting himself, not to mention the rest of us, into."

"Danger?" says Nicole.

"That's their stronghold!" Goldman says, taking her by the hand and leading her out into the parking lot. "I have a plan."

As they start to get into Goldman's red Dodge Dart the young Asian man who fought with Soon Park arrives at Christ the Crowned King and places a small toy TV set on the hood. "This is item," he says. He is accompanied by the fat woman who was with him earlier. They are both out of breath.

"Thank you, Lee," says Goodman, who is now Goldman. He raises the toy to his eye and looks inside. He freezes.

"My god, it's full of dogs," says Ben I. Goldman. He lowers the toy TV. "This is wrong. It's completely wrong. We have to act fast."

"What are you boys so worried about?" says Wilma, still panting. "It's just a harmless toy. The little dogs romp and play and are so cute and color*fule.*"

"This is no toy, Wilma," says Reverend Goodman. "I thought it could be controlled. I was an idiot. This device is the very thing the enemy is using to try and enslave all life forms on this planet!"

"The enemy? You mean Satan?" says Wilma.

"Screw Satan!" says Reverend Goodman. "This is much bigger than Satan! Satan is child's play. This is serious!"

"Nothing is more serious than Satan!" Wilma protests.

"Come off it, Wilma," says Reverend Goodman. "Think! Think about what you told me. You told me that Lee here had said he killed his friend's wife. What made you suddenly forget all of that?"

With a sudden jolt Wilma remembers what Kim Yong Lee told her about the wife of the man at Miss Park's house. "It's true," she says. "He told me that he killed her..." her voice trails off. Then she turns to Nicole and says, "I know where I've seen you before! You're - you're Miss Park!"

Miss Park? thinks Nicole.

"I don't know what you're talking about there," says Reverend Goodman. "But think. Here you are just hanging around with him like nothing is wrong. Why? I'll tell you why, there is nothing in your head except for these damned toys, that's why. Mind control!"

Wilma turns to Kim Yong Lee. "You're a killer! Get away from me!" She backs towards the wall.

"Hold on, now," says Reverend Goodman. "Just hold on and listen to what Lee told me in the car after I picked him up from jail. Go on Lee, tell her."

"I kill Soon Park wife. Is true," says Kim Yong Lee. Nicole's eyes go wide and she steps back.

"Go on," says Goodman, who is now Goldman. "Tell her the rest. Tell her the same story you told me."

"Soon Park wife love me. I love her. But Soon Park my best friend. We in films together. Many films. Soon Park wife want to go away with me. Run to other country. I say no. I do not run. Soon Park wife very sad. In her sad time she drink poison and she die. I kill her. I kill her and Soon Park kill her. If he love her she is alive now. But he does not love. Now I hate Soon Park and Soon Park hate me."

Wilma blinks her eyes in stunned silence. "Then you didn't kill her. Oh, Kim Yong, you didn't murder her at all. It was love," she says and grabs him in a pillowy embrace.

Kim Yong Lee disentangles himself. "I kill her!" he shouts.

"Look. We haven't got time for this now," Goldman says. "The people who are selling these toys have no idea of their power. Neither did I until now."

"Now hold on a minute," says Nicole. "What are you talking about?"

"No, you hold on a minute," Ben I. Goldman, or Reverend Goodman or whoever he is, says to Nicole. "Sinister alien forces are about to launch a full-scale mind-control program throughout the planet Earth. Their base of operations is the Cuyahoga Falls Johnny Teagle's Hyper-Mart. Joe Nofziger was hired by the US government to track down me and the last remaining copy of *Gill Women of the Prehistoric Planet*. Joe assumed the role of a trash sci-fi film fanatic, but eventually succumbed to the role and became the person he attempted to imitate. By going to Johnny Teagle's HyperMart, the alien center of operations, Joe has placed himself, as well as the entire resistance force in grave danger."

"Joe Nofziger? A spy?" says Nicole. "Don't you have to have some sort of intelligence to be an intelligence agent?"

"Not necessarily," says Goldman.

"Joe Nofziger is now being held prisoner in the alien stronghold, the so-called 'Johnny Teagles's HyperMart,'" Goldman says.

"Now wait," Nicole interrupts. "I never said Joe was a prisoner in the supermarket. I just said I think that's where he went. And what is all this crap about aliens?"

"The alien menace is what this whole thing has been about all along!" shouts Ben Goldman.

Wilma raises her hand and says, "I thought the enemy was Satan."

"Jesus H. Christ Almighty," shouts Goldman. "Isn't anybody here paying any attention at all? Look," he says, lowering his voice and speaking evenly now, "the alien menace is real and you had all just better face up to that fact, if we're going to get anywhere."

"Destroy the alien menace!" shouts Wilma, unprompted, smacking the hood of the Dodge Dart with her palm. The others look at her. "Right?" she says sheepishly.

Nicole says, "Come on now. I have to admit to having seen a lot of strange things in the past few weeks, but I'm not about to start believing that creatures from outer space are actually going around Cuyahoga Falls, taking over supermarkets. And Joe Nofziger as a government agent is a bit tough to swallow. You have to admit that."

"How can you say that?" Goldman says. "You must have seen the film of the spacecraft landing. I know Joe has it, and I doubt you'd have come here if you hadn't seen it. How can you doubt that they are among us, ready to lash out at any time with unspeakable power?"

Nicole says, "I've seen the film, but the only space ships I saw looked like pie plates hanging on wires."

"That's their propulsion system! It radiates energy upwards and on film it looks like the craft are hanging from wires!"

Nicole shakes her head.

"All right," says Goldman. "Believe whatever you want to believe, but help us help Joe. As far as I'm concerned, he's on our side now, no matter how he got into this. We're going to treat him as if he is exactly what he appears to be."

*   *   *

Abe is not sure about Carl's plan. In all his years as president of the American Mills Corporation, Abe has steered away from ostentatious publicity campaigns. American Mills has an image to maintain: Wholesome all-American breakfast foods, produced by a down-to-earth company. A company staffed by people of a single mind, devoted to the health and well-being of the nation. Would the president of a solid company with both feet firmly planted on Mother Earth float around in a balloon, dropping toys on people from the sky? Somehow it doesn't seem right.

He decides to have Charlie come along with him when he goes to the Cuyahoga Falls Johnny Teagle's HyperMart to speak with Carl. Charlie is very centered and will tend to ground whatever discussions are going on. Grounding is important.

Rumors spread around the American Mills Corporation that Abe Kidman has some big publicity stunt planned. General consensus among the workers is that this is a good thing. The company is going down the tubes. Already there are rumblings that they should start producing more brightly-colored, sugar-packed, cartoon-based cereals and dump all the slow-moving health food crap.

When further rumors circulate that the night janitor is now attending high-level corporate meetings, this confirms the general feeling amongst the employees that Abe Kidman has finally slipped over the edge into total madness.

Carl doesn't like the idea of Abe Kidman bringing the American Mills Corporation's night janitor to the meeting about the plan to drop Dogs On TV from the skies over Akron. But he does not complain. In business it's important to be tolerant of people's personal eccentricities.

Charlie has no idea why he's been asked to go to the boss's big meeting at Johnny Teagle's HyperMart, but what the hell? Life is a series of unexpected events and unexplainable coincidences.

Abe and Charlie arrive at Johnny Teagle's HyperMart and are shown to Carl Walters's office. Carl seats them on the vinyl-covered couch and begins to explain how the Dogs On TV drop will work. He has rented the Goodyear blimp and hired an experienced pilot to fly it. Carl and Abe, as the top people in both of the companies involved, will personally go up in the blimp and throw the Dogs On TV toys out to the waiting crowds along Main Street, which will be blocked off to traffic for the event. The timing will coincide with the world premiere of a new locally made movie at the Akron Civic Theater downtown. Huge crowds are expected.

Suddenly Carl's secretary appears at the door and calls him out of the room.

*　　*　　*

Charmaine can hear voices outside, coming through the high basement windows. People arguing. One of them sounds like Nicole. The duct tape Goldman stuck over her mouth before he went upstairs to answer the door makes it impossible to shout for help. Think of something, she tells herself. Think!

*　　*　　*

"Me?" I said to the guy in the striped Johnny Teagle's HyperMart vest who was now asking me threatening questions. I needed to buy time. My heart raced. Maybe he wasn't a mindless drone after all, but a highly-paid X-ian agent, merely posing as a drone in order to get closer to the opposition. I had to think fast, to say something clever that would diffuse the situation and throw suspicion off me. After all, they were still human beings, no matter how thoroughly brainwashed they'd been. A clever response and they'd be baffled. "Nothing, nothing at all," I said.

"I don't think so," he said. "I saw you holding that lobster. You were trying to take it without paying, weren't you?"

"Take it without paying?" I said and laughed, though it came out sounding somewhere between a cough and a congested sneeze. "You have got to be kidding."

"I'm very serious, sir," he said, trying to make his squeaky nasal voice sound business-like and hard. "Shoplifting is a very serious matter."

"You think I was trying to steal that lobster?" I said. "Did you ever check that tank before?"

"No," he said. "This isn't my regular section. The Aquatic Pets Supervisor knows all about that."

I wondered briefly about the hierarchy within the organization. Does an Aquatic Pets Supervisor outrank, say, a Produce Manager or a Non-Foods Superintendent? I'm sure they had it all worked out. "I did not take anything from your store," I said.

"Please stay here for a moment, sir," he said, then turned and went down towards the corner of the store. As soon as he was out of sight, I said a brief good-bye to Space Lobster™ and walked swiftly in the opposite direction.

"Code Five, Section 22, Code Five, Section 22," the fat man's voice rang out over the intercom. A secret alert signal to his masters from beyond the solar system. I had to think fast. Sacrifices needed to be made.

I walked swiftly down the cereal aisle. A woman there had left her cart behind and was reading the label on a box of Count Chocula. If I'd had time, I could have said something to her like, "If you're a vegetarian, you should know that there's gelatin in the marshmallow Count Chocula treats. I would recommend buying another sweetened cereal such as Quisp or Cap'n Crunch with Crunchberries." But I did not have time. And besides that, I might end up helping the store make money and thereby fund the alien take-over operation.

I tore off my coat, hat and sunglasses and stuffed them into her cart then walked swiftly down the aisle. I really hated giving up that coat, I'd had it since eighth grade. The pockets were held on with safety pins, but it still kept me warm in the fall and it still looked cool. It was a necessary sacrifice in the service of a greater good.

"Code Orange, please," said a male voice on the intercom. "Code Orange." I had to get out quick. For all I knew "Code Orange" might mean "neutralize the intruder, use deadly force if necessary."

I was past the check-out counters and almost at the door, when two gigantic men wearing red and white striped vests stepped in front of me, blocking my way. "I'm afraid we'll need to talk to you before you leave, sir," said the one on the left, who I immediately recognized as Bob, my security guard friend from a few days before. The other was the guy who tried to corner me in the pets department. He wore a nametag that said "Tom."

I pushed past them and bolted for the door. But they rushed up behind me and one of them jumped on my back, pinning me to the floor. The other one stomped away and soon I heard his voice on the intercom. "Code Nine, please. Code Nine."

That was it. I was a dead man for sure.

Soon a crowd of shoppers had gathered around to watch me being oppressed by the forces of alien tyranny. Together Bob and his associate, the so-called "Tom," lifted me up off the floor. "You again," Bob said, as if he hadn't recognized me before. Then he turned to the crowd of shoppers and said, "It's all right. We have everything under control here. Thank you for shopping at the Cuyahoga Falls Johnny's Teagle HyperMart."

"Fascists!" I screamed. "Alien dupes! All of you! Leave here quickly! This store is under the control of beings from outer space! Run for your lives! Warn others!" A meaty hand clamped over my mouth. At least my final words would be a warning to my fellow human beings.

About half of the shoppers laughed at me. Some of the laughers were plants, no doubt, put there to influence others into believing I was ridiculous. Herd behavior. Fear of independent thought. If other people laughed then it must be ridiculous, right?

I saw a few in the crowd, though, who were not so easily taken in. As long as there were people like that there was hope for mankind yet.

*   *   *

Carl Walters is annoyed at having to deal with this Joe Nofsinger character yet again. "I ought to call the police this time," he says after the security people plop Joe on the couch in front of his desk. But even as he says this he knows he won't really follow through. Every time you involve the cops it just gets more complicated than it's worth.

His store's security is the worst. How did they even let that man back in here to begin with? Carl has had enough. He decides there and then to fire the lot of them.

*   *   *

Nicole already knows where she'll find Joe. She tells Ben Goldman, or Goodman or whoever he is to drop her off. She'll get a ride back from Joe one way or another.

She knocks on the door of the manager's office and, just as she expects, there's Joe sitting talking to the poor manager again. "I'm really sorry about this," she says. "Can I just take him back with me?"

The manager sighs. "See that he does not come back here again," he says.

"I will," Nicole replies, and escorts Joe out of the office.

*   *   *

It's late at night before Charmaine manages to wriggle the chair close enough to reach the telephone on Goldman's desk and knock it to the ground. She uses her feet to dial Nicole's number. There is no answer. Shit.

She tries to leave a message on the answering machine. But the tape over her mouth makes her words largely unintelligible. She manages to get the words "church basement" out just before the machine cuts her off.

*   *   *

On the way back home in the Wheezing Dragon Nicole told me what Ben I. Goldman had told her about the aliens, about the Dogs On TV alien mind control devices and about me. When she got to the part about his believing that I was a spy, it all started to make sense. "Of course," I said. "Before I was transferred from my own Universe into this one, the me who existed in this Universe might have been just that, a government spy sent to track down Ben I. Goldman and his film. It would explain a lot."

Nicole rolled down her window, leaned out and screamed, "Everyone I know is completely crazy!!" Then she rolled the window back up, smiled at me and said, "Please take me home now."

I left her at her place without pressing the point any further, then went back to the Clubhouse where I collapsed on the Couch of Doom, utterly exhausted.

I awoke the next morning to see The Cat With No Name sitting on the back of the couch looking down at me. "Morning, cat," I said. He started cleaning himself, pretending he hadn't heard. I went to the Kitchen of the Forever Damned and made myself some Genuinely Horrible Instant Coffee.

Logan and Mark came thumping up the basement steps, carrying one of the big black speaker cabinets from the Zen Luv Assassins' PA system. "We're setting up a motherhumper of a world premiere party for your movie, dude," said Mark.

"Rock and roll," Logan said breathlessly as he struggled to get the speaker cabinet through the door.

"I'll be there later on!" I shouted after them.

"You better be!" Mark shouted back, then started up the Zen Luv's rusted out old Econoline van. With a two-inch hole in the muffler the sound was loud enough to peel paint off of swing sets as far away as North Howard Avenue.

*   *   *

"It's going to be tough," Carl says to Soon Park, the only person who has answered the ad he placed in the Akron Beacon Journal for people to become part of the new security force at Johnny Teagle's HyperMart. The man looks familiar somehow, but Carl can't quite place just where he might have seen him. "As of yesterday, I have been forced to retire my entire security staff due to gross incompetence. The former security force has threatened to protest against the new hires, that means you. Can you handle it?"

"I handle anything," Soon Park replies confidently. He was worried when he first met the manager, having recognized him from their meeting at the Jade Palace when Soon was pretending to be "Ken Suzuki" of Marutani Foods. Of course, the manager does not recognize him. All Orientals look alike to him, thinks Soon. Typical.

The owners of the Jade Palace opted not to press charges against him, but now he needs a job. As a master of Tae Kwon Do there is no-one in all of Cuyahoga Falls or indeed all of Summit, Portage and Medina counties who can defeat him in hand-to-hand combat. Dealing with a few shoplifters and the former members of a second-rate supermarket security force will be nothing.

"Good," says Carl. "I'm counting on you." I know, he thinks, this fellow looks exactly like the man from Marutani Foods. Then again, all Japanese people look alike...

*   *   *

Lori Nofziger-Feinman's second package of Dogs On TV and the various accompanying contracts and documents arrives early in the morning via Vector Courier Services. She decides to have another go at selling them to her brother Joe. She did so well with selling them to his friend, she can't help but be successful selling them to Joe.

*   *   *

Back at the Anthony Wayne Hotel, Msoto and Ngugi's Interociter buzzes. "The pig's shit! It's him again," says Ngugi and switches it on.

The face of the Controller of Planet X forms on the screen. The swollen purple veins in his massive head throb angrily. Criss-crossing lines of multi-colored static distort the picture. The Controller of Planet X scowls at them across millions of miles of interstellar space with reddened eyes. "I am so sick of dealing with bunglers. I'm beginning to think this whole invasion scheme was a waste of time."

"Are you giving up the conquest of Earth, your lordship?" says Ngugi.

"Fuck off," says the Controller of Planet X. "Of course we're not fucking giving up the fucking invasion of your stupid putrefying fucking little planet! Do you think you are the only fucking agents we have to carry out this fucking invasion? Do you?"

"No, sir," Ngugi and Msoto reply in unison.

"Okay," says the Controller of Planet X, calming down a bit. "I've got a different assignment for you, one which perhaps, just maybe, possibly even you might not completely and utterly fuck up."

"What do you desire we should do, sir?" say Ngugi.

"Look at you, you weasel," says the Controller of Planet X, as static fizzes all around his bulbous head. "You aren't even insulted. Fucking sycophant. Better turn around and see what your friend there behind you is about to do."

Ngugi turns around just in time to see Msoto bring a heavy table lamp down on his head.

*   *   *

"I fart out of that," Milena says to Ljes as he kisses her on her smooth round ass.

"Beautiful farts," says Ljes. "Like a melody by Tchaikovsky."

Milena giggles. "I shit out of it, too."

Ljes continues to nibble at her full round cheeks, moving lower, ever lower, as she bends a little more to give him better access to her wet nether regions. "Fine and wonderful shit," he says, rubbing his face in her wetness.

"Runny shit, sometimes," says Milena, breathily this time.

"Like chocolate mousse, rich and creamy," Ljes says, then plunges his tongue deep inside her. She screams in ecstasy.

*   *   *

Abe Kidman is waiting in Carl Walters's outer office. Charlie has told him that this is a decision Abe alone must make, so he has returned to Johnny Teagle's HyperMart to make his move. After Carl had left to take care of the disturbance in his store's parking lot yesterday and never come back, the meeting lacked proper closure.

*   *   *

Lori arrives at Joe's door just as the Zen Luv Assassins' van peels out of the driveway. The band waves at her and she waves back. They're nice people. A little deranged, but Lori likes some of their songs.

She carries with her a few sample Dogs On TV and a sheaf of papers including the sign-up sheet, the six page Purchasing Agreement contract required to be signed by all new purchasers of Dogs On TV licensed products, in which the Purchaser agrees not to exploit, re-sell or in any other way profit from his Dogs On TV licensed collectible amusement item, and the exciting Xeroxed brochure of all Dogs On TV products. The couch on the front porch is filthy. The skull and crossbones curtains on the living room window make the place look like a house full of death rock worshipers. Which it basically is.

Joe answers the door, looks around suspiciously, then abruptly pulls her inside.

*   *   *

"I'm glad you came to me first," I said to Lori.

"Jesus, Joe, what's wrong with you?"

I grabbed the bag of Dogs On TV away from her. "It's these things! Have you got any idea what they are?"

"Dogs On TV, the hottest amusement item in America today. By the mid 21st Century every home in the Western hemisphere will own a complete set, if current trends continue and I am proud to be one of the Newly Reorganized Dogs On TV Corporation of America's official representatives."

"If current trends continue, with these things there won't *be* a Western hemisphere in the mid 21st century!" I shouted, spilling the bag of alien mind control devices out on the Couch of Doom.

"Joe, stop it! What are you doing?" Lori shouted as I dumped out the so-called "amusement items." Ha! Amusing, if you're an alien being bent on world domination!

"These things are not what you think they are!"

Hands on hips Lori said, "All right, conspiracy boy, just what are these things?"

"Devices meant to control the minds of decent people and make them do the bidding of aliens from a far-off star system, with evil intentions for all mankind!" I said.

"I should have known better than to try and get you involved with anything popular," Lori said. "You are the ultimate nay-sayer. Anything popular is bad. You just hate Dogs On TV because other people like them and derive pleasure from them."

She went to gather up the devices, but I blocked her way. "Come on Joe. Give those back to me. Other people like them. I can earn a lot of money selling these."

"No, you can't have them," I said. "They're dangerous. Don't you understand?"

"All I understand is that you are seriously unbalanced," Lori shouted at me, pushing me out of the way and stooping to gather up her nefarious so-called 'toys'. "Mom is right, you should seek professional counseling. Now give me back my things, I'm getting out of here."

I held her shoulders and said, "Okay, just hold on. Calm down. Ask yourself something. Why do you like these toys? They're not particularly attractive. You're not a dog lover. All that's inside are pictures of dogs dressed up in silly costumes. And yet, for some reason, all kinds of people want them. Why? What is the appeal?"

She thought about that for a minute. "I don't know, it's trendy. It's fun to collect them…"

"But why?" I said. "They have no intrinsic value. You just collect them, that's all. Why do you collect them?"

She hesitated, then said, "To get a whole set?"

"But why do you need a whole set?"

"Because I'm missing one?"

I took one of the so-called 'toys' out of the bag and held it up to my eye. Inside I saw a poodle dressed as a lion tamer, standing on its hind legs, 'taming' a bored-looking striped cat. The poodle's penis was clearly visible. You never see animal penises on TV, but you always see them in real life. Butt holes too. Animals on TV never have butt holes. Real-life animal butt holes and penises are a constant reminder that things in life are not as they are presented on TV.

I put down the toy and looked at Lori. For a split second her face transformed. In that instant I saw my sister with a large bulbous bald head with pulsating veins on top. In my mind the word *Controller* seemed to echo.

*　　*　　*

"Just peachy," says the Controller of Planet X, folding his arms across his chest, his patent leather outfit making a crinkly sound as he does. "And what the hell did you do that for?"

"I have had enough of this!" Msoto shouts at the image of the Controller on the Interociter screen. "If you people are so technologically advanced, why don't you come down to this planet and invade it yourselves? If we are so stupid and incompetent why did you hire us in the first place?"

"You were," says the Controller of Planet X, "a very minor part of a much vaster scheme. You have failed. We no longer need you at all. Go away. Fuck off." Msoto throws the table lamp at the Interociter screen, shattering it.

Msoto stands before the broken remains of the Interociter. Ngugi lies sprawled out in front of the control panel, like a speared wildebeest, the heavy table lamp lolling on its side next to his head. He groans occasionally, but shows no signs of regaining consciousness any time soon. He will live. The Kikuyu scum.

Msoto has had enough. He walks out of the room with no intention of ever coming back.

*   *   *

Milena's portable Interociter has been beeping for several minutes now. She disentangles herself from Ljes, picks her Louis Vuitton purse up off the floor and excuses herself to the ugly bathroom of their room at the Anthony Wayne Hotel.

When she switches the Interociter on, the Controller of Planet X looks angry. The transmission is unclear, full of buzzing static. "What took you so long to answer? Don't you know how much it costs to use inter-dimensional transmission lines? Do you realize that we have a very limited budget for this invasion? Earth is not the only world that Planet X is acquiring this quarter, you know. We have a lot of other planets currently being invaded besides yours. You are not the center of the Universe."

Milena, annoyed, says, "Yes, yes." She has heard this all before. Then the Controller tells her about the plan by the man from the supermarket and the man from the cereal company to drop Dogs On TV toys over the streets of Akron. "The plan to drop the toys from the sky by blimp is not approved," he says. "You are to stop it immediately."

Milena's eyes go wide. She switches off the Interociter. "LJES!!" she emerges from the bathroom screaming.

*   *   *

"Lori, have you ever looked through one of these?" I asked.

"Oh sure, of course," she said. "All true Dogs On TV collectors look at their Dogs On TVs all the time. That's part of the fun. The little dogs are so cute."

"Lori," I said, fixing her with a firm stare. "Who is the Controller?"

She looked confused, like just maybe the word "controller" had some meaning to her. Just as I was about to explain the entire alien invasion plan to Lori in magnificent detail, the Clubhouse doorbell buzzed. I opened the door and Nicole came staggering in, totally out of breath.

"Joe, you've gotta help me out! When I got home last night, I went straight to bed," Nicole said. "It wasn't until an hour ago that I noticed my answering machine light was blinking. I played it back and there was a sound like someone shuffling and I could hear Charmaine's voice. But it was all muffled, like there was something in her mouth. The only words I could make out sounded like 'church basement.'"

"Shit," I said. I could feel the blood rushing out of my face, my stomach clenching and unclenching.

"I think your Reverend Goldman has got Charmaine!" Nicole shouted.

*   *   *

"Get up! Come on, what's wrong with you! Up! Up! Up! Let's Go!" buzzes the voice of the Controller of Planet X from the speaker set in the Interociter's control box. Groggily, Ngugi staggers to his feet. His head is swimming and his eyes are bleary.

"I have one last assignment for you," says the Controller of Planet X. "Go to this address. Have you got a pen and paper? I'm going to read it off to you." He staggers over to the desk, takes out a pen and paper and writes the address down. "Got it?"

"Ung," answers Ngugi.

"Good," says the Controller of Planet X. "There's a man there, one of our agents. Go there and act as his bodyguard. And take a taxi, will you? The bus service in this city is lousy."

"W-where is Msoto?" asks Ngugi.

"How the fuck should I know where that blockhead is?" shouts the Controller of Planet X. "You don't need him, anyway. Now get going!"

*   *   *

Charmaine, still handcuffed to the lawn chair in the basement of Christ the Crowned King Church in North Hill, awakens in time to see Ben Goldman stuff what looks like a brown rubber mask into a plastic bag and then switch off the big electronic contraption with the upside down triangular screen. "I hope you slept well," he says, pulling the tape off of her mouth. "You need to breathe better. I'm sorry I had to do this to you, but you'll understand it's all for the best. Trust me."

Except for a couple of embarrassing supervised toilet breaks, Charmaine figures she has been bound to the lawn chair for at least a full day. She feels groggy and her muscles ache. There must have been drugs in the food he's been giving her or she wouldn't have been able to sleep at all.

"I have some work to do," says Goldman. "But someone is coming over here to take care of you while I'm away."

*   *   *

Carl arrives in his outer office to find Abe Kidman sitting there and waiting for him.

"What a pleasant surprise!" says Carl, shaking Abe's hand.

"Let's do this thing!" Abe says.

Carl has some trepidation about leaving the store unattended with no security force save for a small wiry-looking man from Japan. Or was it China? Carl isn't sure, but it hardly matters. He has a job to do and he's got to press on with it no matter what the cost.

*   *   *

"What are you planning to do, this dropping of Dogs On TV from a blimp?!" Milena shouts at Ljes.

Ljes bolts out of bed. "What is your accusation?"

"You are planning to drop by blimp the amusement items!"

"It is not I," Ljes says.

Milena shouts, "These men will pay!"

* * *

Arriving at the appropriate address in North Hill, a strange little church called Christ the Crowned King with a barn-shaped roof, Ngugi is greeted at the door by a fat bald white man with a beard.

"I'm glad you could make it. Come in," the fat man says ushering him through the door. The fat white man has exactly the same voice as the Controller of Planet X.

In the basement of the church, Ngugi sees another Interociter. This one is much larger than the one at the Anthony Wayne Hotel. Next to the Interociter is a black woman handcuffed to a folding chair.

"What is going on here?" Ngugi demands.

* * *

Ljes and Milena rip through the day's Beacon Journal and find an advertisement for the premiere of a movie called *Jesus vs. Mecha Jesus* downtown at the Civic Theater. The ad also mentions that the Goodyear blimp will be flying overhead, dropping free Dogs On TV on the crowds below. "Come One! Come All!" the advertisement says.

"This is an outrage!" Ljes bellows, ripping the Beacon Journal in two. Milena notices that his tiny penis is starting to rise again. Now is not the time, she decides.

"We must stop them," says Milena.

"We can get a helicopter! I shall bring the blimp down!" Ljes shouts. His tiny penis is now fully erect, standing almost four inches tall just below the rippling muscles of his washboard stomach.

Milena glances at the schedule of the event, decides there's still plenty of time. She grabs Ljes' tiny erection by the roots.

* * *

"This is too much," I said holding my head in my hands. "It can't be true."

"It is true, Joe. You can't deny the facts," Nicole said.

"This Goldman guy, is he dangerous?" Lori said.

"Dangerous?" I said. "How can he be dangerous? He's Ben I. Goldman. He's a genius."

"Look," said Nicole, "I know he's your hero and all. But he's obviously deranged."

"Deranged or under alien control," I said.

"Joe, stop it!" Nicole said. "I don't want to hear any more bullshit about alien invaders! We have got to get Charmaine out of the trouble she's in! Now I need you to help me. I need you to be reasonable!"

"Look into it!" I shouted, shoving the Dogs On TV device into Nicole's face. I had to make her understand.

She stared at me with utter fury, then took the device and looked through the little peephole on the back. "So what?" she said. "It's just a bunch of pictures of dogs

dressed up in stupid costumes." She lowered the device and looked at me again. Suddenly her expression changed. "Oh my God!"

"You see?" I said.

Nicole sat down on the Couch of Doom and took several deep breaths. "Joe, I saw it. I saw you as an alien with a giant head, and I heard the word 'Controller.' Just like someone was inside my brain. Who do you think made these things?" Nicole said.

"Beings advanced far beyond our own Earthly scientific accomplishments," I said.

Nicole sucked on her bottom lip. "OK, fine. It doesn't matter. We've got to get to Charmaine and get her out of that church."

"She's right," Lori said.

Nicole turned to Lori and said, "This is totally irrelevant, but I don't know you, do I?" I made the necessary introductions.

*   *   *

Ljes, far too furious to make love again, pulls Milena's hand away from his tiny member. "We take action now!" he shouts and puts on his clothes. Milena looks on admiringly. She loves it when he takes charge.

Ljes heads out the door. Milena follows.

*   *   *

Charmaine looks over the man Goldman has brought down to the basement. "You've got to help me," she says. "He's keeping me prisoner down here!"

"This woman is the enemy of Planet X," the fat man says to Ngugi, clamping his hand over the mouth of the black woman tied to the chair. "It is your duty to defend me. There are people who may try to harm me, or to free her."

"Why do you have the same voice as the Controller of Planet X?" Ngugi demands.

"Ow! Stop biting me!" shouts the fat man and rips his hand away from the black woman's mouth.

*   *   *

Nicole and I left Lori to guard the Clubhouse and took the Wheezing Dragon to the church, meeting no resistance on our way. "He's expecting us," I whispered to Nicole as we snuck up the front path crouching behind the hedges along its edge.

Abruptly, Nicole stood. "Well, then, let's go ring the bell," she said.

"Jesus Christ, what do you think you're doing?" I whisper-shouted up at her.

She pulled me up by the arm saying, "If we're not going to surprise him, we might as well just make our presence known." Then she pressed the doorbell button.

"We're sure as hell not going to surprise him now!" I said.

*   *   *

The fat man with the beard shakes his hand and stammers, "I have the same voice as the Controller because, uh, because I am related to him. I am a direct, uh, descendant of the people of Planet X."

"You lie!" says Ngugi. "The people of Planet X are black-skinned men. You are a white!"

"Now that's not necessarily true..." says the fat white man. Upstairs the doorbell buzzes. "Aw Christ, who the Hell is that?" The fat man thumps past Ngugi and up the stairs.

*   *   *

Carl Walters drives Abe Kidman to the Goodyear blimp hangar on the south side of Akron, his station wagon loaded with Dogs On TV toys. Huge and black, the hangar looms like the hump of some enormous black whale, rising from the tarmac ten stories high. Inside, the air is icy cold, the two blimps moored there in the semi-darkness float, bobbing slightly in the chill wind. They say the hangar is so big rain clouds sometimes form inside.

Carl leads Abe to the blimp nearest the back. This is against nature, thinks Abe. Still, he has made his decision, he will not turn back now. Together they load sack after sack of Dogs On TV toys into the gondola.

*   *   *

Ben I. Goldman opened the door. "Joe. And Nicole. What brings you here?" he said.

"We want Charmaine back," Nicole said.

"Charmaine?" Goldman said.

"Yes," I said firmly.

Goldman sighed. "All right. Fine, *Noftsinger*. You get your girl-friend when I get my film and the alien creature." He jabbed a fat finger in my face.

"Not before we see Charmaine," Nicole said.

"You'll see her when I'm ready to let you see her," said Goldman. "There's more at stake here than her."

*   *   *

Ljes and Milena take a taxi all the way to Ravenna, where Ljes rents the most powerful helicopter on the lot. Together they climb into the mighty machine and take off for the skies of Akron. "Make sure your parachute is secure!" shouts Ljes.

"Are you not safety driver?" Milena shouts back.

"You must always be prepared!" says Ljes.

In a matter of minutes they have spent all the cash the Dogs On TV Corporation of America has.

*   *   *

Nicole gave Goldman a lightning-fast chop to the stomach. He doubled over with an "oof." Nicole rushed inside, when suddenly a Bblack man in a black suit stepped out of a door to her left and stood in front of her. "Jesus Christ!" I said. "It's one of the guys that attacked me and Mark!"

"That is correct," sputtered Goldman, righting himself with great difficulty. "And he is under orders from me to protect my interests and make sure I get what I want. Now give me the film."

"I am under whose orders?" said the black man in black.

Nicole launched into action without hesitation, knocking Goldman's huge gangster henchman off balance with a swift kick to the back of the legs. He went sprawling on the floor face first. Goldman was barreling straight for me. I grabbed a heavy Bible off a table by the door and swung it, connecting with the side of his head.

Goldman went down. Before he could get back up again I brought the Bible down on his head again. "Yaaahh! I give in! I give in!" he yelped.

Meanwhile, Nicole was punching the henchman in the ribs. He slumped against the wall with a dazed look in his eyes. Goldman knelt down on the floor, rubbing the back of his head and moaning. "Out of my way!" Nicole shouted, pushing Goldman to one side and heading down the basement steps.

*   *   *

"This is going to be great," Carl says to Abe, patting him on the back as they finish loading the last of the Dogs On TV toys into the blimp's gondola. "You just wait and see!"

Abe looks over the Goodyear blimp moored there, inside its huge dark cavernous hangar. It's unnatural. Like a great gray blowfish floating in a sea of steel and rubber.

*   *   *

I followed Nicole to the basement. Charmaine was down there, handcuffed to a folding lawn chair. Nicole ran upstairs and screamed at Goldman to give her the keys to the handcuffs. I heard a few thumps and a couple seconds later Nicole came back down the steps, keys in hand.

"Thank God you're here!" Charmaine said, her voice slurred, her eyes not quite focused. Nicole unlocked the cuffs and eased her out of the chair. Charmaine moved slowly, with great difficulty.

Next to her was an immense device of some sort. It looked like some contraption out of a Frankenstein movie. On top was a screen shaped like an inverted triangle. "The alien communication device!" I shouted.

The black man in black staggered down the steps. "It is a falsehood," he said. "This fat man is behind it all."

"Falsehood?" I said.

Clutching his stomach, Goldman staggered down the stairs behind the black man in black. "It's no falsehood," he huffed. "The aliens are real. It's true that some of the messages were from me, but the device is real. The only missing piece is the alien creature which this man has." Goldman pointed at me. "With the alien creature and the film, the forces of evil which he unknowingly represents will be able to complete the construction of the alien transport device. But they don't understand its power. As soon as they try and use it - Ka-blooey goes the whole world." He turned to his henchman. "You've got to help me stop him!"

"You dare to speak to me at all!" the black man in black shouted and began punching Goldman hard in the ribs. "I should kill you!"

"We've got to get out of here!" Nicole shouted. She and I took Charmaine between us, holding her by the shoulders, and circled around the black man in black, who was still beating Goldman and shouting at him in African. We left them down in the basement and ran out of the house back down the hill to the Wheezing Dragon.

The three of us slid into the front seat of the Wheezing Dragon, the back seat being too full of old magazines and eight-track tapes for anyone to occupy. I was completely at a loss at this point. What the hell had just happened? "Let's get back to the Clubhouse," I said, starting up the car.

No-one answered. I turned to see Charmaine and Nicole locked in a passionate kiss, tears streaming down both of their faces. That's when I knew it was time for me to let go.

*   *   *

Ben I. Goldman pounded on the window of the Wheezing Dragon. I rolled it down half an inch. "What?"

"Listen, it's not what you think," he said. Then he noticed Charmaine and Nicole still lip-locked together on the passenger side. "Oh, sorry. Excuse me."

Nicole pulled away from Charmaine and leaned over me to yell at Goldman: "What the fuck do you want?" Her leather jacket smelled of a complex mixture of tobacco, herb cigarettes and sweat.

"I need to explain," he said. "Will you please let me explain?"

"Explain, then," I said. Nicole glowered at him, then at me and then floomped back in her seat to listen.

"That film you have," Goldman said, addressing me. "It's very dangerous. With that as their guide plus the mechanism in my basement, those in power will have all they need to build an experimental spacecraft. What they don't know is that the power source involved will have a disastrous effect when used in the Earth's atmosphere. The one piece that's missing now is the creature, the only living survivor of a saucer crash thirty years ago. It was safe. I had a very elaborate scheme, involving a dummy grocery conglomerate based in Yokohama, arranged for its preservation. But now I can't locate it."

I opened my mouth, but before I could speak Nicole said. "Shut up, Joe. Don't even try bringing your pet lobster into this."

"Lobster?" Goldman shouted. "You have the lobster?" He slapped his forehead. "That's it! That's the missing link. The alien creature. That creature channels and amplifies the power of the communications machine and the mind control devices."

"Space Lobster?" Nicole said.

"Space Lobster™," I corrected her.

"It's not a lobster. It's a complex intelligent organism of extraterrestrial origin. You've got to give me the creature," Goldman said.

"I don't have it," I said. "But I know where it is. I can get it for you."

"No," said Goldman. "You've got to get down to the Civic Theater with *Gill Women of the Prehistoric Planet* and show the film to the world. Put it on instead of *Jesus vs. Mecha Jesus*. It's important. Tell people it's a double-feature. I'll get the creature and then come down there with it. As soon as the film's over we'll show the creature to the audience, tell them about the footage from the air force and the whole thing will be blown wide open!"

*   *   *

"This is going to be the greatest publicity stunt ever attempted by a Johnny Teagle's HyperMart manager!" Carl shouts proudly, standing unsteadily in the gondola of the Goodyear blimp as it floats and bobs its way northward toward the center of Akron. "This is going to be it! This is what's going to put the name Carl Walters on the lips of every corporate head in the Johnny Teagle HyperMart organization!"

Abe looks at Carl dubiously. "Come on," says Carl smiling. "Don't take everything so darned seriously all the time." He reaches into a plastic Johnny Teagle's HyperMart bag he has brought with him, pulls out a Hostess Ding Dong and hands it to Abe. "Put a smile on your face!"

Abe gives a fake smile, stuffs the Ding Dong in the pocket of his army surplus jacket and goes back to ready the giant bags of Dogs On TV, wondering whether or not this is what the Buddha would have called Right Action.

*   *   *

"Whoa, whoa. Hold on. Wait just one minute here," said Nicole, leaning over me again. "You kidnap Charmaine, drug her, handcuff her to a lawn chair in your basement for 32 hours, and then you expect us to just forget all of that and go and help you out with some scheme that is not only stupid, but completely and utterly insane?"

A tense silence followed. Goldman scratched at his beard and said. "Essentially - yes."

"Fuck me with a broom handle," Nicole exclaimed.

"I think we should help him," Charmaine said.

"What?" Nicole said, spinning her head around to glare at Charmaine. "The drugs have affected your mind. You're not thinking straight."

"But what if he's right?" Charmaine said. "What if this threat really is real? We have to do something. If we do it, it won't hurt anything, but if we don't, maybe something horrible really will happen."

Nicole threw up her hands. "What do you mean 'what if he's right'? You're like Patty Hearst or something, starting to believe what your kidnappers tell you! You believe this crap about crashed spaceship control mechanisms and government operatives and alien lobsters?"

I said, "Before the first atomic bomb tests at Los Alamos, Edward Teller, one of the leading scientists on the project, predicted that the fireball could ignite the Earth's atmosphere. Burn everyone and everything on the planet. And yet the test was carried out anyway."

"That very same mentality is at work even now," Goldman put in.

"But the Earth didn't burn," Nicole said. "We're all still here."

"It could have," Charmaine said quietly, looking Nicole in the eye.

A tense silence followed.

"Then it's settled?" Goldman said.

"Let's go," I replied.

"You people are completely unbalanced!" Nicole wailed, pounding her fists against the dashboard. Charmaine and I patted her comfortingly on the back.

*   *   *

194

Chaos reigns at the Cuyahoga Falls Johnny Teagle's HyperMart. The former security force, pissed off over having lost their jobs and being forced to give up their fake brass nametags and red and white striped vests, have organized a protest. They march outside the store, carrying signs with slogans that make it perfectly clear to anyone who wants to know that at the moment the Cuyahoga Falls Johnny Teagle's HyperMart is utterly without security.

Word of the lack of security at the HyperMart spreads fast. Soon people are coming from North Hill, Black Horse and even as far away as Brimfield and Ravenna to rip off stuff from Johnny Teagle's.

As shoplifters emerge from the store, they hold up their stolen merchandise to show to the ex-security force, who respond by cheering them on and giving them thumbs ups, while simultaneously casting threatening looks at any clerk or mid-level management type who looks as if he might try and stop the thievery. News crews from channel 23 are there, broadcasting the event live in between soap operas and reruns of *Johnny Sokko's Flying Robot*. The broadcasts attract even more shoplifters.

*   *   *

Goldman went back inside the church to get in touch with his people. "I've got to go pick up the movie and then go downtown," I said to Nicole and Charmaine. "I'll drop you off somewhere if you want."

"Are you kidding? I'm with you!" said Charmaine.

Nicole sighed, rolled her eyes and then said, "I'm in."

I stopped by the Clubhouse, went down to the basement, got *Gill Women of the Prehistoric Planet* and launched the Wheezing Dragon in the direction of the Akron Civic Theater.

*   *   *

"There they are!" Milena shouts over the roar of the helicopter blades, passing the binoculars over to Ljes.

"The bastards!" Ljes says, taking a quick look through the binoculars and passing them back. He banks the helicopter in the direction

195

of the Goodyear blimp. The Akron skyline glitters through a steel-gray pollution haze below.

*　　*　　*

Wilma and Kim Yong Lee arrive at Christ the Crowned King. Ben I. Goldman explains the plan to them. They do not understand any of it, but are so taken in by his utter conviction that they agree to help.

*　　*　　*

Main Street was blocked off from the public library all the way to Canal Park Stadium. I parked by the Anthony Wayne Hotel and we walked the next four blocks. In front of the Akron Civic Theater, Mark and Logan had done better than I could ever have expected, setting up a small stage for the Zen Luv Assassins and reconstructing the entire city of Akron in miniature from props salvaged from the shooting of *Jesus vs. Mecha Jesus*. It was a beautiful sight to behold.

I went inside the theater and gave the canisters containing *Gill Women of the Prehistoric Planet* to the projectionist, a friend of Goldman's from way back, explaining to him that this was to be substituted for the main feature, and explaining the development treatment process for the particular 23 seconds. "Ben I. Goldman is nuts," the projectionist said. "But it's his world premiere and if this is what he wants..."

*　　*　　*

As the Goodyear blimp floats over Route 76, coming in low over the old red brick BF Goodrich factory, Carl can already see the crowds on Main Street. A four-block area has been closed to traffic just for this event. "Awwl Riiight!" he shouts, waving his fist in the air. Abe Kidman rolls his eyes.

*　　*　　*

Wilma, Kim Yong Lee and Ben I. Goldman push their way through the crowds of shoplifters and protesters in front of Johnny Teagle's HyperMart. Once inside, they head for the seafood department. The electronics department has already been decimated; the sporting goods section has been cleaned out of all of its air rifles and crossbows. Homeless men are walking out of the pets department with expensive exotic birds squawking happily on their shoulders, or pedigreed kittens mewling in the pockets of their flea-bitten old overcoats. There is no more cereal of any kind.

Finally Wilma, Kim Yong Lee and Goldman make it back to the seafood section. Either the crowds haven't gotten this far into the store yet, or the people of Akron just aren't that into seafood. "We're looking for a lobster with stripes on its back," says Goldman. The three gather around the lobster tank, looking for the lobster's distinctive shape and markings. With dozens of similar creatures all crawling listlessly over one another it is difficult to pick out any one individual creature.

Suddenly there are shouts from behind. Goldman turns around to see a crowd of shoplifters heading down the aisle towards them. "Shit! We've been spotted!"

With the rest of the store almost entirely picked over, groups of people are descending upon any remaining items of value. "Lobsters!" someone shouts. "Only rich folks get to eat them 'uns!"

Goldman gets pushed out of the way by a fat man in a bright orange hunting jacket and goes sprawling into the remains of the Hostess Ding Dongs display at the end of the cereal aisle.

Kim Yong Lee, still not certain what they are looking for, rushes over to help out Goodman who is now Goldman, while Wilma gets squeezed out of the crowd and ends up sandwiched between a woman in a terry cloth robe with curlers in her hair and an empty freezer with an ad on the front for Green Giant Frozen Butter Peas.

*   *   *

I pushed my way through the crowds downtown. It was a scene I'd never witnessed before on the streets of Akron. Main Street was full of people waiting to get a glimpse of the spectacle about to unfold. The media came from as far away as Dayton and even Indianapolis to cover the event. A few rival churches had sent picketers who carried placards, protesting that the portrayal of Jesus Christ as a 200-foot tall warrior who battles a gigantic mechanical replica of himself while smashing all of downtown Akron to ruins was somehow disrespectful or even blasphemous. Some people will never see the Light.

*   *   *

Carl asks the blimp's pilot to veer towards the old O'Neil building, so they can make a dramatic entrance rounding the corner of the building and appearing right above the crowds filling Main Street.

*   *   *

Soon Park, new head of the Cuyahoga Falls Johnny Teagle's Hyper-Mart security force, runs back to see what is going on in the seafood section. "Stop it! Not steal from this store!" he shouts. He has been doing this every time a mob has descended on one section of the store after another, to no avail. Americans have no sense of moral responsibility. They only obey when they are forced to obey.

Soon Park sees Kim Yong Lee standing just on the edge of the crowd that has almost entirely engulfed the lobster tank. "I kill you!" he screams.

*   *   *

Nicole and I helped Logan and Mark into their respective Jesus and Mecha Jesus costumes. Mark said, "Just keep in mind that I can't see a goddamn thing through these little peephole eyes here."

"I'll get you Mecha Jesus," Logan said with a sinister grin, brandishing his glowing Crown o' Thorns weapon - sure to be a great toy license after the film's general release. Charmaine tsk-ed.

Mark looked like a mechanical Samurai warrior in his Mecha Jesus outfit, truly an impressive sight. Logan in white robes and jet-black forked beard was the very image of Christ himself. Twelve big crucifix earrings hanging from both ears enhanced the sacred effect beautifully.

*   *   *

The crowd on the street cheers as they see the blimp overhead. Carl leans out the gondola and gives them the thumbs up. "Switch on the sign!" he shouts to the pilot. Above the gondola the lighted sign goes on. Carl and Abe shade their eyes against the golden glare.

*   *   *

Milena nudges Ljes and points out of the helicopter down at Main Street. Hundreds of people are milling about down there, filling the entire street from O'Neil's at the south end all the way past the public library at the north. Most of the crowd is concentrated in front of the Civic Theater where a movie premiere is taking place. Through the binoculars Milena can see some kind of a stage show going on down there. A rock band is playing.

*   *   *

Taken by surprise, Kim Yong Lee is thrown backwards by the force of Soon Park's body against his. Together they tumble into the crowd surrounding the lobster tank. A chain reaction of body against body results in the lobster tank being knocked over. Dirty salt water splashes over the crowd, and frightened crustaceans scuttle along the linoleum floor, many of them ending up crunched into horrible puddles of exoskeleton and lobster gut guacamole under the feet of the confused mob. Fights break out amongst the slipping and sliding shoplifters. Soon people are smacking each other about the face and body with writhing half-live lobsters and torn and broken pieces of claws and shells.

"Stop it, Kim Yong! Stop it!" shouts Wilma. She can hardly even see Kim Yong Lee through the thick crowd of brawlers.

Ben I. Goldman takes her by the sleeve, pulling her out of the fray. "Come on, Wilma. We've got to get out of here. The creature is dead by now. There's nothing more we can do, God help us all."

"I can't leave!" Wilma shrieks tearfully. "What will become of Kim Yong?"

"Let him go," Goldman says. "He has to deal with this himself." He takes Wilma by the arm and drags her away from the battling throng. Wilma reluctantly follows, tears streaming down her reddened face. A piece of lobster tail flies by only inches from her nose.

*　　　*　　　*

"Let's boogie!" said Mark, fitting the angular metallic-looking Mecha Jesus mask over his head. To the right of the miniature replica of Akron, the Zen Luv Assassins - with Steve from upstairs at the Clubhouse on drums sitting in for Mark - launched into the heavy metal-meets-retro-psychedelia theme song to *Jesus vs. Mecha Jesus*. Logan in his Jesus costume took to the stage and belted out the lyrics:

Gonna wreak some havoc tonight
Gonna smash out all of the lights
Gonna stomp on the city, Gonna smash it all up
Gonna crush and destroy, And I ain't gonna stop
Cuz it's Jesus vs. Mecha Jesus
Jesus vs. Mecha Jesus
Jesus vs. Mecha Jesus toni-hi-hi-hi-hite!!!

The Goodyear blimp bobbed into view, emerging from behind O'Neil's. A roar went up from the crowd as the blimp hovered in position over Main Street like a gorged whale floating through a gray sea. Something that big shouldn't be able to float in the sky.

*　　　*　　　*

A few dozen yards away Carl sees a black helicopter hover into view, angling its propeller blades and moving in closer to the Goodyear blimp. "What the hell does that idiot think he's doing?" shouts the blimp's pilot.

*　　*　　*

Jim Millar, the Zen Luv's guitarist, as if you didn't know that, launched into a crazed solo drenched in Big Muff fuzztone distortion and swimming with spring reverb. Logan tossed his mic aside and assumed the crouched stance of a seasoned Tae Kwon Do warrior. Mark stomped onto the stage in full Mecha Jesus regalia, kicking over the miniature Akron Public Library while a strategically placed series of smoke bombs and flashpots exploded all around him. The crowd went crazy, racing for the stage.

*　　*　　*

"Let's get closer!" Milena shouts to Ljes.

Ljes heads the helicopter in towards the blimp. They take up opposite positions about a few hundred yards away, one vehicle at each end of the closed-off section of Main Street, facing each other like boxers on opposite sides of the ring.

*　　*　　*

Abe stares at the bags of Dogs On TV and then leans over to look out the windows of the Goodyear blimp's gondola down at the hysterical throng below. Right or wrong, he now realizes that he has committed himself to a course of action that must be seen through to its conclusion. He too wonders what the hell that helicopter is doing. It looks threatening somehow. But why?

"Let's drop some of these suckers!" shouts Carls. "That ought to get 'em going!"

*   *   *

By now brawls have broken out all over Johnny Teagle's Hyper-Mart. All Ben I. Goldman and Wilma can do is get out of the store without being kicked or punched or hit by one of the hundreds of soup cans and pieces of desiccated lobster being lobbed indiscriminately around the store.

In Christ the Crowned King's burnt orange "Honk If You Love Jesus" custom-painted Dodge Mini-van, the two head for downtown Akron.

*   *   *

The screen on the side of the blimp lights up with the words "ARE YOU READY (pause) ...FOR... (pause) DOGS ON TV?!"

The words "DOGS ON TV" blink on and off. Down below the crowd screams in unison. The blimp moves in closer to the Civic Theater, the center of the cheering crowd.

"Stop them, Ljes!" shouts Milena.

*   *   *

Then there was another massive shout, this time from the back of the crowd, away from the stage. They were all pointing at the sky. I looked up and saw the flashing message on the Goodyear blimp. *"Stand by... for free...DOGS ON TV!!...DOGS ON TV!!...DOGS ON TV!!!"*

God help us all, I thought.

*   *   *

Ljes brings the helicopter in closer. When they are about fifty yards away from the gigantic gray dirigible, he switches on the PA system. "Stop what you are doing at this very moment!" he shouts.

He can see the supermarket manager along with the man from American Mills Corporation in the gondola. The supermarket manager raises his middle finger at Ljes. Ljes does not fully understand the meaning of this gesture, but he knows when he has been insulted.

*   *   *

"Ignore those twerps!" Carl shouts at Abe and the blimp's pilot.

Abe squints out the window. It's hard to make out the tiny figures in the little black helicopter, but he can just about recognize them as the two weirdo foreigners who sold him the Dogs On TV toys to begin with. "Come on!" Carl shouts. "I said throw some of those son of a bitches out!" He grabs a handful of Dogs On TV's and tosses them out an open window. Below, the crowd goes wild.

*   *   *

The screen on the blimp blinks with the words, "GET READY... GET SET..."

Ljes repeats his warning. "Cease releasing the amusement items! I repeat..."

*   *   *

Another warning from the idiots in the helicopter, thinks Carl. "Let this be a lesson to those who would screw with Carl Walters!" he shouts and begins tossing handful after handful of Dogs On TV's down at the writhing crowd below.

*   *   *

"They are dropping them now!" Milena shouts at Ljes. "Do something!"

Ljes pushes the helicopter to within twenty yards of the blimp. The gigantic gray balloon now dominates the entire view from the front window of the helicopter. The golden lights forming words on the black screen on the side of the blimp are too close to be read now. Each letter is almost as large as Ljes and Milena's helicopter.

*   *   *

The crowd went wild. Dogs On TV started falling from the sky. People were going crazy, trying to catch them all. There was no way our stage show could compete with the commotion. The black helicopter was closing in on the blimp. I could hear the helicopter pilot shouting something through his PA system, but couldn't make out the words.

On stage Logan put down his glowing Crown o' Thorns weapon and said, "What the hell is happening?"

"World domination, that's what!" I shouted back.

"Not again!" Logan replied.

The Zen Luv Assassins launched into a cover of *Oh Bondage Up Yours* by the X-Ray Spex, but it was too late.

*   *   *

Down below, the crowd continues to scream. A gigantic mass of people forms directly below the blimp. From Milena's vantage point in the helicopter it looks like a bowl full of struggling cockroaches.

Ljes switches on the PA again. "This is your last warning! Do not drop any more of the amusement items!" The blades of the helicopter get closer and closer to the blimp's giant gas bag.

*   *   *

"You're too god-damned close!" the pilot of the blimp shouts at the helicopter. Not having a PA of his own, there's no way he can expect them to hear. He waves frantically out the window, but the idiots in the helicopter take no notice.

*   *   *

The crowd goes completely insane. Hundreds of people scramble to catch the few Dogs On TV toys being dropped.

Ljes moves the helicopter even closer to the blimp. Suddenly the blimp lurches forward, caught by a gust of wind. Within seconds the dirigible is only a few yards away from the helicopter. Dogs On TV's continue to rain down upon the frenzied crowd below.

In the street people scramble for the Dogs On TV like locusts in a cornfield. Fights break out. Within seconds a full-scale riot begins.

*   *   *

"I can't hold her steady with all this wind those assholes are kicking up!" the blimp pilot shouts back to Carl and Abe.

*   *   *

"Stop them, Ljes!" shouts Milena. "Do something!"

The blimp is now so close it is nearly touching the helicopter's blades. Ljes pulls back a few yards. "What are you doing?" Milena shouts.

"It is very dangerous!" Ljes says. "We have to pull back!"

*   *   *

Carl continues tossing Dogs On TV toys out the window. Abe finds three parachutes. He helps the pilot on with one as the pilot continues trying to maneuver the blimp away from the helicopter. "Thanks, buddy. We just may need these," the pilot says. Abe tries to get Carl to stop tossing toys out the window long enough to put on a parachute, but Carl refuses. Abe straps his own on and then forces the last one over Carl's shoulders and clips it into place.

*   *   *

"Pull back?" Milena screeches. "No real man ever pulls back!" She grabs the joystick and pushes forward on it. The helicopter plunges straight for the blinking sign on the side of the blimp.

*   *   *

The pilot tries to move the blimp away from the helicopter and head it eastward away from the main concentration of the crowd. Carl notices this and comes running into the control room. "Hey! We were just getting started!" He grabs the steering wheel and gives it a sharp tug.

*   *   *

There is a tremendous wrenching sound as the helicopter's rotating blades make contact with the skin of the blimp. The helicopter starts to pitch and roll violently.

"Get out!" shouts Ljes. His voice sounds like Mickey Mouse's from having inhaled the helium now streaming out of the torn Goodyear blimp. He undoes his safety belt and pulls Milena out the door of the 'copter.

Wide-eyed, Milena looks down at the writhing crowd rushing up at her from below. Ljes pulls the rip-cord on her parachute and it snaps open. Ljes falls away in the opposite direction, his own parachute snapping open seconds later.

Above her she hears a terrible grinding of gears and a ripping of fabric and metal.

*   *   *

There is a monstrous ripping sound and the entire gondola tips, throwing Carl, Abe and the pilot sliding across the floor towards the rear of the compartment.

The blimp continues to churn and sway, now completely out of control.

*   *   *

The helicopter blades slice through the giant gas bag of the Goodyear blimp. A rush of helium gas escapes in a red cloud and the blimp starts to go down, heading straight for the Civic Theater marquee of the.

"Get out!" shouts Carl, his voice two octaves above its normal pitch from all of the helium. "We're going down!" He struggles to the nearest door, opens it and jumps.

The pilot, meanwhile, is crawling towards the control cabin. "There's nothing you can do!" Abe screams in a cartoony squeak.

"I've got to try!" the pilot shouts back, sounding like a 33 rpm record played at 45 speed. Out the window Abe can see the gigantic marquee of the Civic Theater looming into view. It's too late. He grabs the pilot and forcibly ejects him out the gondola door. Then, with the Civic Theater marquee only a scant few feet away, Abe jumps.

*   *   *

By the time Ben I. Goldman and Wilma cross the Y-Bridge from North Hill to Akron, the crowds downtown have become so thick they have to park the car on Market Street and run the next five blocks to the Civic Theater. Overhead, the Goodyear blimp collides with a black helicopter and both vehicles plunge into the heart of the city. "Oh my God!" shouts Ben I. Goldman. "Joe! My movie!" He picks up the pace and leaves Wilma huffing and panting behind him as he races for the center of town.

*   *   *

Milena's parachute catches the wind and she is jerked back and forth, like a yo-yo being played with by a stupid child.

Above her the helicopter continues plowing into the side of the blimp. Sparks fly everywhere as the blimp's nose turns downward and the craft heads straight for the Civic Theater building.

The crowd below scatters from the impending crash. In the sky across from her Milena can see three more parachutes bloom open. It's the imbeciles from the blimp. They are to blame for all of this. If she ever catches any of them, she will kill them with her bare hands.

*   *   *

Floating down towards Main Street, buoyed by the parachute, Carl watches all of his dreams vanish as the great writhing gray shape of the deflating Goodyear blimp smashes through the Civic Theatre, huge chunks of concrete, steel and twisted blimp innards flying in all directions.

*   *   *

I watched in utter amazement as the blimp/helicopter combination plowed into the Civic Theatre with a mighty crash. The crowd halted, turned as one to the scene of mass destruction, then scattered. Mark tore off his Mecha Jesus head and jumped from the stage just before an eight-foot chunk of marquee went crashing through the miniature replica of the WAKR building. The Zen Luv Assassins broke and ran, Jim and Linda with their guitars still strapped on. The crowd scattered for shelter, hundreds of Dogs On TV crushed beneath their feet.

*   *   *

Milena's parachute catches on the marquee of the Hamburger Station and rips in half, spilling her onto Main Street. The ground shakes as the Goodyear blimp smashes into the Civic Theatre.

*   *   *

I stood frozen as the front of the Civic Theatre crumbled onto Main Street and the Goodyear blimp continued to bulldoze its way inside. In the hazy red sky above five parachutes bloomed.

The blimp/helicopter combination, its individual pieces now utterly indistinguishable, came to a stop, its front half buried deep in the Civic Theater, its rear hanging out of a vast gaping hole, rapidly deflating, farting huge red streaming clouds of helium gas from its backside. Nobody was gonna watch the movie now.

*   *   *

As he floats to the ground, Abe watches as the blimp crashes into the Civic Theater. There is a certain serene beauty to it. Nothing will ever be the same.

He pulls the Hostess Ding Dong out of his pocket and savors the smooth chocolate taste while enjoying the explosions and fire.

*   *   *

Ben I. Goldman pushes his way through the fleeing crowds. At the center of the fray he finds Joe Nofziger and Nicole, helping Mark out of the Mecha Jesus costume. He grabs Joe by the shoulders. "The film! Where is the film?"

"It's inside the theater," Joe shouts back. "But you can't go in there!"

"Screw that!" Goldman shouts back. "That's the only copy! It's all the evidence we've got now!" He runs into the burning theater, against the crowds pouring out of the entranceway.

*   *   *

Milena sees the supermarket manager touch down just a few yards away. She scrambles towards him, ready to tear the fat bastard apart.

When she's only a few feet away from the big-butted supermarket manager her parachute, still attached to the Hamburger Station marquee, snags and she falls flat on her face.

*   *   *

"Fucking Christ," I said to Nicole. "He can't go in there. He'll be killed!"

Mark, still in full Mecha Jesus regalia, minus the head, said, "I'll get him! Nothing can stop Mecha Jesus!" Clanking and clunking he stomped towards the entrance of the Civic Theater.

"Shit," I said and raced after him. Nicole followed.

*   *   *

Carl sees two more parachutes open up some yards away. Those idiots from Dogs On TV, no doubt. They're the ones responsible for all of this. If he ever gets his hands on either of them, he'll kill them. His parachute snags itself on a telephone pole and Carl makes violent contact with the ground.

He looks up to see the woman foreigner from Dogs On TV running towards him. He scrambles to his feet and runs at her ready to strangle her to death with his bare hands. Caught by her parachute she trips and falls. Carl bellows with laughter.

He stomps over ready to kick her in the head but his own parachute catches and he slips and falls square on his ample butt.

*   *   *

Ben I. Goldman reaches the auditorium. Already huge steel beams and gigantic shards of ornamental plaster are falling from the ruined ceiling. He tries to get to the projection booth, but his way is blocked by a gigantic chandelier that has crashed into the wide stairway leading upstairs. There's no way in now. Ben I. Goldman falls to his knees and weeps.

*   *   *

Ljes' parachute catches on a flagpole jutting out from the fifth story of the Beacon Journal office building. He swings there looking down at the action below. Fools and imbeciles, all of them, he thinks.

*   *   *

"There he is!" I heard Mark/Mecha Jesus shout as he clanked his way to where Ben I. Goldman had collapsed on the floor in front of the main staircase.

"It's gone! It's gone! Now how will anyone know?" Goldman wailed.

"We've got to get out of here!" I yelled as Mark/Mecha Jesus grabbed Goldman by the shoulders and began pulling him out of the crumbling Civic Theater lobby. Goldman must have known it was useless and gave up, allowing Mark to pull him to the door.

Charmaine came running into the lobby just then. "Nicole! Joe! Are you okay?" she shouted.

There was a gigantic rumble from above and the entire building began to shake. We reached the entranceway just as the elaborately sculpted ceiling of the Civic Theater lobby came crashing down to the floor. As we stepped out, a reporter from the Akron Beacon Journal snapped our picture.

"We did it!" I shouted, hugging Charmaine and Nicole. After a few seconds I began to feel awkward and moved away. Charmaine and Nicole remained there hugging each other for a long, long while.

*   *   *

Not much is left of the Cuyahoga Falls Johnny Teagle's Hyper-Mart. What hasn't been looted has been mangled beyond recognition. The twisted remains of shelving and fixtures, torn out by the ravenous crowds, clutter the aisles. Parrots and cockatoos squawk in the high rafters. Tarantulas and iguanas crawl through the decimated remains of the produce section. In the parking lot outside children play with air rifles and crossbows.

Carl Walters, Manager, paces slowly through the ruins, stopping to examine the corpse of a smashed hand scanner at the end of the canned foods aisle. There is a strange kind of relief here. It's gone. It's finished. A ferret scampers by, carrying half a cinnamon raisin bagel in its mouth.

He wanders around to the seafood department. On the floor near the aquariums section, he finds one lone lobster twitching in a shallow pool of salt water and broken glass. It's oddly shaped and has strange markings. Carl recognizes it as the lobster that the Japanese were so concerned about keeping healthy. It's not very healthy now. The damned Japanese, Carl thinks, I'll never work in retail management again. He picks the lobster up, puts it into a plastic dog food dish, sighs heavily, then walks down the Non-Foods aisle towards the door, whistling.

Ben I. Goldman officiated at Nicole and Charmaine's wedding. I was the Best Man for Nicole, and Charmaine's brother Mark was Best Man for Charmaine. It was decided that the term Bride's Maid was too demeaning.

The Zen Luv Assassins played a heavy metal–inspired version of the Wedding March as Mark escorted Charmaine down the aisle, her traditional-style white wedding dress glowing against her chocolate skin. I had never seen her looking more beautiful or happier.

"We are gathered here today in the sight of the Lord to join these two together in holy matrimony," Goldman said. "The great State of Ohio may fail to recognize the legality of this bonding. But God sees love as love and the bonds that these two share between them are recognized by we who are gathered here and by He who watches over us all."

Christ the Crowned King lost most of its regular congregation the day of the wedding. It didn't matter much to Goldman, since he had no intention of carrying on the "Reverend Goodman" disguise any longer anyway. He had greater things to accomplish. Already several Hollywood studios had called up inquiring about *Jesus vs. Mecha Jesus.*

Most of the attendees were regulars from The Grind as well as members of the V-Nervs, Starvation Army, Planet Log and a dozen other Akron bands.

*   *   *

Left without a purpose, and recognizing a deep, penetrating attraction for the Orient, Wilma answers an ad in the local paper to teach English in Japan.

*   *   *

Kim Yong Lee and Soon Park, who were among the many arrested at the Cuyahoga Falls Johnny Teagle's HyperMart riots, are found to be without proper visas and are deported.

*   *   *

Nicole wore a black gown. She had debated whether or not to wear a tuxedo or some variation thereof, but in the end she decided that she should appear at the event in something more traditionally feminine, in order to emphasize that this was a bonding between two women and that neither one of them would play the "male role" or the "female role" that society seemed to expect of same sex couples.

I fought back tears as I handed Nicole the ring, and watched the happy couple passionately kiss at the end of the ceremony. During the lingering kiss the Zen Luv Assassins launched into an impromptu rendition of *When I Think About You I Touch Myself.* The crowd laughed and cheered.

*   *   *

Back in Kenya, Msoto leaves Nairobi as quickly as possible and heads for his family home in the Ngong Hills. He burns his Western-style clothes and vows never again to try and emulate the ways of the whites.

*   *   *

We all threw puffed rice when Nicole and Charmaine emerged from inside the church. Raw rice is bad for birds. They eat it and it expands in their stomach and can kill them. Mark drove the two of them in the Zen Luv Assassins' van to a special suite in the Anthony Wayne hotel. The happy couple received dozens of cans of Raid as wedding gifts. I gave them a toaster.

*   *   *

Ngugi returns to Nairobi. He gets a job in a construction company. But one day he shall make his name known. One day he shall be a man of importance and influence.

*　　*　　*

I walked back to the Clubhouse alone. The invasion of planet earth by creatures from the Planet X in the Zeta Reticuli system was over. At least for now. The balance of two universes had been restored, although pecan-flavored Snickers bars were still nowhere to be found. Maybe I'd imagined that part.

*　　*　　*

Danny and Skylar groan loudly as Lori places a casserole topped with crushed Goofy Feet® onto the dining room table in front of them. She is quite proud of her newest culinary creation, being determined not to let any of the many boxes of cereal she spent so much money on go to waste.

*　　*　　*

Ljes and Milena have had enough of America and return to their home country where they plan to start a new business. If Dogs On TV was such a big hit in Akron, Ohio, it will surely be a big seller in Europe as well. On the plane home they draw up lists of things they will buy with their money, once it starts rolling in.

*　　*　　*

Dogs On TV had peaked, the fad quickly dying away, now that the alien transmissions were no longer being filtered through the devices. Now people were starting to get into plastic cubes that could recite the names of everyone in their "master's" family. I thought about buying one myself to see if there was any sort of alien influence emanating from them. But in the end I figured it wasn't really my job even if there was. I'd done my bit for the planet Earth.

*　　*　　*

Abe Kidman resigns his post as president of the American Mills Corporation in order to travel to the East and learn the ways of the great masters there. He has spent all of his savings on his ticket and is bound for Tokyo where he will stay in a suite at the Imperial Hotel in Ginza. He will wander the streets of the city until he meets his true Master. There must be true masters all over Tokyo.

*   *   *

In the aftermath of the event, looking for popular support in an election year, and reacting to a wave of a nostalgia in the populace for old movie palaces brought on by the overblown media coverage of the heroic story of the projectionist escaping the destruction with a few frames of film clutched in his hand, Akron mayor Don Plusquellic promised that the ruined Civic Theater would be restored to its original state and not turned into a parking complex as many had feared.

*   *   *

Before resigning Abe has named Charlie the janitor to succeed him as president of the American Mills Corporation. The employees stage a walk-out in protest.

*   *   *

I sat on the Couch of Doom, feeling sorry for myself. What would I do, now that the fight had been won? Maybe I could write a book on the subject. But no-one would ever believe it. It might make for half-decent science fiction, but even then I'd be stretching the bounds of credibility. Science fiction fans want fantasy that seems like it could really happen. This means that the actual weirdness of real life ends up toned down quite a bit.

I figured, what the hell. So I sat down and started writing, beginning with a scene of me going to see The Cramps at The Grind. It's the book you're reading now, in case you didn't get that incredibly obvious hint. But there are still two more chapters to go.

*   *   *

Carl returns to his home on Herbruck Avenue, a huge smile on his face. "Let's have a celebration!" he says to his wife and shows her the lobster he has brought back with him from the store. His wife, realizing that Carl has finally lost his mind entirely, quietly goes and dials the police.

In the kitchen Carl boils a big pot of water. Lifting the lobster out of the dog food dish and holding it before his face, he whispers, "Now you're going to get yours, you little Japanese bastard." The lobster waves its antennae and wriggles its tail lethargically. Carl holds it high above the pot. "Sayonara!" he says and drops the lobster into the boiling water. The lobster screams. Carl laughs.

*   *   *

The lobster's scream is actually a signal sent out by the creature across the vastness of space to its home world in the Zeta Reticuli star system. The signal is an order for the invasion of the planet Earth by an army of genetically-engineered super soldiers, frozen in stasis for just that purpose in a flotilla of flying saucers, parked just outside the orbit of Uranus.

T   H   E   E   N   D

?

37430918R00135

Made in the USA
San Bernardino, CA
17 August 2016